PRAISE FO[R]

'A knockout new talent
—Lee Child, international bestselling au...

series

'It really had me gripped.'
—Marian Keyes, international bestselling author of *Grown Ups*

'The definition of an utterly absorbing page-turner. Richly drawn-out characters, a compelling plot, and a finale that will keep you guessing.'
—John Marrs, bestselling author of *What Lies Between Us* and *The One*

'Claire McGowan has such an incredibly consistent track record of writing thrillers that hook readers from page one, and *Truth Truth Lie* is another hit. Perfect for fans of Lucy Foley, *Truth Truth Lie* explores the power of guilt, paranoia and envy, with a group of friends coming apart under pressure.'
— Jane Casey, *Sunday Times* bestselling author of *The Killing Kind*

'A real nail-biter of a thriller that gets darker and more twisted with every page. If you liked *What You Did*, you'll love *The Push*.'
—Erin Kelly, *Sunday Times* bestselling author of *He Said/She Said*

'A genius premise and a truly hypnotic story that had me hooked from the very first page. Intricate plotting and breathless pace – a masterpiece.'
—Andrea Mara, author of *No One Saw a Thing*

'A roller-coaster read, full of thrills and one spectacular spill!'
—Liz Nugent, bestselling author of *Skin Deep*

'*What You Did* is a triumph, a gripping story of the secrets and lies that can underpin even the closest friendships. Put some time aside – this is one you'll want to read in a single sitting.'
—Kevin Wignall, bestselling author of *A Death in Sweden* and *The Traitor's Story*

'Hitting the rare sweet spot between a satisfying read and a real page-turner, this brilliantly written book deserves to fly high.'
—Cass Green, bestselling author of *In a Cottage in a Wood*

'I absolutely devoured *What You Did*. Claire McGowan has created the ultimate moral dilemma in this timely and gripping psychological thriller. I can't recommend it highly enough.'
—Jenny Blackhurst, bestselling author of *Before I Let You In*

'McGowan writes utterly convincingly in three very different voices and she knows how to tell a cracking story. She will go far.'
—*Daily Mail*

'One of the very best novels I've read in a long while . . . astonishing, powerful, and immensely satisfying.'
—Peter James, bestselling author of the Roy Grace series

'Funny and perfectly paced . . . chills to the bone.'
—*Daily Telegraph*

'Plenty of intrigue makes this a must-read.'
—*Woman & Home*

'You'll be desperate to know what happened and how everything will turn out.'

—*Sun*

'An excellent murder mystery.'

—*Bella*

'Plenty of twists and turns keep you hooked.'

—*Crime Monthly*

'With a great plot and brilliant characters, this is a read-in-one-sitting page-turner.'

—*Fabulous*

'A keeps-you-guessing mystery.'

—Alex Marwood, bestselling author of *The Wicked Girls*

'A brilliant crime novel . . . gripping.'

—*Company*

'A compelling and flawless thriller . . . there is nothing not to like.'

—Sharon Bolton, bestselling author of *The Buried* and *Now You See Me*

'Ireland's answer to Ruth Rendell.'

—Ken Bruen, author of *The Guards*

THE
FIRST
GIRL

ALSO BY CLAIRE McGOWAN

Crime fiction

The Fall

What You Did

The Other Wife

The Push

I Know You

Are You Awake?

Let Me In

Truth Truth Lie

Other work

This Could Be Us

Non-fiction

The Vanishing Triangle

Paula Maguire series

The Lost

The Dead Ground

The Silent Dead

A Savage Hunger

Blood Tide

The Killing House

Writing as Eva Woods

The Thirty List

The Ex Factor

How To Be Happy

The Lives We Touch

The Man I Can't Forget

The Heartbreak Club

You Are Here

THE FIRST GIRL

CLAIRE McGOWAN

THOMAS & MERCER

Text copyright © 2025 by Claire McGowan
All rights reserved.

Published by Thomas & Mercer, Seattle

www.apub.com

Amazon, the Amazon logo, and Thomas & Mercer are trademarks of Amazon.com, Inc., or its affiliates.

ISBN-13: 9781662513886
eISBN: 9781662513893

Cover design by The Brewster Project
Cover image: © Dave Wall / Arcangel

Printed in the United States of America

THE
FIRST
GIRL

Chapter One

The first time I ever laid eyes on Aaron Hughes, I had a sense that he would change the course of my life. A shiver along the spine, a hint of the horror to come, as rain ran down the windows of the prefab classroom on a wet Tuesday in September. I knew at once things would never be the same again. I just didn't know how.

These are the first lines of the book I wrote about you, your crimes, and how I helped to send you to prison for them. It's a good enough opening, if a little cheesy, but it isn't true. Of course I didn't think anything like that. Does it ever happen in real life, that sort of premonition, such a foreshadowing of doom? It didn't for me. The first time I saw you, you walked into double maths in my school in a small town near Doncaster, in the north of England, and I thought very little of it. The year I suppose was 2004. Moving schools in the middle of the term, with A levels already underway, was enough to mark you out, so I noticed you, yes – in the absolute tedium of a school afternoon (I can't actually recall the day of the week or what the weather was like) any distraction would do. But I had no sense of anything beyond mild curiosity. You were a tall, skinny boy, with long lank hair in a ponytail. I turned back to my algebra and I'm not sure I even took in your name. *Aaron.* The double vowel, so rare in English. A biblical priest. Just a boy. Later, infamous.

That was the first time. The last time I saw you sticks in my memory more. It was at the Old Bailey, on the last day of your trial. I had been sequestered until I gave my own evidence, then allowed into the court for the verdict, to hear that you would die in prison for what you'd done. We were probably only three metres apart, but I couldn't bring myself to meet your eyes. Emelia was there too, of course, drawing the press attention so I could slip away in big sunglasses and a baseball cap. Without quite knowing why, I went to a pub and ordered a Smirnoff Ice, like we used to drink back then, or rather like I used to drink while you made fun of me. I forced down the sweet liquid and told myself I would never think of you again after today, that I would reset back to that moment I met you first, start my life over as if I had never known you. I would delete my email account and all my social media, choked with death threats and insults, and I would begin again. Afterwards, I was sick in the loos, crying on my knees in a dirty stall, but I told myself that was the end of it, that whatever had begun in maths class back in 2004 was finally over.

Of course, that wasn't true either.

I learn the news while I'm on stage. Not really a stage so much as a small area in a bookshop, with four chairs set out for me, two other authors, and a member of the shop staff who's interviewing us. I don't think I'll ever forgive the person who tells me, though they are a total stranger to me – a twenty-something in granny glasses and a deliberate mullet, overalls. The usual true-crime fanatic. I'm good at spotting them now. The event is supposed to be promoting my last novel, the one about female screenwriters in early Hollywood, but so far all the questions have focused on the memoir, due out in a month. *Karen, can you tell us why you're breaking your silence now, after all these years?* I don't think 'My last two books didn't sell and I can't turn down that much money any more' is a good answer, so I speak some platitudes about giving voice to the victims, countering the false narratives of podcasts and documentaries. The ones who don't believe you even were the killer known as the Bagman, or that not all the victims were yours, or that, if they were, you still shouldn't be in prison for life as you were clearly suffering from mental health problems at the time. Who could kill eight women without being mad, after all?

Then a girl speaks up from the audience. 'Karen.' How rude, as if she knows me. 'Have you seen there's like, a copycat case back in England?' She's thumbing through her phone as she speaks, typical of her generation.

What? 'I haven't seen anything.' I flatten the shake in my voice. 'People like to dream up stories about him, you know, make it twisty and mysterious. But the reality of murder is messy and grim, and whatever people say, the court had enough evidence to put him away. He's definitely guilty.'

'But, for like, all of the murders . . . ?'

'Next question please.' I don't care that I'm being rude and will likely feature on a critical TikTok any minute. I have limits to what I'll talk about. I need to.

As soon as we're clapped off stage, unenthusiastically, my face stony, I rush to the 'green room' (a folding table and jug of water in the stockroom) to ring April. I see she has already tried to call me five times, nothing if not plugged in to the news.

'What's going on?' The voice shake is back. I may even cry. 'Someone just ambushed me with a question about a copycat?' What did she mean? How could there be one?

3

April's accent is nasal, very New York. 'Oh, just some disappearance back in the UK that people are linking to him. But don't worry, this can only be good for the book.'

'That's not actually what I'm worried about!'

She pauses, resets from agent mode. 'Karen, he's been in prison for ten years. It's nothing. Some unconnected missing girl that people are getting all spun up about, that's all.'

'But what if it's—?' I don't even know what I fear. Someone copying you, a new predator? Or worst of all – that there's some truth in the persistent rumours you didn't in fact commit all those crimes back then? But you aren't innocent. I know that better than anyone – I helped put you in prison, after all. I use the calming breathing techniques I've been taught in countless bullshit workshops led by taut thirty-something women in yoga pants. In out. Hold. In out. Hold. This can't be anything to do with you. It just can't.

'Karen,' April says again. 'You're gonna get questions like this, babe. You did write a book about it.' I promised myself I wouldn't do anything exploitative to promote the memoir. I would talk about your crimes, but only in a sensitive way. I have to be careful – I didn't receive the blessings of all the families, and of course not Emelia's, but she has her own project in the works, and she can hardly stop me anyway. The living are not afforded the same respect as the dead.

'I know. Just wasn't expecting it. I need to read up on this, see what's what.'

'OK, hon. Did your car arrive? I asked them to get you one.'

'I live here, April. I'll take the subway.' And I need to get away as soon as I can. The signing queue can wait – in any case, it's rarely a queue so much as a huddle. A peculiar torture for an author, to sit with a forced grin and unused Sharpie, while people approach with handfuls of books for the other panellists and none for you. Also at the event today are a number-one bestselling writer of romance, and a twenty-something with long blonde hair and a slight, hipster novel that's all over TikTok. And there's me, Karen Cruz. Or Karen Walker, as my publishers have insisted I call myself on the cover of the memoir. My old name, old personality. The one who survived Aaron Hughes, who put him away. Who didn't call the police in time. Who had no idea. Or who knew it all. A heroine, a monster, an idiot, a victim. I have been all of these things.

As soon as I'm out on the busy, blaring street, I go online. The BBC site loads with ads. A woman is missing in Yorkshire. I start sucking in air. The annoying Gen Z-er didn't say that the case was in our actual hometown. Marebridge. I scan quickly. It says that a woman disappeared from her home three days before, signs of a struggle, 'suspicious activity' in her flat. I zoom in on the map and hyperventilate more. They don't mention and likely don't know that the apartment block she vanished from is ten minutes from my mother's house, where as far as I know she still lives. And five minutes from where you grew up. This is close to home. Much too close.

I find a more detailed story on a local news site, complete with user comments, which are more informative than the article, not being tied by any burden of actual proof.

POLICE PROBE MISSING WOMAN CASE

Concern is growing for a missing woman, last seen entering her flat in Marebridge, South Yorkshire after a night out. Lara Milton, 29, was returning from drinks with her colleague and friend Melissa O'Donald, also 29. When Lara didn't arrive to work the next day, Melissa went round to check on her. Her last sighting of Lara had been climbing the short flight of steps to her flat in a Victorian conversion, so Melissa had not felt much alarm on her behalf. But on arriving at the house, she found that the door to the top-floor flat was ajar, and no sign of her friend. Police have reported signs of a struggle and are treating the disappearance as suspicious.

Below, someone has commented: *I heard there was a symbol on the wall. In her blood.*

And someone else has linked to the Wikipedia article about you, the Bagman. *Didn't he leave a symbol at his kill sites too?* Someone else reminds them you have been in prison since 2013. Maybe a copycat, someone says. Or maybe they got the wrong guy the first time?

I put my phone down on my lap, the subway shaking around me. I feel like I could throw up neatly between my feet. This being New York, no one would notice. There's an old man asleep opposite with a puddle of something suspicious beneath him. Poor guy. No, I tell myself. This isn't true. It's like one of the weird vivid dreams I have where you are somehow in my flat, like that last day, except it's now and here. You smile at me in that gap-toothed way which used to blast my heart. *Kare-bear. Did you miss me?* In the dreams, my arms don't work, they have no strength to fight you or grab a weapon, and so you come for me, and I can do nothing to stop you.

I unlock my phone again. The story is still there. A prank, I tell myself. A misunderstanding, where she's just gone away and forgotten to lock the door. But her blood? On the wall? And I wonder about this supposed symbol. It was never made public, your symbol, the crime scene photos all locked away and suppressed. There are no copies that I know of – you destroyed them all. It was only my testimony that even linked the one found at six murder scenes to the one you liked to draw all over your notebooks when we were at school. Maybe this is just speculation and there's nothing at the new site. Or at worst it's a copycat, thinking they're paying some sick homage, inventing a symbol of their own. You wouldn't give the time of day to such people, but they're fascinated by you. Symbologists, Satanists, sad teenage goths, incels. I need to see it to know if this is anything. But how can it be real? You're in prison.

There's a box outside my apartment when I reach it. Heavy and cumbersome. Books. With impeccable timing, the first copies of my memoir have arrived. After locking the door behind me, the first thing I do is check all the rooms, stupidly. It doesn't take long as there's only two and a half. My cat, Jane Pawsten, tail swishing angrily, emerges from under the bed, yowling in rage at being disturbed. She'd be little use against an attacker. I should have got a dog, a big, big dog.

I boil what Americans annoyingly call a 'tea kettle', bought online as such things aren't available in shops here, and make a cup. The milk is vile, but needs must. The tea-drinking shows I haven't left Britain behind altogether, though I get my hair highlighted and my teeth bleached and I raise my voice at the ends of sentences so that everything becomes a question. *Hi, I'm Karen?* Am I Karen? Who can say? I have Santiago to thank for my new surname and my green card, my right to remain more or less anonymous in this ocean of a city, but underneath I'm still the same person I was back then. With you.

I find my Stanley knife, what they call an 'exacto knife' here, and I weigh it in my hand for a moment before realising I've slipped back into thinking of things as weapons. I don't have a gun as this is New York, and in any case madness has not set in as far as that. I use the knife to open the box and there's my book, my advance author copies. *Becoming Bagman* by Karen Walker. My face on the back, in black and white, resting on my fists. I look like someone to be taken seriously. This is heartfelt true crime, not schlocky sensation. I open it, marvelling at how clean it is, breathe in the paper smell. I turn to the first line. *The first time I ever laid eyes on Aaron Hughes, I had a sense that he would change the course of my life . . .*

I flip to the middle, glossy sheets of photographs. A parade of pictures, the faces of the dead. Emelia, papped walking away from your trial. On the page facing her, Jen, caught forever at seventeen, dressed up for a party in her slutty angel costume, the one that made all the papers. And there's a page of smaller pictures, the very few I took of you over the years, or that my editor found from other sources, distant acquaintances claiming you as a friend, kids at our school, the aunt you never saw but who doles out baby snaps in return for cash. You didn't like to have your photo taken. A tall boy with a ponytail or shaved head, usually in Army fatigues or the long black leather coat you wore. But handsome, undeniably. You had something. It's what made the women talk to you in the first place, and by then it was too late.

I shut the book again, sick with guilt and fear. How much of what I've written is actually true, or just a cobbled-together narrative of my best impressions, warped by time and denial and the bits I don't want anyone to know? Narrative non-fiction. A story I am telling. I walk to the shelves, stuffed with copies of my other books. April sometimes describes them as 'quiet', or 'powerful', little literary stories about small, shattered lives. I've poured everything I have into them, and yet all anyone wants to talk about is you. The Bagman I knew. If I had any inkling, at seventeen, of what you would become. If I knew, during those years when you were killing so many women. If I suspected it was you, the spectre that had haunted the north of England since the early 2000s. All of it will rise up again now, just in time for my book to be published next month. April must be rubbing her hands in glee. I slide the new book into a free slot on my shelf. Three years of work between artfully designed covers. It means nothing to me.

I have to do something. I try to pick the cat up for a cuddle but she has always scratched and run from affection, something I can identify with. Outside, it's not the grey skies and brown hills of South Yorkshire, it's the skyscrapers of New York, the endless blare and frazzle of the city. A good place to avoid thinking. Suddenly I'm scrabbling on my desk, looking for a notebook. A typical writer, I have dozens to hand, pens in pots everywhere. Can I remember how to draw the symbol? No, I never really could, though I tried, tracing the curves I first saw all those years ago in maths, a sinister parabola, the lines eating themselves. Would I still recognise it if I saw it? Yes, I'm sure I would. I would throw up, likely, also. But how can I get a glimpse of it? Would they send me a picture, risk having it out in the world, that evil? You never believed that – the symbol is just lines, curves. It means nothing without the actions behind it.

I google the South Yorkshire police department. A confusing mix of numbers, and I can't remember how to dial the UK – I haven't spoken to anyone there in years, and even if I did I would use video chat like a normal person – but eventually I get through to the main desk. The woman's flat vowels take me right back. *Ey-up, our Karen.* 'What's the reason for your call today?'

'Hi, um – I was hoping to speak to someone about the investigation. The missing girl.'

She sighs gustily. 'There's a separate press line.'

'No, I'm not – um, you see, I knew him. The – Bagman.'

'Oh.' I can hear her working it out – the New York noises in the background, the Yorkshire accent emerging from the American vocal fry I've buried it in. 'Are you—?'

'I was wondering about the symbol. I need to speak to someone working on the case. Please.' I can hardly breathe around the words, gulping in air.

She pauses for a moment. 'I was at school with your mum, you know.' Her voice has turned cold.

This is why I live in the biggest city on earth. To avoid people knowing me. Knowing what happened, or what they think happened.

'I just need to know if it's real. Please.'

'Hang on then.'

A dial tone, an empty space where I hang, across oceans. Then a man picks up. He sounds younger than the woman, impatient. 'Hello? This is DS Chris Donetti.' His accent is not Yorkshire – Lancaster, maybe. Bolton or thereabouts.

'Hi, I'm someone who used to know—' I can't say your name. Even alone in my apartment. 'I used to know him.'

'I know who you are.' His tone is also unreadable. 'You heard about the new case then. That leaked out fast.'

'Is it really new? It's – connected?'

He is guarded. 'There were signs of a struggle. We don't know much else.'

'And the – drawing? The symbol? It's the same?'

A sigh. 'That's got out too, I see. We aren't sure is the answer. Need to check it against existing records.' Of course, there are pictures from the older crime scenes, locked away somewhere in archives. 'I was going to call you, actually. Hadn't tracked you down yet.'

'I could look at it?' It's out before I can think it through. Why would I want to see this symbol again, the one I used to be so terrified of I couldn't stop it swimming before my eyes when I tried to sleep?

'You'd come over?'

I hadn't considered going back to the UK. 'Um. I don't know. Would I have to?'

'It's policy not to release any copies of the image. We've managed to keep it out of the public eye all this time, if it is the same.' Symbols take on meaning with time, like a rock rolling down a hill. It was thought best to keep the Bagman symbol a secret, but that's only increased the fascination. 'So you'd have to come and view it in person.'

'I – I don't know.'

His voice shifts. 'Do you have further information about the case, ma'am? Or the Bagman cases?'

'No! I told the police everything at the time.' As I have so many times, I wonder at his tone. Cold, accusing. I'm a victim here too. I may not be dead, like the rest of them (Emelia aside), but you left your wounds on me also. *You must have known.* The phrase I can always hear people thinking, even if they don't say it.

'I just – don't get how someone could have known about the symbol,' I say weakly. 'Someone else, I mean. No one's supposed to have seen it.'

'And you've been out of the country all this time?'

'I haven't set foot in the UK since the trial.' Apart from me, and the police from last time, and some of the family members maybe, the ones who viewed the bodies, no one living has ever seen it. Not even Emelia has seen the full thing, since you didn't get that far with her.

'If you were prepared to help us with our investigation, Ms Walker, that would be very useful. But we're trying to keep publicity to a minimum, as the chances of a connection to the Hughes murders is very low. In fact, my superiors don't want to direct any resources to that theory at all. And I understand you have a book coming out soon.'

'Yes, but I wouldn't – I wouldn't want anyone to know I was there. Christ, it's the last thing I want, to come back.'

'But you would?'

'If it could help.'

And by help I also mean help me. To dispel this terrible fear, not felt since you went to prison. To know the truth. To check

11

under the bed, make sure you are locked up safely in your cage. And more than that. To stop it all coming out.

'It would help. I'm afraid we can't fund flights though.'

'That's OK. I can – I'll do it.'

A year ago I could never have afforded a last-minute transatlantic flight, but the advance for the memoir was healthy. Blood money, of a sort.

Am I really going home to Yorkshire, to Marebridge? To the past and my mother and Ash Rollason and Gareth Hale and all the rest? It looks as if I am. You were right about that too – most people have no idea what they are capable of, in the right circumstances, and I'm no exception.

But I am getting ahead of myself.

Chapter Two

From *Becoming Bagman* by Karen Walker

'What are you doing?'

I looked up from my activity to see a snub-nosed girl with chestnut hair in pigtails. It was 1992 and, like me, she was wearing the uniform of our local primary school, but unlike mine hers was clean and ironed and actually fit. What I was doing was lifting up a rock to examine the worms underneath – something about it sent a thrill through me, the secret world beneath, the way they writhed and shied from the light, like people caught doing something they shouldn't. When serial killers are caught, everyone likes to look for clues. Oh, he had that dog he killed, or he used to squash ants, or he teased a cat. The truth is most children are little psychopaths, crushing living things in our curiosity to see how they tick.

'Research,' I said.

The girl laughed out loud. 'You're weird.'

I heard this a lot growing up. *I know you are, but what am I?* The childish response that somehow still had the ability to drive people insane, as there was no comeback. 'What's your name?' I said instead.

'Jennifer Rollason.' She said it proudly, as if I ought to know it. And years later many people would know it, of course, but not for the reasons she'd have wanted. The little girl with pigtails would be dead before her eighteenth birthday, the first victim of a serial killer, though no one knew it for a long time. The first girl, as she's often described, but to me she was Jen, my friend from this moment in the playground when we were five.

She crouched down beside me. 'If you use a spade you can lift up more worms. For your research.'

I have ten emails from April when I hang up the phone, forwarded media requests mostly. A demand to talk strategy. She uses the word *leverage* a lot. April is excited, and I suppose that's her job, to promote my work and look for openings. God knows I've moaned enough about my lack of success. *Call me!* she says.

I don't call her. Instead I go to a comparison website and start looking up flights to the UK. I can fly direct to Manchester, it transpires, and it's not expensive enough to put me off. I've always wished I were a writer in a rom-com, where everyone seems to be loaded and travels around with big sunglasses and private drivers. Where your agent doesn't seem to have any other clients and exists only to coddle you and pour you wine. In reality, I've never even flown business, and only premium economy once when a literary festival was paying for it. But for some reason I now stump up the extra £500 for the more expensive seat with the legroom and the little glass of sparkling wine. Maybe because I want to come home convincing at least myself that I've made it. To refute the words my mother threw at me as I left that day ten years ago. *You'll never manage, Karen. You always were delusional.*

Doing something makes me feel better, gives me an anchor. I take down my wheely case and stare into it. I have no idea how long I'll go for – the return flight is booked for a week but it's transferable, which was extra again. What will I need? It'll be cold in Yorkshire in February, it's always cold. Like the day Jen died, so wet and miserable, howling with rain and wind. But I can't think about that, and as it rises up in my gorge I shove it down and put in jeans, T-shirts, toiletries. A blazer. Big sunglasses, because why not play the role. Phone charger. Most of my clothes are very simple but luxe, ironed beautifully by my cleaner, Marisol. My mother used to clean from time to time to make ends meet, and now I pay someone to do it for me. Passport. Still British. Despite my love for New York, something in me is always rolling my eyes at this country I now call home. I throw in a copy of my book at the last minute, unsure why. To get my own story straight, perhaps.

Next, I need to figure out where to stay. Absolutely not with my mother. Even if she would have me, I would die if I had to spend one single night in that box room with the peeling wallpaper and built-in plywood wardrobe. There aren't any good hotels in Marebridge so I book an 'inn' out by the ring road. That means I'll need a car so I'd better hire one too. I only learned to drive in America, and even then barely, when Santiago taught me on holidays. You'd have to be nuts to drive in NY. No money for lessons in my teens, not like the ones Jen got for her seventeenth birthday. She had her own car, even, almost unheard-of in our town. The pink Mini. I wonder what became of it.

15

Soon, there is no more busywork and I have to actually do something, leave my apartment, commit. I feel like a character in one of my novels, rushing to the airport on a whim, called back to the past by nothing more than a rumour and a missing person in a town thousands of miles away. For all I know the girl will have turned up by the time I arrive, and it will be a wasted flight.

April has left me three more missed calls. I can't face her now, so I tap out a WhatsApp as I stand on the street waiting for my Uber. *Going to Yorkshire for a few days. I need to look into this case.*

I see her typing, then her immediate reply. I wonder if April ever actually puts her phone down, even to pee. *What the hell? Why?*

I need to see if this is real.

Of course it's not real babe he's in prison.

But it could be something. Anyway I'm already heading to the airport. The Uber has drawn up, so I wave it down, holding the phone in one hand and the case in the other, a tote over my shoulder.

OK. We can use this. I'll ask the PR firm to set up some interviews there. Famous writer returns to scenes of crimes etc etc.

I send her an eye-rolling emoji. She sends back a thumbs-up. Maybe she's right. After all, I did write a book about you. If I'm willing to use that part of my past to sell books, I can hardly retain any moral high ground.

The cab smells of smoke, hidden by a cloying floral air freshener. I say hi then nothing else. The driver has headphones in, no interest in me. Our bodies share the same space but we may as well be on a bus together. I send a message to Santiago, asking him to feed the cat. He'll be happy to, though Paloma, seven months pregnant, will kick up a fuss. We've been divorced for three years but his new partner – still not his wife – keeps a beady eye on me all the same. I can't call him, or he'll want to see me, and he'll tut with sympathy and try to feed me up and I won't be able to bear it. I just have to go. I need to find out if it's really your symbol and

16

if so how it got on the wall of a missing woman ten years after you went to prison. If there's any chance someone knows what I have kept hidden all these years.

◆ ◆ ◆

I've always found airplanes comforting. The whoosh of chill stale air, the endless background hum, the passivity of sitting there and being brought nuts and little bottles of wine and packaged food in compartments. Neat. Numb. My flight to America ten years ago, though the cheapest economy I could find, was exactly what I needed after the month-long circus of your trial, the unwanted attention it brought to me, the newspaper front pages, the death threats. And the years before that, of living with a fear so constant I had stopped noticing it. But now I am going the other way. Each step in the ritual of flying makes me more and more nervous. Arrive at airport, surrender my hastily packed case at the bag drop. Queue for security, decanting toiletries into a bag, take off my belt and watch. Root through my handbag for forgotten lip balms. Raise my arms to show I have no weapons, I'm no threat. Set it off with my bra underwire and submit to a pat down, a buzzing wand waved over me as if searching out the rot within. Then I shuffle off, around the airport shops under cold, muzaked air, filled with pointless longings to buy make-up in clean packaging, perfume, new underwear. I don't buy anything. Old Karen had no truck with such things, and it's her whose eyes meet mine now when I catch myself in mirrors, despite the New York gloss I have applied to myself.

Ever the masochist, I check for my books in the bookshop. I find one on the shelf, forgotten. It's *You Weren't There*, my first, the one that sold modestly well. There are twenty copies of Emelia's book on the island. *Survive and Thrive: how to overcome trauma and build the life of your dreams.* A big smiling picture of her on the front. She's such a good victim. In the hierarchy of her and me, the two who lived, she's always top, since you never actually tried to kill me. Everyone believes Emelia survived through cunning and determination and sheer physical fitness, but I'm uncomfortable with that narrative, because what does it say about the others, the ones who didn't make it? They weren't strong or fast enough? They let you take their lives, and Emelia just refused to? Maybe you had a rough night, slipped up. Or maybe some sliver of compassion and pity had got through to you. We'll never know, because you've never talked about any of the murders. You've never actually admitted you killed anyone at all.

Soon it's time to get on the plane for the long journey. I cried, on that long-ago trip from London to New York, tears spilling easily in the pressurised environment. But that time it was with relief because I was free and you were never getting out.

I don't feel free any more. I navigate the herds who seem to have never been on a plane before and can't figure out how to put a bag in a locker and sit the hell down. My seatmate is an older lady in Crocs and pedal pushers. The kind of thing my mother would have worn, though tighter for her, with a fag dangling out of her mouth. She never got frumpy, Arlene. Although maybe she has now.

'I sure hope we take off on time,' says the woman. Midwestern accent, ridiculous pink neck pillow. Tucked into her seat pocket is a book by a thriller writer I once slept with at a conference, until I realised he just wanted information about you.

'I don't,' I say, shutting down further chit-chat by putting on giant headphones.

When the seat belt sign is off I take out my laptop and plan who to contact. Assuming they will even speak to me. Emelia, of course, is first. There's Wi-Fi, which I slightly regret as it stops me shutting out the world, but it lets me track her through the hall of mirrors that is social media. She's speaking at a conference in Germany at the moment, on trauma and resilience, and the TV series about her is due to start filming soon. In Manchester, in fact, at the studios there. Sometimes on Instagram she lets herself be shiny-faced and dowdy, vulnerable in a calculated way. Sometimes she is made-up and styled, thanking companies for their brand partnerships, as if a hoody or a water bottle or a CBD supplement can protect you from a disintegrating brain. Emelia Han. Such an inspiration, is the general agreement. An icon, a heroine. And Karen Walker? You know, the girlfriend? Well, we've never been too sure about her.

My seatmate gets up to pee for the second time and I have to stand to let her out. Then I realise I'm not peeing enough and should have brought a bottle of water. Maybe one of Emelia's branded ones, that read HYDRATE AND THRIVE. Emelia would never get dehydrated. She's even done a viral reel of her 'top five plane tips'. She gets on every nerve I have, but all the same I need to talk to her, so I click on her DM button. *Can you meet me in Manchester? On way over. Very important.* It's likely she won't even see it among the flood of praise every post brings. I wonder if she knows about the missing girl. About the symbol. If, like me, she heard the story and every moment of safety from the past ten years seemed to melt away like ice in the sun.

Who else can I talk to? Most of the families weren't keen on being involved in the book, ignoring my messages. I should contact my mother but I can't bring myself to. Ash, same. Gareth, I can't even think about him without my entire body clenching in shame. I find myself thinking again and again of Jen. What I wrote in the book about her is so anodyne, doing nothing at all to sum up how she was, how we were as friends. It never made sense to people. Her dad was a lawyer and they lived in a nice house with a stable in the field behind, where Jennifer's pony, Applesauce, roamed. She went

19

skiing. She took speech and drama lessons. Whereas I was the girl from the council estate, whose dad left when she was a baby, whose mum could sometimes be seen around town drunk and falling off the sky-high heels she bought second-hand from the town's charity shops. More than once she brought home a pair donated by Jen's mother.

The truth is Jen Rollason and I were that great and terrible thing – lifelong friends. Of course I couldn't write the truth, of our rivalries and affections, our small hurts, big hurts. I could hardly say that she wore bras a size too small to give her more cleavage, that she bounced when she walked and she knew the boys looked. That sometimes I hated her. That she was cruel, often, self-obsessed, a snob. You can't say such things about a girl who was murdered before she'd even left school.

I wonder every day how life would have been, if she was still alive, if she'd made it to her eighteenth birthday. No doubt she would be a yummy mummy, with several cute kids, an interior-design side hustle, a handsome rich husband in banking or law. Skiing, the Caribbean, yoga, paddle-boarding, baking her own bread. The phantom Jen I sometimes still hear in my head. *Karen, what are you doing? Your flat is a tip. Your split ends are dreadful. And when was the last time you went near a nail salon?* I will never not think of her first thing when I wake up and remember all over again that she is dead. I will never forgive myself for my part in it.

That last bit is true, even if nothing else is.

A long time later, but still too soon, we are approaching Manchester. Beneath us rolling hills. Satanic mills, England's green and not-so-pleasant land – that's where I'm from. And I wish I could cancel it all, go back, because I'm not ready, I could never be ready to go back there. I've made a terrible mistake.

Marebridge. That's the name of my hometown, a huddle of grey stone houses at the foot of a mountain, in what's called the Peak District, in the north of England. There are big houses and wealthy people in the valley, some doctors and even a few bankers who work in Sheffield, or old mill families grown rich off the labour of the poor. For the most part everyone struggles, everyone knows each other, everyone drinks in one of the same ten pubs. It's hard to escape, in Marebridge. A black river runs through it that floods most springs. No reason to ever go back there. And yet here I am, driving badly in a hired car, crossing the snowbound Snake Pass. Here I am, back.

There's a place I have to go before I do anything or see anyone. It's like ripping off a plaster – it will be painful, but at least it won't loom over me the whole time. Here is the bus stop I got off at every day, a ten-minute walk from home. There's where Gareth's Jeep was waiting that day. I find a place to park on the road, almost fall over a man with a dog as I walk to the steps that lead down to the woods, a dense pocket of trees and stream bisecting the town, where generations of Marebridge kids have got up to no good. He shoots me a curious look, glancing at my unsuitable footwear. 'Muddy down there, love.'

'I know. I used to play in it.'

'Used to be good for that. Then things happened. A girl got hurt, you know.' He meets my eyes, as if suddenly twigging that I might be one of the death tourists. The podcasters and ghouls. It's important to me to be different to them, for all I am releasing a book about the cases, for money. I have a right to do that, I tell myself.

I sidestep him and head down the slippery, mossed steps, realising how alone I am. The woods on a weekday, completely deserted,

21

not even the sound of birdsong on this gloomy morning, rain dripping from the branches. The path is worn and muddy, new handrails installed. Security lights. Signs about ringing the police if you see anything untoward. As if a phenomenon like you could strike again. As I scramble along the path, mourning my suede boots, I can see discarded cans in the undergrowth, vapes glinting in the dark, and I wonder if modern-day kids have found the same fun as we did here. The thrill of a space where no one will come looking for you. The place must not be haunted for them, too young to remember the fear of the years before you were caged.

I find the spot that used to be ours. A ring of flat stones on the bank of the stream, the remnants of a fire, though it's not allowed. We used to build them too. I wonder if the kids who drink and vape here now know what happened in this place, that Jen's body was found half-in half-out of the abandoned electrical hut over there, sunk into the mud, her hands clawed up around her neck, desperately trying to breathe. Not even buried, not even hidden. Left out in the rain, a necklace of bruises coming up on her throat. And yet her murder went unsolved for almost ten years, the wrong man in prison for it. Because of me.

I sit down on a stone, though it's damp and cold, and breathe in the wet woodland air. Can I conjure her spirit here with me? I don't think Jen would choose to linger in this spot, if she had a choice. Not where her body was left splayed out and discarded, not even arranged in a semblance of beauty. She never really liked it here. More of an indoor girl.

'Are you here?' I whisper, as a gust of wind bends the trees, showers water on my head. Stupid. I don't even know if I'm talking to her or to you.

Chapter Three

From *Becoming Bagman* by Karen Walker

The first time I ever saw the symbol was at school, scribbled in a leather-bound notebook Aaron carried everywhere that year. A couple of weeks into the autumn term, he was still just the new boy, briefly interesting in the sense that he was novel. He wasn't hot, even if he was good-looking, and he seemed odd, talked to no one. He had been seen reading a book about Charles Manson once. He wasn't sporty or funny or cool. Just a boy. Then it was maths class, sometime in late 2004, and we suddenly had to work in pairs. I was only taking maths to keep my options open, and I have a deep dread of groupwork even now, but Mr Higgins, our teacher, liked to set it so he could slide next door and chat up Miss Coxon, the young and pretty French teacher, just out of training college. I had chosen to sit alone at the start of term, and when weird Aaron arrived, so had he. Now there was no other choice. With a deep sigh, I picked up my cheap backpack and lugged it over to him.

'I think we have to work together,' I said. Radiating annoyance, no doubt.

'Oh, I did the sums already.' He was drawing in the notebook with a calligraphy pen, a sharp curved nib. That pretention was enough to get you thrown into a bin in our school.

'What?'

He looked up at me as if startled, as if he had forgotten entirely where he was, or fallen asleep with his eyes open, so deep was his concentration. 'I solved them. Do you need me to show you?' He met my eyes then, staring right into mine with his, blue and endless, and I felt for a moment like I'd been punched in the throat. He smiled. 'No, you don't need that, Karen.'

I didn't, but even I could not have done them that quickly, in the time it took me to stand up and sit down again. 'What are you drawing?'

'Oh. It's just my symbol.'

This was not long after *The Da Vinci Code* came out and amateur symbologists had a field day, just another weird quirk of a weird boy. But I was interested. And there were not many things in my hometown that could interest me. I saw that his hands had ink on them, and that they were thin and sensitive, with long fingers. He was a delicate boy. That's what people don't imagine. There was no sense of violence from him. He had filled in more of the symbol now. It was a collection of loops and whorls, something a bit like a Tudor rose, but spikier.

'What does it mean?'

'Nothing. I made it up. After all, a symbol is just anything with agreed meaning.' He met my eyes and I caught my breath again. Here was something – someone – entirely different to what I had known before.

◆ ◆ ◆

I can't remember the name of the hotel I booked, and my phone isn't working in the UK, but after missing the turn off the round-about a few times I figure it out. The Farrier's Arms, a pub that's been given a bit of a spruce-up and offers some rooms to rent. When I arrive, the place is empty, tinny music playing in the bar and restaurant, which smells strongly of chips. I'm relieved not to recognise the receptionist, a young Asian man with accented English. I don't want word spreading that I'm back.

I've stayed in a lot of hotel rooms in my adult life, mostly cheap three-star ones with tiny kettles and little packets of biscuits wrapped in plastic. I like them, in a way. Anonymous, sealed-off. A place to disappear. But this is Marebridge, so I can't do that. I shower, the white plastic curtain clinging to me unpleasantly, and brood about what I'll do next. Visit the police station, obviously. Hope very much that this is all nothing, that it's a different symbol altogether. Go and see Arlene, assuming she's still there. I'm certain that she will be, because giving up a council house round here is like shooting yourself in the foot and then the other foot too. Whether she'll let me in or not is another matter.

Stomach growling with confusion at the time shift, I brave the breakfast room, which is now playing a tinny muzak version of what after a few minutes I judge to be the Vengaboys' 'We Like to Party!'. I help myself to wrinkled sausages and solid scrambled eggs left in silver tureens, and then I remember why it is I don't come to Marebridge.

A woman comes in carrying two plastic jugs of juice, and she stops at my table. She wears a black skirt and white shirt, slightly stained, and slops some of the juice at my feet. 'Karen? Is that you?'

Oh no. Recognised already. I can't place her prematurely lined face, and then it's overlaid by the taut one of a sixteen-year-old, a high ponytail, and a sneering face. Sinead Cowden. In my year at school, a bully and occasional ally of Jen's when it suited, though way too downmarket for her.

I force a smile. 'It's me. Hi, how are you?'

She's working in an inn in our hometown, so she can't be doing all that well, but she starts telling me how she married Gary Graham, if I remember him, and they have three kids, the oldest fifteen already. I find this mildly shocking but I smile along.

'Not staying at your mum's?'

I remember too late that Sinead was an inveterate gossip, and that Jen only made nice with her to get at what she knew. It was Sinead who corroborated my evidence against Gareth. The bruises, the broken wrist. It was also her who told the police Jen and I had fought that day in school, and at the party too.

'Didn't want to get under her feet.'

'I saw her last week down at bingo. She never mentioned you were coming back.'

'Last-minute thing. Some book stuff I had to do.'

She inclines her head. 'Oh yeah, you write books, don't you. I don't have time to read.' One of my least favourite things for people to say. 'You should get one adapted for Netflix.'

Another of them. 'Um yeah, great idea, Sinead, I'll get right on it. So what's been happening in the area?' I want to know if there's talk about the missing girl, the possible link to your crimes. If there is, me being spotted here will only fan such rumours.

'Same old Marebridge. I saw you on telly a few times. Documentaries. Here, you're not back to see *him*, are you?' Her eyes goggle.

I think about pretending I don't know who she means, but I'm doomed to have only one 'him' in my life. 'I've not seen him since he went inside, Sinead. Why would I?'

'You two were always thick as thieves.'

'Well, that was until I found out he murdered eight women, including my best friend.'

She's chastised, and carries on her way with the juice and some platitudes about grabbing a drink with 'the girls' while I'm back. I'm relieved she's gone, but wonder if I'll feel Jen's wrath from beyond, describing her as my best friend. We would both have disputed that at times, back in the day. Certainly in the days before she died we could barely stand the sight of each other.

I've always shunned Facebook, maintaining a skeleton account under a semi-pseudonym of Kay Cruz, a profile picture of a sunset instead of my face. I hate the way social media stirs people up, scries mysteries from the runes of normal behaviour, finds crimes where none exist, pillories the innocent, forgives the guilty. I'm thankful that we didn't have it when everything happened with Jen, but even so there's no way to truly remake yourself if you're online. However, I have to admit it comes in handy for tracking people down. When I finally make my phone work I click on to Instagram, debating a cover-story post about being home for 'research', and see that Emelia has replied to my message from last night. *Fine. I land in Manchester at 1pm and I will come to your town first.* Wow. She must be really rattled to come somewhere as unbougie as Marebridge. Probably not an iced latte to be had within five miles. I also have four more messages from April about PR opportunities, which I ignore. I google cafés in Marebridge and suggest a place to Emelia. Then I can't avoid it any more and have to go to the police station.

DS Chris Donetti is exactly as I've been picturing him. A muscled poser, his shirt straining over his gym-shredded arms, tie buttoned tight over a prominent Adam's apple. Olive skin, dark hair buzzed short, nice-ish suit, glowering expression. Unfortunately, he is quite hot and clearly knows it. 'I was expecting you sooner.'

'Well, it takes a while to get here from New York,' I say snappishly, as he buzzes me into the police station. It's a different building, not the one I spent three days in back in 2004. They bulldozed that, built this new one that has cream walls and navy carpets like an airport hotel. It's a Saturday but the place is busy, everyone perhaps called in to try and find Lara.

'This is quite time-sensitive, Ms Walker.'

I want to say it's Mrs Cruz, but the feminist in me won't allow it. I never called myself Mrs. Only took Santiago's name at all as a shield against the world. 'I know. Is there any news?' Any sign of Lara Milton, I mean. I imagine him saying, *Oh yeah, she's fine actually, turns out she went on a no-phones yoga retreat*, and I can just turn around and go home to New York. Not that it's home, not really.

'No. That's why we need your eyes on the scene. But let me brief you first.'

I follow him down a windowless corridor that smells of photocopier ink and bad coffee. 'But it can't be him,' I say. 'He's in prison. Isn't he?'

He shuts the interview-room door behind us, placing a plastic cup of water in front of me without asking. 'Of course he's in prison.'

'Did you actually check?'

'How could he get out of . . . ?'

'But did you check? With your own eyes?'

'As it happens, I did. And yes, he was there in his cell, very much enjoying all the fluster.'

'You spoke to him?'

'Routine questions. I didn't want to stay in there longer than I had to.' I like him more for this. I too would like to see you behind bars with my own eyes, if I could bear to see you at all, that is. 'He did kind of – hint that he knew something about this case.'

My heart falters. 'What? What did he say?'

'Oh, just stupid riddles. Likely just wants attention.' Donetti hesitates. 'He asked if we were talking to you.'

'I can't see him!' I snap.

'I'm not asking you to. But he did indicate he wants to.'

I shake my head to clear it. 'So – how can this be connected, if he didn't do it? If he's locked up?'

'That's what we need to figure out. Sit down, please.'

I feel like asking, *Am I under arrest, Officer?* the way a TV character would when they have something to hide, but I know that I'm not. I sit and he opens a manila file and slides it over to me. The smell of his cologne fills the narrow, bare room. 'Tell me if anything sticks out.'

I look up at him. 'Is there—?'

'Nothing graphic. We haven't photographed the symbol, of course. Access is strictly limited.'

I turn over some pages. There are pictures of a young woman with long dark hair and a choppy fringe, printed off social media. The usual shots of holding up cocktails, cheeks pressed to those of other young women, running a 10k, blah blah. So far, so Emelia. Lara works for the local council, lives alone in a second-floor flat in town, no family except a grandmother who died last year. Nothing that stands out in any way. 'What am I looking for?'

He gives me another scowl. 'Anything you notice. A connection to Hughes.'

'But how could there be a connection?' I say again. 'At most someone's playing a prank, right? I mean, a few people have seen the symbol, so someone could have reproduced it. If it is the same one.' And I'm still hoping it isn't.

'There's a significant amount of blood in the apartment.' He pulls the file back. 'It goes beyond a prank. I've already been over to Sheffield to check the old crime scene pictures.'

'And? The symbol matches?'

He shrugs. 'It's hard to be sure. It's . . . messy. That's why we need you to look. You're the only one who saw Hughes's original symbol.'

'There's no CCTV or anything?'

'Not from the flats. She was last captured walking past the Tesco Express about a hundred metres away, along with her friend Melissa. And none of the other tenants saw or heard a thing that night. So it's up to me to figure out how a young woman can vanish from her own flat without making so much as a sound.'

I can see they don't have much to go off. 'Anyone in her life – boyfriend? Ex?'

He glowers further. 'We do actually think of those things, you know. It may not be like in books . . .'

Oh, here we go. He knows who I am, he's researched me.

'. . . but we aren't totally incompetent. Lara didn't have a boyfriend, didn't date, and there was no one in her life of any concern, according to friends.' But would they know? I have thought of this often over the years, when going on dates, inviting random men to my place or going to theirs, unfamiliar apartments in unfamiliar parts of the city. If I vanished no one would have any idea where I was. People might tell the police the same thing: *no, there was no one.*

'So what's your theory – a copycat?'

'It could be. He has his fans.'

'A copycat who knows how to draw the symbol?'

He shrugs. 'It seems abduction is the most likely explanation, unfortunately. We're tracking her bank cards and she didn't just slip away or have a mix-up about a holiday. That much blood – she'd be badly injured. Also, her phone was left behind in the apartment. Her friend said that was massively out of character – and leaving the door open too, and the lights on. She was taken, almost certainly.'

My mouth is dry, so I drain the little plastic cup, hearing it crack under my hands. 'Nothing in the file means anything to me. He often chose dark-haired women, but not always.' You were varied in your tastes, shall we say. I never knew what motivated you. What made you choose Emelia, the one with the strength and luck to get away. Why you never chose me. I heave a sigh. 'OK. Take me to see it.' I may as well get it over with.

'First we need to get some elimination prints. Obviously you should try not to touch anything, but just in case. It's hard not to.'

It feels churlish to complain, so I let them roll my fingers over an ink pad, and a female officer comes to swab my cheek for DNA comparison. As I breathe in her cheap shampoo, I'm starting to feel like a criminal again. They took my prints back then, my DNA too. Not that it would have done much good. Jen and I lived in each other's pockets, we borrowed each other's clothes – of course my DNA would be on her. Or rather, I borrowed her clothes. She would not have been caught dead in any of my New Look rags.

Urgh. Bad joke.

Donetti just stands there the whole time with his arms folded. The female officer, who has a jaunty little ponytail, keeps glancing at him. 'All done, Sarge.' She loved saying that, I can tell. *Arrest me, Sergeant, I've been a bad girl.* Yuck. 'Can we go then?' I say ungraciously.

'Thank you for your cooperation,' he replies, with an equal lack of grace. He leads me out, not to a squad car, but to a normal saloon, a hybrid of some kind.

'Am I allowed in the front or are you going to push my head down into the back?' I'm being a bitch to cover my nerves. Because what if it is the same symbol? What does it mean?

He sighs in response and starts the car. We don't talk for the first ten minutes of the drive through town, snarled in lunchtime traffic. I see more Jeeps and BMWs than I could have imagined, more evidence of money.

'Place isn't what it used to be,' I remark without thinking.

'Meaning?'

'More cash about, I suppose. It was a right dump when I lived here. You're not from the area?' He must be about my age, and I'd have remembered someone handsome like him at school. Jen would have been all over him like peanut butter on toast.

'Burnley.'

'Why'd you move here? Good schools and all that?'

He blinks. 'No. I'm not married – I mean, I don't have kids. A job just came up and I wanted to work in Major Crimes.'

'Do you remember hearing about it, at the time? Him?'

'Of course. Our very own serial killer.'

'Hardly the first.' The Yorkshire Ripper was who really put us on the map.

'No. It gave me some flavour of what that was like, I suppose, for my mum, when she was young in the seventies and eighties. The terror. That there was like this – ghost, just coming out of the darkness, impossible to stop. Body after body piling up and no one could catch him.'

I bite my lip, almost hard enough to draw blood. Your reign of terror was the same, if with a slightly lower body count. You were caught sooner, because of me. But not soon enough.

He says, 'I remember you too. From the trial. And before.'

'Before?'

'Your friend. When they found her.'

I frown. 'That was hardly reported.' I was a minor, and never charged with anything in the end. Outside of Marebridge, it wasn't widely known that I had been a suspect.

'Dad was on the force too. They all knew about it, talked about it down the pub. You remember the Amanda Knox thing – when that happened, he said it reminded him of you.'

I roll my eyes slightly. The only similarity is that we were both young women and both had a friend die. Amanda Knox barely even knew poor Meredith Kercher. I had known Jen for almost thirteen years when she died.

'Yes, well, a certain sexist narrative always wants to blame a young girl for things. Not the obvious culprit, you know, the man who actually did it.'

'It wasn't like that. He felt sorry for you.'

I'm shocked by this. 'What? Why?'

'They were making you a scapegoat, Dad could see that. Trying to pin it on you, and you were terrified. Probably why you gave the evidence about the boyfriend, that Gareth Hale.'

I look down at my hands. 'I blame myself every day for that.'

'You shouldn't. You only told them what you thought, what you knew, and the CPS made the case. It was just unlucky.'

Unlucky. Not the word I would have chosen.

He puts on his indicator and pulls neatly into a parking space on a tree-lined road, large Victorian houses on either side. A primary school is on its break further down the street, the children as loud as birds chattering. 'Come on.' He puts something on the car and I glance at it. 'Police permit. Saves hunting for a parking space.'

'Is that – strictly what you're meant to do?'

He throws me a look. 'I think investigating an abduction trumps some middle-class mum's need to not walk ten feet to her Range Rover.' Oh no. He's not a twat after all, or he is, but he's one I might like. Annoying.

We walk a few paces and I recognise the building from the news article. Those steps, the ones Lara was last seen going up. A nice enough house, but with the neglect of a shared space, old post in the hallway, paint peeling from the doors. He knows the entry code, and leads me up the stairs to the second floor. It's the only flat on that level. No one would ever be up here except for Lara and her visitors, and it's cleaner, no dried leaves blown in. He has a key to unlock the door and then we're in.

The flat is musty and hot. Skylight windows overlook the town and the moors beyond. It feels intolerable to be here, walking among Lara's things, when she isn't. I would hate it so much if people had to look around my flat without me, deciphering clues about my life. The half-burnt Yankee Candle on the mantelpiece, the underwear drying on a rack, mostly practical cotton sets, which tells me she wasn't currently sleeping with anyone. The unwashed pan in the sink, that she probably intended to do the next day. High heels kicked off by the door, indicating she came in safe from her night out. Plastic bags pulled out from under the sink, littering the floor, and that gives me a jolt too.

'These were left like this?'

'As you see.'

You used bags. Hence Bagman. Does it mean something? I want to rifle through her clothes, unstopper all the bottles in the cupboard. I want to run my hands over her life and try to answer the question of why her, why now, what is going on.

I'm deliberately not looking at what is on the wall.

A small flat, kitchen/living room, one bedroom, bathroom with shower but no bath. I bet she hated that. I bet she said to her friends all the time, *Yeah, it's OK but I want to move somewhere with a bath, ideally some outdoor space.* And maybe now this is the last place she'll ever live.

'Is that the symbol?' says Donetti impatiently.

I have to look. I turn my head slowly, fill myself with breath as if to cushion me. On the blank white wall is daubed a pattern in dried, rusty brown. And suddenly I'm back in that prefab classroom sometime in 2004. I couldn't say what date or time it was, but I recall exactly the texture of the leather notebook it was drawn in. In pen that time. Not in blood. The curves, the lines. Is it? I think it is.

'It's the same?' He can tell from the way I'm hyperventilating, I imagine.

'How?' I gasp out. I realise that I didn't truly believe it could be the one, not deep down, not until this moment. 'How can it be?'

'That's what we need to find out.'

'He's definitely in prison?'

I realise I have groped for Donetti's arm and am clinging on tight, like someone drowning. He pats my back, surprisingly kind.

'Yes. He's safely locked up, I promise.'

'Oh God.' Maybe I'm going to be sick? Contaminate the crime scene? I breathe heavily and watch the play of sunlight on the frayed carpet until it stops.

'So that's a positive ID. As far as you can tell this is the same symbol used by Aaron Hughes, left behind at his murder sites.'

'Yes. Yes, that's the one.'

Chapter Four

From *Becoming Bagman* by Karen Walker

How well do you remember the things you do in an average day? Exactly what time you left the house, which neighbours you saw in the hallway, what you had for breakfast? You might think that you would, but the truth is you live most of your life on automatic pilot, and if you don't know something is going to prove significant, you likely won't remember it at all, or you'll remember it wrongly. I learned this when I was questioned over the death of my friend Jen Rollason, at the age of seventeen. The police seemed to find it suspicious that I didn't recall all the details of my day at school, the journey home, the exact last time I'd seen her and what she said to me. Our conversation in the school lobby, witnessed by several people. The bus she took home, if she told me where she was going and who she was meeting. My memories were jumbled, it's true. But I was scared and worried, which also affects your recall, and I hadn't known I would need to remember any of it. If you are ever unlucky enough to find yourself a witness to a crime, you will likely realise the same.

◆　◆　◆

When I finally manage to breathe again, Donetti looks at his watch.

'Alright, thank you, Ms Walker. Did you want me to arrange a flight back for you?'

'What? I can't go now. I have to know what's going on.'

I will need to tell Emelia that it's the same symbol, feel the same cold fear spread through her that is now into my fingers and toes.

It can't be. But it is.

'There were other clues that linked it to him? Please. I need to know everything.'

He walks me through it again, showing a patience I would not have suspected he had. Maybe he's the kind who's good with victims, with the vulnerable. Arsey to everyone else. 'So her friend, that's Melissa O'Donald, says she left her on the street down there, at the base of the steps. Melissa called herself a cab and Lara watched out the window till she got in, waved her off. That's been confirmed by the driver and Melissa's parents, who she lives with. But Lara doesn't turn up to work and doesn't answer Melissa's texts all the next day. And these girls are used to sending a lot of texts, so Melissa calls round. The door was open, not just unlocked but ajar. Lara's shoes were kicked off like this, but the bed hadn't been slept in or the shower used, which suggested she made it back in here, but not into bed. She cooked herself something to eat before bed. The TV was on standby so maybe she watched something. The dress she was wearing is over the chair in there, and her pyjamas look to have been taken out from under her pillow, but they're gone. Her phone was plugged in by the bed so, wherever she is, she doesn't have that. And the lights were left on, which her friend said she'd never do.'

'So then what? She let someone in, at that time of night?'

'We don't know.'

'Or someone came over? She invited them?'

'It's possible. Melissa gave us the impression Lara was going straight to bed though, after they said goodbye.' And that's what it looks like. You don't come in and eat beans and take your dress off if you're planning a hot rendezvous, do you? So did someone get in here and abduct her, in her cosy pyjamas? Were her feet bare when they took her? I shudder at the idea.

'What did – that?' I gesture to the sign.

'Like I said, it's her blood type and DNA. It was dry when the first officers arrived, less than twenty minutes after the alarm was raised, so we feel confident it happened several hours before, likely not long after Lara returned home.'

'Was there a weapon?'

'Not that we found. Melissa thinks there's a knife missing from the kitchen, but she can't be sure.' It might not have been a knife. Scissors, or a Stanley knife like I used to open my box of books.

'He used a calligraphy knife,' I say, staring out the window. 'For the – exactness.'

'I'm aware.'

I'd held it. The same tool you used on some of them, playing with it while I sat at the desk in your flat. My prints were on it when the police searched the place. 'Were there any fingerprints?'

'We only found hers. She was something of a clean freak, her friend said, and didn't invite people over often.'

You never left prints either. It isn't hard, if you're careful. I suck in more air. They should open a window, it's so stuffy in here. 'Please. I need to know what's happening. Can I sit in on some interviews, talk to people? Maybe there's some link between Lara and him.'

He twists his mouth, drawing attention to his cleft chin. 'It's not really allowed.'

'You said your bosses, they don't believe it's linked to him. That it's not the same symbol?'

'Well, maybe they'll change their mind now you've IDed it.'

'Or if we can find a link, maybe we can help Lara.' Eight women you killed. Eight. I cannot bear it if it becomes nine.

He thinks about it for a moment. 'I suppose we could talk to the neighbours again, if they agree.'

'OK. So who else has seen it? The symbol?' Who could possibly have done this, since it can't be you?

He lists them for me. 'Anyone who found a victim or viewed their body. The police from the time, the CSIs and so on. Emelia Han. Perhaps some other kids from your school, friends of Hughes.' Then there's the copy Jen claimed to have, which may or may not have been real. 'And of course, you.'

Me. Here's the thing I remember most from before, about when you're the key witness in a crime – you'd better solve it quick or people are going to start to think you did it yourself.

Donetti ushers me down the stairs, carpeted and rarely hoovered, clearly. The next floor down brings a thirty-ish man with large headphones, his flat full of tech but with bare walls, no cushions or rugs. 'Good afternoon, sir, do you have a few minutes to talk to us?' Donetti is stiff but polite.

The neighbour glances at his phone clock. 'I have a few seconds, I suppose.'

'That's kind of you.' So Donetti can be sarcastic when the occasion demands.

The man – Jonathan Kremer is his name – doesn't ask us to sit down, just leans against his fridge. The place has a chill, uncared-for air, and smells of burnt toast.

'I told you everything I know – I was here that night, yes, but I usually have headphones on for work or gaming.'

I ask, 'And your job is . . . ?'

'Sales. I work remotely.' What a closed-off life, to not even notice the girl upstairs being abducted.

'And you really heard nothing at all?'

He shrugs. 'Nothing that I can remember anyway.'

'Was she noisy?'

'All upstairs neighbours are noisy,' he says with a slight smirk. 'We had a chat about it once, and she said she'd get a rug, not wear her heels in the house.' I think of her shoes removed by the door. 'Honestly, we didn't talk much. It's not that kind of building. Might take a parcel for each other sometimes, that's all. Mostly me taking for her. Christ, she gets a lot, flowers, takeaways, all kinds of things. A right pain, to be honest.'

I'm trying to think what possible connection there could be between you and Lara. 'Did she have visitors, ever? You would have heard, probably?'

He screws up his face, as if trying to remember. 'Sometimes, I guess. I can't say when exactly.'

'A date? A man?'

'Mm, yeah, I think so. But like I said, I didn't exactly take notes. So sorry, I don't think I can help.'

I have one more question. I want to make him care that his upstairs neighbour, who lives just metres away from him, might be dead or fighting for her life.

'The front door – is it easy to get in?'

40

'It's on a code, but our entry phones don't work, and it often doesn't close properly. The woman downstairs never shuts it right – she's always carting this massive buggy. One time I had a new router nicked right out of the hall. So yeah, easy enough.' So someone could have gained entry, and then it just would have taken Lara to let them in her flat door. But she had a security chain – surely she would have used it?

'You didn't buzz anyone in that night? No deliveries or take-aways or anything?'

He shakes his head. 'I answered all these questions already. Can I get back to work now?'

Donetti looks at me with a clear message – *not much help.* 'Alright, thank you, Mr Kremer.' Back in the hallway, he throws me a little side glance. 'Nice to be so untroubled by life.'

'Isn't it.'

Oh no, we are bonding. I didn't want that.

In the downstairs flat is a harassed woman with a baby in a sling and a loud toddler, who has thrown baked beans all over the table and floor. Marianne Cooper, Donetti said.

'Oh hi, come in, come in. Um . . . God, sorry, it's such a mess.' She hurriedly wipes off the kitchen chairs and I sit gingerly on one. The toddler is liberally smeared in bean juice, and stares at me, suspicious.

The mother raises her voice over the racket of the children. 'I'm sorry, I didn't think of anything new.'

Donetti raises his voice too. 'Could you just tell it all to us again, for Ms Walker? She's a – new witness.'

'Um, well, let's see, we would have been long in bed by the time Lara came home, but I heard her on the stairs, clumping in her heels. It's a wonder she didn't break her neck, bless her. And she was on the phone, I think, I could hear her voice – she never thinks to keep it down at night. But she's a nice girl. Always says hello to Charlie, doesn't she, Charlie?'

Charlie – gender unclear – is picking avidly at their nose.

She goes on, 'So awful what's happened. I've been on at Nick, that's my husband, to install one of those door cams for us. I'm always buzzing deliveries in without asking for ID.'

I had seen a towering stack of Amazon boxes in the recycling bin by the door. 'So you didn't hear anyone else come in that night?'

She also adopts an expression of intense thinking. 'Um, I was up with Saffron at some point. I looked at the clock – it was about half twelve, I think? I did hear a car outside actually, now that I think of it. Did I tell you that before? They were going too fast, that's why I noticed. We're thinking of starting a campaign to get humps. People come down the street so quickly!'

Donetti is making a note. 'You didn't, but that's very helpful.' Half twelve was too late to be the friend's taxi leaving, so it could be relevant. Could have been Lara's late-night visitor. Her abductor.

I say, 'Did you ever notice Lara having visitors, a boyfriend or anything like that? Dates?'

'Sometimes, yes. There was this one who was quite rude though. Almost shoved us out of the way in the hall, didn't he, Charlie? I mean it takes time to move the buggy, I can't help it.'

'When was this?'

She shakes her head. 'Sorry, I don't remember exactly. A few weeks ago, maybe? A month or so?'

Donetti says, 'Might you be able to do a photofit of the man?'

She frowns. 'Mm, I don't remember much, to be honest. He was big is all I know. Big and rude. White guy, local accent. One of those bomber jackets. I thought he seemed like a right thug, I was pleased he didn't turn up again. She could do so much better.' The present tense seems to clang in the room.

42

'What time was this?' I glance at Donetti, who's making more notes. Did he not think to ask any of this before?

'Must have been a weekend, if she was home. Let's see, Nick was at the football, so it was probably a Saturday afternoon, a few weeks back, a month maybe.'

So maybe there was a man, one who had been given the elbow by Lara. Maybe we are getting somewhere after all. And maybe it is nothing whatsoever to do with you and I can go back to pretending that those years of my life didn't happen.

◆　◆　◆

Donetti drops me back at the police station to collect my car. 'So you'll be staying in town for a few days?'

'I guess so. I want to help, if I can.'

He thinks about it. 'Look, the higher-ups are pretty clear this is a non-starter. It's hard to see a match with the old pictures. Too much – dripping and that. And he's been in prison ten years, so how can he be involved? They want to focus on other leads.'

'But you don't agree.'

'If you say it's the same symbol, I believe you. But I can't think how.'

'Me neither.'

After a moment he says, 'You could come with me to interview some of the witnesses again. Off the books, if they agree. There might be something that leaps out at you.'

'If you think it would do any good.'

He shrugs. 'Honestly, I'll try anything. We're really hitting a dead end on this case so far.' The word *dead* seems to resonate.

'Whatever you need.' At least then I will know exactly what's going on. 'I'll leave you here. I'm going to walk a bit, clear my head.'

43

It seems crazy I have no idea where my own mother even lives, but I'm assuming it's the same place I left her, a pebble-dashed council monstrosity in a row overlooking the moors. Grey skies and almost dark already at two in the afternoon. I head there on autopilot, my feet remembering the journey from the woods to our house, less than ten minutes. I used to feel I would actually die of boredom if I had to walk this route ever again, day after day after day exactly the same. It's so horribly familiar.

The dank cottage where you lived with your crazy father, that's only a few minutes away, edging on to the moor, and I go the long way to avoid it. The row of depressing shops, a bookie's, a chippie, a closed-down tattoo parlour. I fought so hard to get out of here. Now I'm back and I blame you for this along with everything else. Our house was number 17, and how many hundreds of days I spent walking up the hill to it, trudging with the wind in my face, dreading the cold and dark house, where so often she'd let the electricity meter run out and I'd have to hope the emergency bit would last until the morning so I could shower for school. I couldn't always. Which Jen never let me forget. I realise I'm gasping, and not from the climb, since several years of ruthless New York SoulCycle classes have left me fitter than when I lived here. From the weight of the past.

She won't be home. Some other family will surely live there now. Or maybe she did remarry or maybe she's dead. No, I would have heard if she was dead. One of the local busybodies or her many relations would have tracked me down and told me.

I stand in front of the door with its peeling paint. Outside, an empty plant pot filled up with fag ends, and a battered wheely bin I can smell even in the cold. I have to ring the bell. I can't. But I have to.

There's no answer for a while, and I'm drawing in a big breath, preparing to walk away, when I see a dark shadow behind the bubbled glass, and it's opened and it's Arlene. Fag in hand. Smell of cheap perfume and hairspray. Burble of daytime TV up loud.

She's aged. Her hair is dyed an approximation of its original red, showing grey at the roots, and her face and cleavage, exposed in a too-tight top, are wrinkled.

She doesn't know me for a second. I see it, and then her face goes blank. 'Heard you was in town.'

Were, I used to scream at her. Were, were. How could I ever amount to anything when my mother could barely speak English?

'Yeah. How are you, Mum?'

It feels weird to call her that when I so rarely did. I'd always felt more like she was the kid and I was the mother. But Arlene is not stupid, despite her poor life choices.

She takes a drag on her cigarette and exhales. 'Back cos of that murder, are you?'

'There's no murder.'

'Well, whatever it is.'

'Can I come in? It's freezing out here.'

'Suit yourself.'

She stands back to let me in. It's not much warmer inside – she always preferred to save her coins for more important expenses, like vodka – but I note that it is clean and well-maintained, in as much as it can be when it's all built of MDF and peeling apart. There are photos on the fridge of kids I don't recognise, likely the children of some of my many cousins from her side, and a few cheap *Live Laugh Love*-style plaques scattered about that make me roll my eyes with cynicism. *Home is where the love is.* Yeah, right. There are no pictures of me, as if she never had a family at all. Dad wasn't around much – him and Arlene had been kids when they had me, barely twenty, and he soon skipped off to work as a builder down south, later leaving the country for projects in Dubai and Saudi. Back then I met up with him maybe once every two years at Manchester or Liverpool airports, where he would give me expensive presents meant for a much younger child. When I was fourteen he got married to an air hostess. I wasn't invited and we haven't spoken since.

That's not entirely true. He sent me a message after the trial, when I was in the news all the time, a rambling late-night email that made me think he was drunk, though it's supposed to be hard to get booze in Bahrain, where he ended up. *I never done right by u Karen but y did u have to go and do this.* So that was nice, my own father believing the rumours. That I abetted you somehow, that I had known and let you kill anyway.

Once in the kitchen, in the familiar smell of fried food and smoke, I feel like I'm having a minor panic attack. Throat closing over, breath shallow, the works. She leans against the kitchen counter, not offering me tea.

'So you're back.'

'Looks like it.'

'How'd you find out? It make the news over there?'

'No. Someone told me.' I won't say it was at a book event or I'll sound snooty, even though barely thirty people were there.

'They're saying on Facebook it's just like him. What he did.'

'Well, it can't be, can it? He's in prison.'

I hold my breath for a second in case she tells me you aren't, that you've been released already, didn't I hear, or escaped. But no. You're serving eight whole-life tariffs, you will never be released.

She takes another drag. 'My mate Sandra works up there, you know. Prison. You wouldn't know her. Friend from book club.'

I must have gaped at that because she bridles. 'Well, I never had time to read when you were about, did I? Working all hours. But I always liked it, when I were small.'

I want to ask what they read, if it's the Booker shortlist or more Colleen Hoover, but now is not the time. 'Your friend, she works with him?'

46

'Oh yeah. Got to know him fairly well, she has. Only a few of them on his wing. High security. Pays better. She's saving for a static caravan.'

'And?'

Another drag. 'And what?'

'Are you telling me this for a reason?'

That makes her smirk, that I showed temper. 'Charming. She says he talks about you. About your book.'

'Which book?' Another snooty question.

She chuckles. 'The one about him, Karen.'

'The memoir? It's not out yet.'

'All the same. She says he talks about it. What you might have said about him.'

'I guess he'll disagree with my account.'

'Course he will. Still saying he never did it, isn't he.'

After eight life sentences. 'Well, that was probably inevitable.' I'm hit by another tranche of memories of that week, the one after they found Jen. The police station, the endless questions. Passing you in a corridor, on the other side of reinforced glass, meeting your eyes. People thought we must have been involved, to be questioned for so long, but we were never charged. We alibied each other, and then I incriminated Gareth and we were home and free.

Gareth. Where is he now? He got out of prison, of course, when you were caught, but not before he'd served almost ten years. Not my biggest fan, it's safe to imagine.

'Do people still talk about me?' I can't help but ask.

Arlene picks a bit of tobacco out of her mouth. 'What's done is done, Karen. What matters is you don't stir it all up again, with this book of yours. Why did you come back? You only just got away last time, didn't you.' She means the trial. Or maybe the time before that, after Jen.

'That's not why I'm here. The missing girl . . .'

'Oh, come on, we don't even know she's missing. Like as not she's just gone off with a fella, or she's trying to make someone jealous, cause a scene. Get a few days off work.'

I wish this to be true so much I respond with anger. 'Mum, her door was open. There was blood on the wall.' She stares at me. 'What?'

'Nothing. You called me Mum.'

'Well, that's what you are.' I resist adding *not that you'd know it.*

'You believe what they say then, about the blood, and the symbol? That it's the same?'

'It looked the same to me.' Donetti said they were planning to keep this out of the press as much as possible, to avoid 'misunderstandings'. I know what he means. To avoid people saying you weren't the Bagman after all.

'You'd really remember? Years since you saw it.'

'Of course I do.' It was only my testimony that linked your symbol to the one left by the perpetrator of seven murders, drawn on to walls, carved into human skin. No copies of it could be found in your possession, and you'd never let anyone else have one, or so you said. I didn't even have one myself, relying on memory alone. It was shaky. There was never much evidence against you, and that's why I'm so afraid now.

'Well, I hope for everyone's sake it's a lot of nothing.' She shifts, throwing her fag end into a bowl on the counter. 'Suppose you don't drink tea any more? All that "coffee to go"?' She affects a surprisingly good New York accent.

'I'd love a cup of tea,' I say. 'It's all muck over there. They don't even boil the water.'

'How do you live?' But she has softened, and I have softened. She busies herself with water, teabags, mugs, while I move into the hallway, eyes roaming over things. True enough, there is a small bookcase, which we never had when I lived here. And there are copies of all my books. *You Weren't There*, *Family Ties*, and even *Desert Orchids*. She comes up behind me, with the tea steaming. 'Go on through.'

I can't resist saying, 'Looking at your library here.'

'They weren't bad. Your books.'

'Thanks.'

'Bit boring, mind. I prefer murders and that.'

I sniff. 'You wouldn't if you'd been involved in one.'

'Was I not then?'

I don't answer that.

After a while of awkward chat about New York, her job in a pub, and news of her various friends, cousins, and siblings (marriages, babies, custodial sentences), I ask if I can use the loo. She gives me a withering look. 'It's your home, Karen, you know where it is.'

That's a loaded statement if ever there was one, but I let it slide because I want to get upstairs. I push open the door to my old room, which smells of warm dust, and find it mostly unchanged. The same nineties wallpaper with shiny accents, the same navy shagpile, the rickety white wardrobe, covered in scraped-off stickers and bits of Blu Tack. The desk where I tried my best to study my way out of here. I wrench open the bottom drawer, which still sticks on its runner. There's everything, just as I left it. Old essays crammed into files, my curly handwriting, red ticks from various teachers. *Well done, Karen. Another triumph*. It was almost too easy to be the best, at my school anyway. But that isn't what I'm looking for.

I quickly tear through all my old schoolwork, trying to remember when I last saw it. Not since I moved out, I'm sure. Long before your arrest and trial. Suddenly there it is and I catch my breath, as if I'm looking at a picture of an atrocity, an obscenity. It's not the actual symbol – you drew it for me once, but you wouldn't let me keep it, however much I begged. Instead, it's the ghostly imprint it left on the paper below, torn off my file-block. You didn't lean hard enough for me to be able to trace it, or for this to be any use as evidence, and in any case I never gave it to the police. I rub it with my fingers. I could never truly forget it, but time has clouded my judgement, and I wonder if I'm really sure about this new one, drawn with blood on a missing girl's wall, whether it's enough to know if I need to be scared again.

Chapter Five

From *Becoming Bagman* by Karen Walker

I'm aware that the writing of this book will bring some judgement on me, but I've lived with judgement since I was seventeen years old and my best friend died. I'm also aware that accounts of what happened will differ. My experience of Aaron Hughes is a unique one, as perhaps the person closest to him in the world, who all the same never saw the side of him that his victims did, in their last moments. I'll never know why I was afforded that privilege, of being the one to survive.

Someone else who survived, fighting for her life against all odds, is Emelia Han. Emelia is aware of this book, of course, and has chosen not to talk to me for it – a decision I respect, though I regret it. Emelia has built a wellness business and become a successful motivational speaker after her escape from 'the Bagman'. I have nothing but admiration for how she has risen above her ordeal. You will all know the amazing story of her survival. It's being made into a TV series as we speak, and in any case she has spoken about it widely, both in person and on her Instagram. She's a true inspiration to women everywhere, with her grit and tenacity.

◆ ◆ ◆

As I'm walking to the coffee shop to meet Emelia, I'm surprised to note a few nicer shops around and that the café offers avocado toast and shakshuka. All those middle-class couples moving back here during Covid, seeking space for their precious offspring. The café windows are steamed with breath, cosy and lit up on this dreary day. It used to be a greasy spoon, where you and I would huddle in a booth to share metal pots of tea and traybakes. As I scan the room for Emelia, my gaze pauses at the counter and I stop dead, because there is Jen.

It's Jen. *Jen!* Her glossy hair, her swishy ponytail, even her clothes – a slip dress over a T-shirt and DMs. Finally, my brain catches up. It isn't her. Jen has been dead for almost twenty years. *Get a grip, Karen.* But this girl – the waitress – looks so like her that I'm just standing there goldfishing. She spots me and gives me a surly look that is also pure Jen.

'Did you need something?'

'Um, I'm meeting – someone. I'm sorry. You just look . . . like someone I know.'

Her expression changes. 'Oh my God, you're *her*, aren't you. You're back?'

I'm so confused. 'Who . . . ?'

'She was my sister.'

I don't understand because this girl can't be more than eighteen, and Jen didn't have a sister, unless you count me.

She rolls her eyes. 'We have the same dad. I was born after she died, obvi.'

Of course. Ash, the area's most eligible widower, did remarry after all, but not my mother. Some younger woman, probably, capable of bearing him a second daughter. A new Jen. Her nametag reads *Rosalind*. A pretty name. I wonder if she lives in the same house with the pony paddock, if she sleeps in Jen's pink princess bedroom. I calculate how old Ash must be now, if he was in his late thirties when I knew him. If this girl is seventeen or eighteen, then she was born not long after Jen died. A replacement family.

God, she really looks like Jen. As if her mother had almost no genetic impact at all. 'I'm sorry. I didn't know about you.'

'Dad didn't want me in the news. The true-crime people still get in touch, sometimes. You're here because of that missing girl?'

She's sharp. 'Yes. I – needed to see what was going on.'

'And you have your book coming out too.'

'Yeah. But that's not why.' She gives me a sceptical look. 'Will you tell your dad I'm in town and I – I don't know if he'd want to see me, or . . .'

How does Ash feel about me? I have no idea. After your trial I distanced myself, running from the idea that Jen might be alive if not for me. Does he blame me? Does he too think I should have known what you were?

'I'll ask. But I dunno what he'll say. He doesn't like to talk about her, always starts crying.'

'Do you I mind if I ask – I'm sorry, what's your mum's name?' Please God it isn't someone I went to school with.

'Lucy. Her maiden name was Coxon, not that we should be using terms like "maiden name" any more.'

Lucy Coxon. Who . . . ?

'Miss *Coxon*?' I exclaim. 'He married her?' Of course he did. Our pretty young French teacher, maybe five years older than Jen and me. That makes perfect sense. I try to recover from this shock. 'Well, I'm pleased he found happiness.' I wonder does this girl know about my mother, the marriage that might have taken place, had Jen not died? 'I'll just – I'm waiting for a friend.'

At that moment, the door jangles and I can instantly tell, without even looking, that Emelia has come in. She gives out that Kardashian aura, the conviction that she is so famous everyone will be looking at her, which ironically draws more attention than just behaving normally. She has sunglasses on indoors, and a baseball cap over a bun, a grey tracksuit I know will have cost hundreds of pounds despite looking like something you can get in the market for a fiver. Her nails are long and nude, filed into pointed spikes. I hate them.

I move towards her, gesturing to a table by the window.

'Too public,' she grouches.

'There aren't any others free.'

With a deep sigh, she sits down and picks up the wipe-clean menu. 'Urgh. What even is this place?' Her mid-Atlantic twang is stronger in person than on her videos, of which I have viewed every single one. I believe the term is *hate-watching*.

'It's a café, Emelia. And it's a lot fancier than it used to be, believe me.'

A different waitress has come over, I'm relieved to see, this one with piercings and dyed blue hair. Emelia lets out a deep exhale. 'Do you even have like, nut milks, non-dairy milks?'

'Of course; we have oat, soya, or coconut.'

'Huh.' She wasn't expecting that. 'An oat latte, one shot, skinny oat if you have it.' She looks expectantly at me, though she hasn't let me so much as see the menu. But I know my order.

'A pot of tea, please, and a rocky-road slice.' What you and I always got, cutting the cake into cubes and sharing it.

'So, I'm here, in this godforsaken rainy dump. What did you want to talk about?'

'Emelia.' I look at her across the table, this woman I can't stand, the only living person who might have an idea what things are like for me. 'You read the news reports?'

'Well, yeah, but they didn't say very much.'

'The symbol was there. On the wall.' Written in Lara Milton's blood, but I don't say that part out loud. Emelia knows better than anyone how you did it.

'But it could be anything.'

'I'm pretty sure it's the same.'

'I don't believe you.'

'Ask them to let you see it. They'd probably be glad to have it confirmed.' Though she likely would not recognise it – she never saw the whole thing, after all.

'How could it be the same?' She slumps back and I see why she has come all this way. She needs to know what's going on as well.

'Well, some people have seen it. The police officers on the old cases, some of his friends before, maybe the families, with the bodies . . . It's not no one, is my point.'

'But why would someone do this?'

'I don't know.' Neither of us wants to vocalise the two terrible options. A copycat, repeating your crimes. Or even worse than that. I don't even want to formulate the other option. My brain keeps running over the meagre evidence offered at your trial, most of it provided by me. Was it enough?

Was it right?

'Did you ever tell anyone what it looks like? Apart from the police?' I hate to ask her this. I hate the fact you tried to draw it on her, into the taut flesh of her stomach. She ran before you could, got away and saved herself, but not before you had started.

55

'Why shouldn't I, if I did? It's my story to reclaim. Anyway, it's not the whole thing. I never saw it.' She is fierce as the waitress brings our drinks and my cake. I slice it into small squares and push the plate to the middle. I take a bite, choking on its sweetness.

'OK. Question is, what do we do now?'

She stares at me and her eyes are huge and for a moment I see the real her, behind the Instagram filters and hashtags and make-up. 'It means . . . someone has this girl. Someone took her.'

'Yeah. Probably.'

Emelia shivers, as if monsters might emerge any minute from the bright corners of the bustling café and seize her. I can't blame her for feeling that way. I do too, and I didn't even experience what she did, running down that deserted country lane, as fast as her track-star legs would carry her, breath tearing in her lungs, blood pouring from her, every second she could pull ahead of you the difference between life or death. Emelia was at a conference in Harrogate when she was attacked, at the edge of the town where it becomes moors, so quickly you can blink and be in the wilderness. She had grown up in California and Hong Kong, with banker parents, truly international. Lacking access to a gym, and needing to keep up her training for the half-marathon she was about to do, she had driven to the countryside to go for a run, not anticipating how quickly it gets dark in the north in winter. A forest track, idyllic in the light, terrifying at night.

She had stopped to get her bearings and do some sprint-shifts. That's when a man stepped out of the bushes and flagged her down. He had lost his dog, he said, brandishing a collar and lead by way of proof. Any chance she could help him track it down? Emelia loved dogs, and would do anything to help one. She had no reason to doubt this man, who seemed so believable and nice. She wasn't from here. She didn't know about the murders that had terrorised the north for years before. She didn't know she had just run blindly into the path of the Bagman, and he was planning to make her his ninth victim.

'It's not him,' she says now.

'No.'

'He's in prison.'

'Yeah.' Though I still need to see that for myself, because people do escape, don't they? Ted Bundy escaped twice. He wasn't the brilliant predator he's made out to be. The police were just mind-numbingly incompetent, fooled by a handsome young white man with a law degree. That's the truth of serial killers. They don't succeed because they're fiendish, but because we let them. 'What's your plan? Are you going back to the States after your filming?'

She shrugs. 'I was. But if something is happening . . . I don't know if I can.'

I understand that urge. Terrifying as it is to be in your orbit, it's worse to not be here, not to know. It must be terrible for her. To me you are a real person, with a past, a family, but to her you are just a bogeyman. 'I'm going to stay. Try to look into it.'

'I can't stay here.' She looks around the café as if it's a refugee camp.

'There are some nice hotels in Manchester.'

'I have things planned, you know. Events, travel.'

'I have a book coming out in a month.'

She narrows her eyes. 'I had heard. After it was written.'

'I contacted you. You didn't answer.'

'I don't know why you think it's acceptable to profit from—'

'Oh, come on. You don't make any money from your Insta? You talk about it constantly. Your trauma.' I do my best not to put air quotes around that, because it was trauma, and I know that, and why shouldn't she make something out of it? I know her posts help people too, I see the comments. 'And what about this TV show, you aren't being paid for it?' *Survivor: The Emelia Han Story.*

She purses her lips. 'Your version of him – it's not mine.'

'I know that. We were friends for years, it's always going to be different.' The person before, and then, when we knew what you did, after. The truth is we both have a right to our views on the subject. She and I and all the dead girls in between, who don't get a say.

She sits back, gathers her Chanel bag to herself. 'Fine. I'll stick around. I guess the TV people will be pleased if I stay longer. Keep me updated on what you do.'

'Don't post about it, OK? They don't want it getting out that it's the same symbol.'

She huffs. 'Well, you don't post anything about me either.'

I can't help but roll my eyes. 'I never post anything, Emelia. Much to the annoyance of my publishers. Believe me, I'm not about to start now.'

She drums her nasty nails on the table. 'I want you to talk to someone. He's this like true-crime expert, worked on the TV show with me. He did a really successful podcast about the murders. He knows everything about – him.' She won't say your name. 'If anyone can find a link, it's Matt.'

As if I don't know everything? But I'll take all the help I can, so I nod. 'Stay in touch.'

'Urgh. OK.'

After Emelia goes, climbing into a taxi I can only assume she pre-booked, since Uber is but a twinkle in a tech bro's eye in this part of the world, I sit for a while. The cake has made me feel nauseous, and I don't know what to do. Or rather I do, but I can't face doing it yet. Instead I obsessively google everything I can about Lara Milton. People do this with the dead girls, and with me too. I used to get emails from those who had tracked me down via some old forum post or Tripadvisor review, to the point where I now change my email address every two years. I recommend it – very freeing. And of course I'm not really on any social media, much to April's chagrin. If she doesn't post on Insta at least once a day I think she's died. She's the kind of online person who feels the need to announce when she's 'unplugging', as if she's a beloved news anchor or the lead in a Broadway show.

But Lara Milton. Ordinary. Even boring. She works in marketing for the local council, she likes dogs though she doesn't have her own, she claims that nothing beats her late gran's roast dinner. She loves Taylor Swift, of course she does, and she pouts in her photos. She takes girls' holidays to Tenerife or Greece. She is twenty-nine years old and appears to never have had a proper boyfriend. Her best friend and 'work wife' is Melissa O'Donald, also twenty-nine. They go on a lot of spa days and drink Aperol spritzes. I've never had a friend like that. If Jen had lived, there's no way she would have gone on a spa day with me.

Not unless you got a pedicure first. Her voice in my head. I wonder what she'd have to say about this new sister, a mini-Jen full of attitude. She hated the idea of her mother being replaced, so I can only imagine what she'd feel about it happening to herself.

The thought haunts me all the way back to my downmarket hotel, picking up my car from outside the police station on the way. There's a new guy on reception, who eyes me frankly in a way that makes me double-lock my door. I flop down on the bed and mindlessly eat both packets of little shortbread biscuits. Maybe I can talk to Arlene's friend at the prison, get some intel that way. Donetti said he would inform the families I identified the symbol, and I can only imagine the pain that's going to cause. Maybe they won't believe it either. Speaking of the families, I need to visit Jen's dad. I remember him clinging to me at her funeral, crying into my hair and all down my school shirt. *Oh Karen. She was all I had left. What do I do now?* The worst I have ever felt, maybe. Or was it worse the day I made the phone call about you, to the police tipline? The audio was played at your trial. My halting, northern-accented voice.

Uh – I think maybe there's something up with my boyfriend. Um. Just some strange things. His name is Aaron Hughes and he lives at . . .

I had called you my boyfriend, yes, and that's how the world thinks of me, but the truth is that, like with Jen, our relationship was many things. Friend mostly. Best friend. I would have said soulmate at times, though not to your face. *Boyfriend* is both too big and too small for what you were to me.

I have to do something, filled with jittery energy that feels like electricity torching my nerve endings. If I sit still, I'll burn up. A ding announces that I have a message from Emelia, a shared contact. *Matt Podcast.* My annoyance with her feels like an old friend, a balm. Not yawning horror. *This is my crime guy, talk to him.* No please, not even a request. Her crime guy means the true-crime nut, the dark-web-diving weirdo. I sigh. I'm annoyed that she's ordering me about, as if I'm one of her 'team', but the truth is I'm grateful for any sliver of knowledge I can get, so I will do as she asks. Anything to prolong what I really came here to do and cannot face. Seeing you.

Chapter Six

From *Becoming Bagman* by Karen Walker

When you don't know that you're in a story, you don't know that you should try to remember things. I didn't know that, over the course of September to December 2004, I was getting to know, becoming best friends with, and if I'm honest, falling in love with a boy who would go on to become one of Britain's most prolific serial killers. How could I? He didn't even know it himself then. After maths class, the next time we would interact was in the Dale, which was a name we gave to a small wooded grove that ran through the middle of town, with steps down to a river. It was a place local kids went to drink, but I'd found my own little spot a bit further along from that, where a flat rock made a seat by the river. I went there a lot, sometimes writing in my notebook, the kind of anguished diary entries you make when you live in a small, depressed town and have never done a single interesting thing in your life.

One day I was there when the strange boy from maths class turned up. I heard rustling in the trees and jumped to a crouch – my mother had always warned me about 'dirty old men' and I was smart enough to realise being alone in the woods was a risk. Then I saw it was him, in his long leather coat, carrying a notebook like me.

'Oh. Hi.'

'Hi, Karen. How are you?' I liked how he talked, instead of just grunting like the boys at school.

'Eh, you know, bored out of my skull.'

'What are you writing?'

I shielded my cheap exercise book, embarrassed. 'Oh. I write sometimes.'

'Like a book?'

'Like a book.' I had never admitted this to anyone, though I was sure my mother had gone through my things, always asking what I had my nose stuck in. It was a thing we shared, he and I, our secret worlds. Of course I didn't know his was full of murder and madness. At least mine was only imaginary.

'Do you mind if I join you? I'll go if it makes you uncomfortable, just us here.'

That's one thing no one understands about him. In that era of casual groping and no means yes, he was uncommonly attuned to women's safety. I suppose that should have made me ask questions. How he knew so well that women could be afraid of men. 'Of course. I'll scream if you try to murder me.'

Yeah, I said that.

Then he was looking at me, with his luminous eyes. 'Tell me about yourself, Karen. You seem more interesting than most of the kids at school. Like you can talk about something that isn't football or *Big Brother*.'

'Tell you what?' I was bashful. Talking about yourself was not encouraged in Marebridge, and even having ambitions would bring instant ridicule.

'Your dreams, your hopes.' He leaned closer, his voice soft under the noise of the river. He smelled like cheap soap and old leather from the coat, a faint hint of grease from his hair before he started shaving it off. 'I want to know everything.'

I have to talk to Gareth. God, I don't want to talk to Gareth, and I'm sure I'm the last person he wants to talk to either. My book is not kind to him. But apart from Emelia and I, he's the one who knows the most about you and your crimes.

After your first trial, for the seven 'Bagman' murders, there were calls, most vocally from Gareth, that Jen's case be re-examined. What were the chances she'd known a serial killer but been murdered by someone else, after all? It had taken another year, another trial, and a vigorous campaign before Gareth was released and her death added to your toll. By then I was in New York and refused to give evidence again, though I did sign a statement that I might have been 'mistaken' in what I told the police back in 2004. Who can remember times and dates ten years later? You didn't even appear in court and the whole thing had the feel of a rubber stamp. Gareth out, you already in, so what difference did it make when you would die in prison anyway? But maybe it did, if there's another killer loose. After all, if anyone knows about insecure convictions, it's Gareth. And so I agree to the meeting DS Donetti has set up, the day after I arrive in Marebridge.

I crashed out hard in my nasty hotel room around 8 p.m., waking several times through the night with no sense of where I was, having nightmares about you being in the corner of my room with a knife in your hand, getting up over and over to check the door. It must be a strange situation when you're exonerated after a long prison sentence. You're in the same situation as any convict, where you've lost all your adult life, you have no skills and no money and probably no friends, and you also have the rage of knowing none of it was your fault. At least Gareth's parents, the Jeep-driving mother and lawyer father, who could not help his son in the face of my evidence, had stood by him, taken him back into the family home on the large farm they own. I gather he's still living there, though he'll be nearly forty now, and has been out for as long as you have been in. Ten years.

I put on my uniform of black jeans, white T-shirt, leather jacket, studded boots to kick away any accusations. Yes, I put him in prison, but it wasn't my fault. The evidence was unfortunate, and anyway, I have to remind myself that Gareth really was a creep. He'd pressured Jen, who was three years younger than him, into sex, and then of course there was what he did to her, the bruises, the broken wrist. Not a good guy. But that didn't warrant ten years in prison, getting constant aggro from the other prisoners as a 'paedo' because his girlfriend was technically underage when they first started sleeping together.

Donetti has suggested we conduct the interview in the police station, perhaps in case Gareth kicks off. I remember him punching a kid at school one time, his rage at Jen's party. I arrive late again, because I don't want to be there, and the uber-punctual detective is pacing in reception. His tie seems even tighter today, his forearms bulging even larger. 'I thought we said nine?'

'It's like, five minutes after.'

'He's jumpy. We can't give him an excuse to walk.'

He buzzes me through, giving me a 'visitor' sticker for my jacket. It's one thousand degrees inside but I won't take the jacket off. Armour. There are carpeted corridors and a nondescript door and a room with no windows, and there's Gareth, at the scuffed table, hunched over it.

My first thought is that he's maintained his muscle mass. I guess that was all he had in prison, a rugby player's heft to counteract his posh voice and the terrible crime he was accused of. But he has lost his hair, and he looks older than forty. I smell cigarettes too. He never used to smoke, except a bit of weed. 'Here's Karen,' says Donetti. 'It must be some time since you two met?'

'Since court,' he says bitterly, fixing me with a look of pure loathing. I gave evidence at his trial too, confirming what I had seen, what he'd done to Jen.

I try to remember my little prepared speech. 'I . . . Gareth, I could only work with what I knew at the time, what I saw. The police agreed with me, remember, it wasn't just my evidence.'

He stares for a moment then looks at the table. His hands are big, scarred. 'I wish I could take back what I did to Jen. But I never meant to hurt her, I swear. I just – didn't understand about consent. I was jealous and couldn't handle it.' Someone's been to therapy in prison.

'Anyway, the real fault lies with Aaron Hughes,' says Donetti, smoothly. 'And we all want to make sure he can't hurt anyone else. So that's why you're here, Gareth, and you, Karen, to see if we can decipher the meaning of this symbol appearing now. Or find any links between Lara Milton and Hughes.'

'I never saw the symbol,' growls Gareth. 'Never wanted anything to do with that freak.'

'I know. But Jen – she didn't necessarily feel the same.' I have to speak delicately. How strange that I barely knew Gareth Hale back then, and yet I have influenced the entire course of his life. He and I are forever linked through Jen and through you, the opposite sides of a square, never touching.

Gareth looks away. I wonder if he has a girlfriend now, or a wife. There's no wedding ring. He's no longer a convicted killer, but he carries that stench all the same. Warped by prison, life in a cage. 'I never saw it,' he repeats.

Donetti is taking notes, maybe just for something to do. 'Was there anyone else who might have – was it known about in school?'

'No,' I say, glancing at Gareth for confirmation. 'He only showed close friends, and he really only had me. Maybe Jen, after a fashion.' I wish I could ask her why she did it. Was it only to hurt me, or did she feel it too, the pull of your gravity, the dark undertow that was you?

'OK, that's useful, narrows it down. And Lara Milton – do either of you have any knowledge of how she might be linked to the older cases? A parent, a friend, someone from school or the local area?'

I shake my head. 'I've been through her social media fairly thoroughly – I don't recognise any of the names of her Facebook friends.'

'Gareth?'

He shrugs, arms folded, each one as broad as my thighs. 'Never heard of her or anyone she knows. But like I said, I didn't know that freak. Maybe there's some connection to him, I don't know. But listen, have you thought about what else this could mean?'

Donetti plays along. 'What's that?'

'Well, all those years in prison, I knew I didn't kill Jen, so someone else must have. So when they said it was Hughes, I was just glad to get out. But it didn't match his MO, did it. No symbol. No cutting.'

'It's not uncommon for serial killers to try out different MOs before they—'

Gareth interrupts me. 'What if someone else killed Jen, and they're still out there? And now they've taken this other girl?'

I can't help but say, 'I thought you were the one saying he did kill her.'

He glares at me. 'I was in prison for something I didn't do. I just wanted out.'

He has a point. I stare down at my hands as Donetti nods. 'It's one theory, yes.'

'Or go further. What if Hughes never did any of them? Evidence wasn't overwhelming, was it? Just – circumstantial.'

Gareth looks at me as he says it. He knows it was largely my testimony that sent you to prison, as it did with him.

Donetti says, 'I think it's more likely someone has reproduced the symbol, for some reason.'

'But no one's seen it, hardly. You said so yourself.'

He's not wrong, but I can't bear to think of that. That some other unknown killer left those symbols on so many dead bodies, and is still free now to take Lara. But why nothing for ten years then? It doesn't make sense. I believe you are guilty. I have to.

And Jen? I've managed to find a way I can live with it. You're a killer, there's every chance you murdered her too. But now it's all in doubt again and the certainties I've built my life on are slipping.

'That's all useful thinking, thank you. We'll keep looking. I think we can let you go now, Gareth.' Donetti stands up, gesturing to the door. Gareth looks at me for a moment, steadier now.

It seems he has prepared a speech too. 'Karen. I just want you to know, I had a lot of bad thoughts about you, for a long time. Sitting in jail all those years knowing I didn't do it, knowing someone else was out there who actually killed Jen. But I understand now. She was your best friend, your sister, almost. You wanted someone to pay for her death. And I probably seemed the most likely culprit. I blame myself for that every day.'

It takes me a while to be able to speak. 'Thank you, Gareth. And if you blame yourself every day, imagine how I feel?'

After he walks Gareth out, Donetti comes back for me. 'Thoughts?' he says.

'Did you look into him for Lara?' I can't help asking. 'He has form for hurting women. Even if he didn't kill Jen, he beat her up.'

'Gareth volunteered an alibi – he was drinking in a bar in town, seen by at least ten people and captured on CCTV. Stayed there till well after twelve. About as solid as you can get.'

'Oh. OK.'

The guilt for what I did to him is so raw I shy away from it. I have to remember it wasn't based on nothing. It's true that some passages in my book are largely fabricated. How could I remember exactly what I said to Jen twenty years ago, and what she said back? But I did see marks on her body – she still had them, fading to yellow and grey, when she died. They are logged on the autopsy report. Her wrist was broken, a hairline fracture. And I did see Gareth's Jeep parked up the woods that day, where he so often picked her up after school. He said he was waiting for the school bus, and when she wasn't on it, having got the earlier one, he left. That he didn't go into the woods. But when the parts of a story are all there, who wouldn't draw lines between them, connect them up? What lies did I really tell? I only said he'd hurt her, which was true. Evidence is not facts. It's just a story and how you tell it makes a difference. It just so happened that even then, that's something I was good at.

68

♦ ♦ ♦

We find Lara's friend Melissa in the living room of her mother's house, haggard, eyes red and raw, tissues up the sleeve of her cardigan. Leaking tears, like a tap that doesn't turn off properly. She's visibly trying to hold herself together. The TV is tuned silently to 24-hour news; perhaps she's hoping for some answers. 'I'm sorry. You're with the police?' She has a strong Yorkshire accent.

Donetti says, 'I'm the lead detective, but Ms Walker here is – helping us out. If you're happy to talk to her?'

'Just Karen is fine,' I say. 'I – know something about the old cases. The Bagman.'

The tears begin in earnest. 'It can't be owt to do with him! He's in prison, in't he?'

Donetti soothes her. 'Of course. Our current thinking is that someone copied the symbol, drew it on the wall to throw us off, or cause fear.'

Her eyes are huge and damp. 'So, what, like – a new serial killer?'

'That's extremely unlikely, Melissa. But you can help us understand Lara better. You two were very close?'

She nods vigorously, shoving the tissues back up the cardigan sleeve. Under it she wears a floral tea dress, thick black tights. She's a nice, normal girl, and her friend was most likely the same. Is. 'She has no family, see. Well maybe like some cousins in Sheffield or something, but her mum and dad are dead.'

'And she's only twenty-nine?' That seems unfortunate.

'Yeah. Her mum died of cancer a few years ago, and her dad, he were killed in a car crash when she were little. Her gran helped look after her, but she died too last year. That's how come Lara has such a nice flat.' She looks round the living room, ruefully. 'Don't pay us enough at work to buy our own places, that's for sure.'

I lean in. 'Can you tell us more about Lara – is she trusting? Would she have opened the door to a stranger, say?' I realise I'm having to work hard to use the present tense, and I'm not sure why. Do I assume she's dead, like the others are? There is no reason to.

'I don't think so. She had a chain on her door like, and her grandma were always dead scared of burglars, wouldn't even answer the door once it were gone nine.'

So maybe someone tricked their way in, pretended to be a gas inspector or building maintenance – there was speculation you'd done the same, to get some of your victims to let you in. Or it was someone she knew.

'How did she seem that night – you were out together?'

'Yeah. She were good – happy. We were going on holiday, to Tenerife. I walked her back and she watched out the window till me taxi came, so we could both be safe.' She shakes her head. 'We were always right careful. I don't know how someone could have got her once she were home.'

Neither do I. But killers can be very convincing – you asked Emelia for help finding a lost dog, and maybe you used that line on other women too. We have no way of knowing. Aside from Emelia, none of them lived to tell the tale. I ask, 'Did Lara have a boyfriend, or anyone she was dating? She used the apps?'

'Um, no.'

But Melissa casts a nervous glance at Donetti, filling the room with his bulk and his knock-you-down aftershave. I force a smile. 'DS Donetti, maybe you could – go find Melissa some water? Or a cup of tea?'

He seems to take the hint. Once he's gone, I lean in closer. 'I get it. We all have things we might not want strangers to know about us. But it's really important, Melissa. Was there a guy?' Maybe the large rude man the downstairs neighbour described.

She nods slowly. 'They went on like, three dates, I think, but she said he got weird. She wouldn't talk about it, even, and normally she told me everything. I think he freaked her out.'

'Like he hurt her?'

'No. Don't think it was that. Scared her, maybe.'

'Did she tell the police?'

'Oh no. Nothing like that. Just a weirdo, you know. You can't report every weirdo you meet dating, can you? You'd never stop.'

She's not wrong about that.

'Where did she meet him – online?' My mind is racing. If the app will release the records, we can perhaps trace this guy. Then all we have to do is prove he's somehow seen the symbol – he could be the son of one of the old officers, perhaps? – and this nightmare will be over and I can go home. But Melissa is shaking her head.

'That were the funny thing, she met him in real life! In some pub. Said he were right nice at first, charming, hench.'

I make a mental note to google what that means. 'Did you find out his name?'

'John something. She was shy, kind of, about it. Didn't say much. But I think he were local like, lived in Marebridge.'

'You don't know when she met him? Or which bar?' If she does, they might be able to view the CCTV.

'No. I wish I did but she never said, or else I forgot. I'm sorry.'

I sigh. We can hardly view the CCTV from every pub in the area. Then I have a thought. She'll have been texting with this John, at least. Her phone was left behind in her flat. If Donetti's team can get into it, the answers might be there.

Melissa is crying again. 'I'm just so worried, like. She must be hurt, or even if she's not he must have her somewhere, or she'd never stay away like this, never never. She's never even missed a day of work.'

I take her cold hand in mine. 'Melissa, do you know who I am? Years ago, my best friend was killed by the Bagman.'

I see understanding dawn. 'Oh! You're that – you're a writer, yeah?'

'I am now. Back then I was just a frightened teenager being bombarded with questions by the police. They kept asking me things about Jen, about her life, that she wouldn't have wanted anyone to know. So I kept her secrets, and they got the wrong man for it. I made a mistake, and her killer went on to hurt a lot more women. I have to live with that. If I could go back, I would tell the police everything I knew, no matter how small or embarrassing it seemed. Because you never know what will be the right answer. OK?'

She bites her lip, blinking back more tears. 'I'm trying.'

'Were there any other boyfriends? Hook-ups?'

'Look, I don't – she sometimes would have, like . . . a booty call. A random. Might not even know his real name, just give him the address on an app and he'd come round.' She sniffs again. 'I kind of said I didn't think that were safe, like – so I don't know if she told me everything.'

It seems insane to me, but I know from friends in New York that it's common in this era of apps, to get chatting and invite someone over to your flat right away, or even go to theirs. Even women who are conscious of safety, who walk with their keys in their hands on high alert, might do this. A total stranger, who could be anyone. Fuck them, leave, never find out anything bar what brand of hand soap they keep in their bathroom. I would never do that, but perhaps I am more fearful than most. 'So it's possible she matched with someone that night, after she went home?' I think back to the flat, the saucepan in the sink, the missing pyjamas and shoes on the floor. It didn't seem like she was expecting anyone over. But what do I know?

Melissa is nodding reluctantly. 'Yeah. She did do that, now and again. I told her not to but – I think she thought I were jealous. You know, I'm still in with my mam here. Can't afford a place of my own, so I can't really bring lads home.'

'I get it. It's OK, no one will judge Lara.' That definitely isn't true, but needs must.

Donetti comes back then, balancing a mug of tea and glass of water in his big hands. 'Alright?'

I look at the girl. 'Melissa has some very useful information, it seems. About a possible man in Lara's life. If she'll share it with you?'

'Anything to help find Lara,' she says staunchly, before dissolving into tears again.

Chapter Seven

From *Becoming Bagman* by Karen Walker

One mistake about Jen's murder that's often been repeated is that she and I were stepsisters. We weren't, but it's true that my mother Arlene, perennially single since my dad left when I was a baby, had started going out with Jen's widowed father, Ash, a few months before Jen died, after getting to know each other at the golf club where he played and she sometimes waitressed. Jen's mum, Patricia, had died of cancer when we were fourteen, the one dark spot on Jen's charmed life. It's also true that Ash proposed to my mother the weekend before the murder.

There was some talk about that at the time, the coincidence of the timing, the unexpected speed of it. That I hadn't wanted them to be together, that I'd been jealous of Jen, not wanted to be overshadowed by a pretty, popular stepsister. Of course, that isn't true. Jen and I had been best friends since we were five. We loved the idea of being sisters. It was just like *The Parent Trap*, we agreed, as we planned what our side-by-side bed-rooms would look like if Arlene and Ash made it official.

◆　◆　◆

Donetti drops me back at the police station where my car is, and I've barely even started the engine when I get an update from him. He writes his email in neat bullet points. They have analysed Lara's phone already, though they're still waiting for the cooperation of the dating apps she was on, but found no texts suggesting a meet-up the night she disappeared. There is indeed a John in her blocked contacts, but he seems to have been texting her from a burner phone, plus the messages have been wiped. They'll re-examine any surveillance cameras near her house and circulate a description of the rude man on the stairs, though there's little to go on. In news reports I've seen the existing CCTV from the corner of her road, which doesn't cover the stairs to her building. She and Melissa, matching each other's steps, apparently laughing at something. About ten minutes later a car sweeps by – Melissa's taxi. Her driver had a dashcam, but it showed no one nearby, loitering in the shad-ows, and he noticed nothing unusual. No one did.

Donetti has also made a long (again bullet-pointed) list of everyone who worked on the cases back then and might have seen the symbol. Although there were hundreds of staff working on the murders, the police were very careful not to release pictures of it, and access was strictly controlled. All the same there are over forty people on there. I scan the list of names – mostly men, more than a few called John. Many of them must be retired now, so 'John' could even be a son or a nephew or younger brother. How can we ever trace every person each of these people has met? It's impossible. I just have to keep pulling at my own threads, so here I am.

I can't believe that Ash Rollason still lives in the same house, after losing both the wife and daughter he shared it with. Now he has a new one of each, a luxury that's available to men but not women past the age of forty or so. The house doesn't look as nice as when Patricia was alive. She loved gardening, would never have let weeds grow up between the gravel like this. But there are three expensive cars parked on the driveway, a Range Rover, a Maserati, and a hybrid Toyota. I wonder if that's for the daughter. Jen was bought a car for her seventeenth too, the little pink Mini. Not that she got much time to drive it. Only months later she was dead.

The gravel makes a crunching noise under my feet, like walking through sand, and I'm breathing hard again despite the flat surface I'm walking on. He may not want to see me at all. I'm a reminder of painful things, of Jen and his disastrous liaison with my mother. This was the one family I didn't contact about my book, despite April's urging. I just couldn't face it. All the same I have to talk to him now, and so I ring the bell. The front door is navy with a heavy brass knocker, but they both need cleaning. The sound of a TV comes faintly through. Then it's thrown open by Ash, in a striped shirt, holding a glass of red wine. He's lost his hair, put on a little weight, but his face softens when he sees me. 'Karen! You're back?'

'Um, yes, hello.'

He hugs me violently, spilling wine on my shoulder. 'Oh, it's good to see you, love.' A hitch in his breath that tells me Jen has not been forgotten. 'Come in, come in. Lucy, look who's here!'

It's Miss Coxon. My brain doesn't allow me to think of her as *Lucy*, and she doesn't look best pleased to see me. She's in athleisure, ears and fingers glinting with diamonds, and she's had something done to her face, fillers or Botox or both.

'Karen. What a surprise.' No warmth. She never did like me.

'Yes. Congratulations, by the way. Talk about surprises.'

She scowls, but Ash comes to stand beside her, arm about her shoulders. He was always a demonstrative man, and didn't I envy Jen that as well, a father who cared. Any parent who cared. 'We got close after everything. Lucy was a huge help. And we have Rosalind now. Ros!' He raises his voice and I see Miss Coxon wince.

'I met her actually. In the café.'

'Oh yes. Just a part-time job, but I think it's good to learn the value of money.'

'Not if it gets in the way of her studies,' mutters Miss Coxon. She pastes on a smile. 'Tea, Karen? What brings you over?'

In other words, *How long are you going to be in my house?*

'I couldn't not come and say hello. I'm back because – well, you know the news, I'm sure.'

His face darkens. 'Someone messing about. I don't know who'd do such a thing. Here, sit down, sit down.'

He pulls out a kitchen chair for me. The decor is very cold, marble and white with ornate flourishes, giant vases with silver twigs in them. I don't like it. 'Mr Rollason . . .'

'Ash, please! You're all grown up now.'

'Right. It's just – it is the symbol. The same one.'

I hear a crash and muffled curse from the kitchen, as if Miss Coxon has dropped a cup. He frowns. 'You're sure?'

'As sure as I can be.' Same question the police asked me back then – *Are you sure, Karen, that this is the same symbol Aaron Hughes used to draw?* How I wished for a copy to check against, for it to be truly, truly watertight with no doubt at all. But you'd been careful to destroy them all. You must have known the net was closing.

His brows knit slowly, trying to puzzle it out. 'Oh. So then – someone who saw it before . . . ?'

'It must be, yes.'

'But the girl – it's surely just a hoax, isn't it? She can't be really – missing.'

77

'I think she is, Ash. I'm sorry. That's why I'm here. To help find her.'

Ash sits down too, heavily. 'But he never took them away. He just – he did it right off.'

'I know. But it can't be him anyway, he's in prison.'

'Of course. So who . . .'

'Someone copying him maybe. But if she's in danger, we need to find her fast.'

He nods slowly, assimilating it. 'What do you need from me?'

'I wondered if you had any of Jen's things still. There might be something the police missed?' I'm being delicate. He doesn't like to think of the fact his daughter knew you. Willingly spent time with you, and perhaps more. That isn't the Jen in his head, pretty and popular, sunlight and smiles. But it is the Jen I knew.

'I don't know, love. You can look in her room, if you like, it's all as it was.'

'That would be great. Thank you.'

Miss Coxon has returned with a mug of anaemic tea. 'We don't allow food or drink upstairs.'

'Fine.' I give her a fake smile. 'Still teaching?'

'Not since I had Rosalind.' She puts down the cup and twists her rings, the spoils of war. This could have been my mother, never needing to work, living in this lovely if slightly sterile home. Maybe she could have given him another child too – Arlene was only thirty-seven when Jen died. But it wasn't to be. Their relationship was over before Jen was even buried. I always assumed he'd ended it after I'd been questioned over his daughter's murder, though Ash never seemed to blame me. Arlene wouldn't talk about it so I don't know. It's festered there between us all these years, the life I cost her.

I scale the wide, sweeping staircase, and Ash directs me to Jen's room, as if I could ever forget the way. He doesn't come in with me.

'Look at anything you want. We didn't move a thing.'

Is that weird, to keep a whole room as a shrine to a girl who died nearly twenty years ago? I suppose they have plenty of spares. I push open the door and I'm hit by a hint of Charlie Red and enough hairspray to choke a cat. Jen. A ghost rising up from the pink shag carpet and princess furniture. Miss Coxon must hate that she can't minimalise this room too. Everything is as I remember. A wall of posters and pictures, stuck up with old, yellowing Sellotape. Robbie Williams and Justin Timberlake.

Her vanity, ruffled and prissy. Ash bought her this suite when she was eleven, and at seventeen Jen did not fit it at all. She kept her weed under one of the drawers and stashed vodka bottles in shoe boxes. The wallpaper is silky and pink drapes hang around the bed. I remember the first time I came in here, I first felt awe, then anger. Why did she get a bedroom like this, when I had a box room with a single bed and damp Jackson-Pollocking the walls?

Where would she have kept the drawing, if she had it, as she'd claimed that day? She'd wanted to hold it over me, that you had shown it to her as well. Drawn her own copy for her, even, which is more than I ever had. I don't know if it was true, but I have to look. I kneel down and start shamelessly going through her things. Make-up, old and dried up, watery nail polish. Brushes with her hair tangled in it, that glossy chestnut shot through with gold. A few trashy novels and magazines. Not a big reader, our Jen. I used to make fun of her to you, with a panicked sense that maybe it didn't matter after all that she wasn't bright. Or rather, she was bright, she just cared about different things than I did. Status and gossip and being the best. There's her underwear, washed and folded by the housekeeper Ash employed to come each day after Patricia died. A vast rack of clothes. I remember that red dress, scandalously short. Those baby-doll tops and gypsy blouses, all back in fashion now. DMs and ridiculous strappy heels, the kind you can't walk ten steps in, unless you are seventeen of course. I find a box of files and folders – school stuff. It would be here, surely, if anywhere. Old essays, in a loopy hand I would always recognise as Jen's. Funny how I never see the handwriting of my friends now, except on the odd birthday card. But I saw hers all day every day, at school, on notes passed in class. In her diary.

That's what I really need. But there was no sign of it at the time, even though the police searched her room. Ash must have made them put every single thing back where they found it, though this schoolwork is disordered, English mixed in with history. Doodles on Jen's folders and in the margins, those little white rings we used to reinforce our hole-punched paper. A smell of ink and old paper. A note passed to and fro with someone whose writing I don't recognise: *God I'm so bored.*

I know dying here. K is such a know-it-all.

A frisson goes through me. K, that must be me. The note was to Sinead Cowden perhaps. I remember her crying on me at the police station, me watching the detective over her shoulder as he watched us. Watched me, how I reacted, if I cried like Sinead was crying. It's hard to cry when you're desperately saving yourself.

I sit back on my heels, sinking into the thick carpet. I know the diary existed, once. It's possible she destroyed it before she died, but why? She had no idea what was coming for her. Or who. I remember Sinead found me in here after the funeral, in my too-short black dress from a market stall. Arlene had given me a pill that day, taken two herself. I don't know what they were but they would help us get through the day, she'd said, downing hers dry in front of the bathroom cabinet. I felt like I was walking through water the whole time.

What are you doing? Sinead had frowned.

Mr Rollason says I can take something to remember her by, I lied.

Oh? I want something too, then. What are you taking?

I don't know. Nothing really sums her up for me.

Sinead snatched at a pink leather jacket on the back of the door. *I want this. She loved it, someone should get the wear of it.*

I faked a deep, blubbering breath then. *Sinead, would you give me a minute? It's just really hard, you know?* I hoped she wouldn't hug me again.

Ash did not notice that the jacket was gone, of course. He lacked such knowledge of the details of his daughter's life. But Sinead wore it to school the next week and some of the comments were interesting. I remember her crying in the toilets. *But you said she'd want me to have it!* A small stab of satisfaction, drawing the attention from me, who had been questioned over Jen's murder. Released by then, Gareth charged and locked away on remand already.

I never found the diary then and I didn't dare go back after that day. Maybe I can find it now. I feel around the edges of the carpet, in case it's loose, and run my hand over the top shelf of her wardrobe, finding several hair ties and a lot of dust, but nothing else. I take out each drawer from her vanity in case it's underneath, but there's nothing, not even old weed. Where could it be? Same with the bedside table. There's a book about grief slipped under the table itself, the feet wearing years-old grooves in the carpet, but nothing else. Where can it be? I stand up and survey the room, running my eyes over every inch, until they alight on the wide pelmet above her window, swathed in pink fabric. I drag over one of the white curved chairs and feel around in the dust. My fingers close over something. A small leatherbound notebook, also in pink. The front is embossed with five letters – DIARY. I can't believe I've found it. I found it, after all these years. Did the police miss it? They wouldn't have known what they were looking for, or even that a diary existed.

Just then I hear a scuffle at the door, and, half inside the wardrobe, I shove the book down the back of my jeans. *Sorry, Jen.*

It's Rosalind, wearing a grey tracksuit similar to Emelia's, with one of those pink silk curlers you see on TikTok twisted in her hair. 'Eh, what are you doing in here?'

'Your dad said I could look around. In case there's something that might help this case.'

She tenses. 'Did you find anything?'

'No.' But maybe there's a clue in the diary.

She narrows her eyes. 'I don't think it's right you're like, going through her stuff.'

'We were best friends, Rosalind. I know what she had.' *And you've cleaned out the weed*, I wanted to add.

'She wouldn't have wanted that. She'd hate it.'

I could ask how she knows that when she never even met Jen, but I don't. Because she is right. Jen would have absolutely hated this, but it has to be done.

Ash and Miss Coxon – Lucy! – must realise something's up, as I barely drink my tea after that, hurling myself out of the house, afraid all the time that the diary will slip from my waistband and on to the floor. Jen's diary. Evidence in a long-ago murder. A murder that has been solved, twice, and yet is somehow still haunting me.

As I walk out to my car, Ash waves from the doorstep, silhouetted dark against the lights. I think – I could have lived in this house. It would only have been for a year before university, but I could have benefited from Ash's largesse, given up my part-time job in the petrol station to focus on my exams, learned to drive like Jen did. At first, neither she nor I had thought it was going anywhere, stolid Ash with his good job and wine cellar and Arlene with her dyed red hair, vodka-glittered eyes, and twenty-a-day habit. But after the proposal, things changed. The stakes were high. Of course, Jen didn't want a stepmother, especially not Arlene, a world away from sweet, nurturing Patricia and not above clouting you in the face if you crossed her. But me? A rich and kind stepdad would not have been the worst. And so I left Jen with no choice but to make her play. And everything unravelled after that.

◆ ◆ ◆

Back at the inn, I make myself walk to the room before I look at the diary, which is stupid. No one would think anything of a pink notebook, totally innocuous. But when I get upstairs, I see the door is ajar. Weird. Maybe the cleaners didn't close it properly. Inside looks normal, the bed made up, new teabags and little wrapped biscuits, fresh towels. My laptop is there, and nothing seems to be missing. I sit cross-legged on the bed and open the diary. The lined pages are flimsy, the date written at the top in Jen's loopy writing, her bright blue pen. I remember that pen, nibbled by her lip-glossed mouth. I soon realise it's more of a calorie record than anything else.

> *September 14th. Ryvita and Dairylea single. 112 pounds. Maths, ugh, and PE (kill me now). S being annoying. New boy at school. Goth weirdo. But not totally hideous. Something new at least.*

That was you! I hadn't known she thought that. Usually other people were beneath Jen's interest.

I flick on, up to December of that year. The words take on a new meaning, her last diary entries. She had no idea what was coming. She doesn't write anything directly about you, but there is evidence here all the same. *G rang but I didn't pick up. Can't feel the same about him now, after YKW.* (You know who?) *Dad out with the hag again.* That must be Arlene, and I feel angry on her behalf. She has manifold flaws, but back then she was pretty at least. Sexy,

83

rough around the edges. *Never mind, I have a plan to get rid of K and her.*

Was that why she did it? To make me angry, hoping the row would lead to a rupture between our parents? And it did, but at the cost of Jen's life. Does this mean her words to me in the school lobby that day, the day she died, were true and not just well-calculated lies? Then, I realise the end of the diary is torn out. I run my fingers over the sheet below, seeking the indentations, the ghost of whatever was written there, but I can't decipher it. Someone has removed a page. Was it a drawing of the symbol? Jen? Someone else? No way to know. Restless, I get up to retrieve my laptop, then pause. It's on the desk, but I'm fairly sure I left it on the bedside table, from where I was using it in bed. I touch the screen and my password box comes up. Has someone tried to get into it? I look around at my things. Does the case look disordered? Even more disordered, that is (I'm never very tidy in hotel rooms)? I stand over it. There's a certain foreign dishevelment. But what can they . . . Then I realise. My book. The newly minted copy, not yet on sale. It was in the zippered pocket of my case and now it is gone. Someone has been in my room.

I don't know why, but the first person I think to call is Emelia. She answers right away.

'Did they get you too?' she says.

I'm jolted. 'What – someone's been in your room?'

'Of course they have. I'd never have left my leggings in such a heap!' I feel this is an ongoing row she's been having with the hotel.

'Did they take anything?'

'I don't think so. My valuables were in the safe, of course.' Emelia has done videos about travel safety. She always uses the door chain and places something over the handle too, in case staff let themselves in while you're sleeping. I think she is paranoid, or I did, at any rate.

I ask, 'Do you have anything with you, any info about him, about your case?'

'Well, there's the TV scripts. Not hard copy, and I carry my devices with me all the time. You know they can be hacked if—'

'They took the book. My copy of it, fresh from the publishers.'

'Oh.' She hesitates. 'So you think it was to do with—'

'It must be, if they targeted both of us.'

My mind is racing. Who could have done this? How did they know where we're both staying – especially her, in central Manchester? And in what rooms? Suddenly my skin is crawling. We're being watched, Emelia and me. You may not be hiding in the wardrobe but perhaps you have eyes on us, you've sent someone as your proxy. Who else would want a copy of my book?

She says, 'Ugh, I can't believe this, I'm going to sue.'

'Did you post about where you were?'

'Um . . .'

I hear her hesitation and grab my phone to go to Instagram. There it is, a post about being in Manchester to consult on her TV show, with a shot of her room and the hotel's name clearly visible on a bottle of water by her bed. 'For God's sake. I thought you were some kind of safety guru?'

'I had to explain why I'm here, OK? People ask questions.'

I sigh. 'You should change hotels, Emelia.'

'Oh, I will, believe me. You too?'

I should. But where can I go? There aren't any other hotels in Marebridge, and anyway, nowhere in this town is anonymous, everyone knows me. And if I'm honest with myself, I don't want to be alone while I'm trying to unravel all this.

'I've got a place to go, it's fine. But we need to be careful. Someone's watching us.'

Chapter Eight

From *Becoming Bagman* by Karen Walker

As I was getting to know Aaron Hughes that autumn, Jen was dating a boy called Gareth Hale, who was twenty and worked part-time on his parents' farm, but still hung out with us all the time. We looked down on him as he was a grown-up chasing after schoolkids. But he was handsome and rich and drove a Jeep and so Jen liked him, or convinced herself she did.

It must have been early November, sometime around then, when I saw the bruises. We still had to do PE once a week in the sixth form, though I did my best to dodge it. On that day we were playing netball, despite driving rain and sleet. I spent the whole lesson hiding from the ball and being yelled at by the teacher, Miss Dudley. Jen was good at netball, good at most things, if not actual schoolwork. When she pivoted up for the ball, her pleated skirt flipped, and I saw them – a ring of small bruises round her thighs. Like the smudges of ink when you get fingerprinted, I would later learn.

'What's that?' I blurted.

She looked down. Smirked. 'Oh, Gareth likes to hold on tight. You know when he – no, I guess you don't know.' My virginity was a source of great amusement to her.

'He did that to you?'

'Chill, will you? It's normal.' A few days after that, she had her school shirt buttoned to the neck, but when she swept her hair up into her hands I saw bruises there too. Big ones, darkening red to purple, the colour of ripe plums. Then there was the day in English when she couldn't pick up the pen.

'Take notes for me,' she hissed. She was cradling her wrist in her lap, and I could see bruises there too, like a dark bracelet.

I just looked at her. 'This is normal as well?'

She rolled her eyes. 'He loses his temper. He saw me talking to someone. He's jealous. Passionate.'

'Wanker. Abusive wanker.'

She said nothing, but I noticed her wince as she moved her arm on to the desk, pretending to write. A lot has been written about the fancy-dress party held at Jen's house on the Saturday before she died, how Aaron and I dressed up as ghosts and ghouls, even though it was Christmas. Pictures circulated of me in a witch's hat, Aaron with white skull make-up. I thought I was being ironic, dressing for Halloween at a Christmas party. The symbolism of that, if we planned ahead to murder Jen in some kind of ritual. Jen had angel wings and a wire halo, her body encased in a tight white bodysuit. Tutu skirt. No tights, despite the cold. She looked beautiful, and very happy. As if she had a secret.

Gareth Hale, in the extremely poor taste that was typical of him, was dressed as the Twin Towers, because he thought that kind of thing was funny. Something was different with him and Jen that night. As if she'd grown out of him, and he knew it, and he wasn't happy. Is it any wonder I thought he'd killed her, when I'd also seen his car parked near the woods, when it was picked up by several traffic cams in the area? I wasn't the only one who'd noticed the bruises on Jen – several of her other friends backed up my evidence. It was bad luck. Not just for him, but for the women who would die later because the real culprit wasn't caught.

The inn doesn't seem too disturbed to see me check out, the slack-jawed receptionist unable to understand what I'm saying about someone being in my room.

'Like, the cleaners go in every day.'

'I know that. Someone's been through my things – are you saying that's one of your staff, or that you let someone else gain access?'

Gain access. Fear is making me snooty.

Her brow creases. 'I don't know, like.'

'Do you have CCTV?'

'In the car park, like.'

'Well, can I see it?'

She heaves a deep sigh, then gets on the phone and mumbles to, I presume, the manager. 'Yeah, it's her in twenty-five. Says someone got in her room. Aye, I told her about the cleaners!' She looks up. 'Has owt been nicked?'

'A book of mine.'

'A book?' She says this in the tone of *a unicorn?*

'An important document.' I'm getting snappy now. 'Look, I need to see your CCTV. I could be in danger.'

She sighs and goes back to mumbling. 'Says she wants to see it. I don't know how, like – OK. Right.' She hangs up. 'He says we best get police in.'

I'd wanted to avoid Chris Donetti – not sure why, something about him unsettles me, and I don't want him to know where I'm staying – but I suppose she's finally right about one thing. It is time to call him.

He arrives in less than twenty minutes, which suggests to me he doesn't have a lot going on in his personal life. He brings a sharp smell of aftershave into the stale, soup-scented lobby of the inn. Within seconds he has flashed a warrant card and cajoled 'Brenda' into unlocking the CCTV cabinet. She has no clue how to work it, of course, but he soon figures it out. It's incredibly boring for the most part. A few people coming and going in the car park, lights sweeping over the moor behind. I recognise most as members of staff I've seen about. It could easily be one of them, of course. Everyone knows everyone here.

After a while, Donetti starts and points at the screen. 'There! See that one – why would they park all the way at the edge of the car park, where it's darkest? It's not busy, there's no need.' I peer at the screen, where a nondescript Jeep-style vehicle has appeared. A hulking figure gets out of it, wearing a black hoody with the hood up. 'Any member of staff that tall?'

I try to remember. 'I don't think so.'

'Customer maybe?'

'The pub's closed today. And no one else seems to be staying.'

He nods, satisfied. 'That's our man then. Can't see a reg on this, but we can check any nearby traffic cams.'

I can't make out anything on the screen. Who can this be? Did someone really come into my room and take the book?

'But why would they do this?'

'I suppose there must be something in the book that's interesting. That someone wants to know ahead of time.'

I shake my head in confusion. 'The information is all in the public domain, for the most part. I guess I give my side of what happened with – my friend. Jen.' I've never spoken about it publicly before, or about how I came to accuse Gareth and alibi you.

'We'll interview the staff, see if someone let this man into your room, who he might be, who was working that day and so on. In the meantime, you should stay somewhere else.'

'Of course. But – can this be *him* too? Do you think he's somehow behind it – does he have some kind of network on the outside?' Donetti knows which him I mean.

'We're following up on all his outgoing mail, and the prison staff are meant to be frisking the cells for phones. Some do get in, of course.' I imagine you texting people, sitting in your cell cosy and connected, orchestrating this all.

I can't put it off any longer. 'I have to go and see him. Don't I?'

He speaks carefully. 'It would be very helpful if you would, yes.'

I stare at the hideous carpet in the small room. 'I can't.'

'He'll be carefully guarded – he won't be able to hurt you.'

But there are other ways to be hurt than physically. You taught me that. 'I – I'll think about it.'

90

'Thank you, Karen. I know it's not easy.' At least he's dropped the *Ms Walker* business.

'No news on Lara? Nothing at all?'

'Oh, all manner of sightings that we have to chase after like bloody Pokémon, but nothing concrete. Now, can I drive you somewhere safer? That ideally smells a bit less like soup?'

'I've got my car.'

'Give me the keys and I'll drop it down tomorrow. You shouldn't drive after a shock like this.'

I sigh. 'OK. Give me five minutes.'

I throw my things into the case, and, as an afterthought, take the little packets of biscuits too. I glance in the mirror and consider make-up, then dismiss that as ridiculous. He's just giving me a lift, after all. I hide Jen's diary in the bottom of my suitcase. I can't tell anyone I've found it, at least until I know everything that's inside.

Ten minutes later we're on the ring road. When his radio came on it was playing a motivational podcast, which he quickly switched over to local radio. Lara is still top of the news, though no updates are to be had. 'What do you do in cases like this, when there's just – nothing? No clues?'

He shrugs. 'It happens all the time. You want to depress your-self, look at the list of long-missing people in the UK. If no one saw anything and there's no CCTV and the friends and family are stumped, well, we kind of draw a blank. We can monitor the phone and bank accounts, but sometimes people just start over. Walk out of their lives.' I hope that's the case for Lara, but that wouldn't explain the bloody symbol on her wall. Wordlessly, I rip open the biscuits and hand him one.

He looks puzzled.

'Eat it. It's not bad.'

'I don't do sugar.'

'We aren't going to get through this without sugar.'

He hesitates, then takes it, putting the whole thing in his mouth so he can dutifully return his hands to the steering wheel. He lets out a faint whimper. 'Oh God. That's the first sweet thing I've had in months.'

'How do you live without it?'

'Right now I don't know,' he mutters, crunching. 'Don't give me any more. Seriously, I used to be five stone heavier. Lost it all to join the force. It's a slippery slope, you know.'

But nothing else makes me feel OK right now, and it's better than vodka, I reason. Soon we are back on the streets of my youth, huddled houses, bleak moorland, feral children eyeing the car, clocking it as police despite the lack of markings. 'Am I gonna lose my hubcaps?' he says, pulling over.

'Can't promise you won't. Number seventeen.'

Likely he already knows which house I grew up in, but he doesn't say anything, just parks up. I lean into the back to get my things, then sit for an odd moment. It's like neither of us wants to part.

'Um – cup of tea maybe? Probably with more biscuits?'

'I'll see you safe to the door anyway.'

My mother has always appreciated a handsome man, so when she opens the door, her face first crunches in confusion at the sight of me with a suitcase, then clears into a smile. 'Oh, this is a surprise.'

'Can I stay here a bit? Something went wrong with the inn.'

I don't want to tell her someone might be after me. Am I putting her in danger, being here? I remember the firecrackers through the letterbox, the dead rabbit on the doorstep, when it came out about what you'd done, how I'd helped you stay free. Not that I even lived here then.

'Not surprising, that place must be crawling with bedbugs.' She flashes Donetti a smile. 'Hello – I'm Arlene Walker.'

92

'DS Chris Donetti. I'm working this Lara Milton case.'

'Oh, not in uniform? Shame. Still, come in, get a cuppa.'

He's too big for the small hallway, but he stoops to go in, awkward. Arlene mouths OMG to me and I ignore her.

'He has things to do, Mum. Quick cup of tea is all.'

He's all charm. 'Thank you. Always appreciated. Milk, no sugar.'

Arlene fishes out some good biscuits for him, ones in a tin that weren't offered to me, and they get into an enthusiastic conversation about weight loss, with her insisting she only keeps these for 'visitors'. Arlene never had trouble keeping weight off, since an all-tobacco and vodka diet is very slimming, if not containing any actual nutrition. I'm surprised to hear them compare notes on the local gym, where she allegedly does Pilates and HIIT. 'That's wise, Arlene, get your weight-bearing exercise in. Staves off osteoporosis, all kinds of things.'

'Our Karen wants to start, at her age.' They both stare at me and I scowl. I do SoulCycle and yoga – I live in New York, after all. I'm not the bone-idle teenager she's imagining.

'Look, Mum, someone broke into my room, stole a copy of my book. I'm worried it's *him*. That he sent someone to get it, maybe.'

But who do you have left to help you? Your dad is dead and your mum long gone, and I was your only friend. One of the prison staff, maybe? You hear about such things.

She swallows her black coffee. 'Well, that would make sense. He's been wanting to have it out with you for ten years, Karen.' She can be surprisingly astute, I forget. I have demonised my mother to the point I no longer see her good points. Or she has changed, or I have changed, or both. 'You know, I kept all the news stuff around the first trial, clippings and such. Jennifer and that Gareth. In case it's useful.'

'You think it's connected?' Donetti's huge hand dwarfs the mug she's given him, which has a faded Mars bar logo from a long-ago Easter egg.

'He always said he didn't do it, didn't he, Hughes? Any of them. Said so in court.'

I retort, 'Well, he would say that.' I had refused to talk to Arlene the day she came to your trial. *Karen, you can't shut me out*, she'd yelled. *I am your mother*. But I did. I told her I was moving to America, then fled after she threw her comment at me about being delusional. I hadn't thought about how it was for her, to see me vilified. I was not only convicting you, I was clearing myself of the idea I had known anything about Jen's death. That I had sent Gareth to prison deliberately. That I had lied.

Donetti is nodding along like she's Jessica Fletcher. 'You're saying it's possible he didn't do all of the murders? I know some people believe that. Maybe he's setting this up to try and reopen the cases?'

'Not the maddest idea of all time, is it?'

'It's certainly *an* idea.'

I can't believe they're even entertaining this thought. I don't dare to myself. 'But then how is Lara Milton connected? Why take a random girl, and who actually did it? It wasn't him.'

'That's what we need to know. I'd bet whoever was in your hotel room could tell us. Maybe they even took her too. It's a lead, anyway.'

It does feel good to have a plan. Perhaps this case can magically be solved in time for me not to face you. He drains his tea, thanks Arlene politely, and is gone, leaving me with her. Instantly, she lights up a fag and takes a deep draw. So much for her health kick. 'So, you were keeping quiet about Officer Sexy there.'

'He's trying to find a missing girl.' I sound like a cross teenager.

'Well, she ain't here, love, but he was. So, you're stopping with me then, are you?'

'If that's OK. Someone broke into my room, you know. It might not be safe.'

She just shrugs. 'Wouldn't be the first time, would it. I'm able for it, don't you worry. Got one of them door cameras and all after my burglary last month.'

'What burglary?'

'Oh, just some local twats, I'm sure. They didn't take owt. Nowt to take.'

I have to tell her something else. 'I went to see Ash. Met the new daughter. Rosalind.' Rosalind Rollason. It sounds like a superhero's alter ego.

Another deep inhale. 'Yeah. He married your little teacher about six months after you left for uni. Patricia would be spinning, the state she's made of that place. Wall to wall beige, it is, apparently.'

'I'm sorry,' I say awkwardly.

She waves it off. 'What's done is done, Karen. You just worry about what you're gonna say to him, up at that prison. Cos I reckon he'll have plenty to say to you.'

I used to think my mother was wrong about everything, terminally deluded, embarrassing. It's somehow even more annoying that she's turning out to be right about a fair bit.

'So what's happening over there?' April's raspy accent seems even more pronounced over the line from America. I can hear the honks of cars behind her, a New York symphony that makes me homesick, even though I am home.

'I'm just helping the police investigate the disappearance.' Not that we have learned anything of value so far. Plenty of clues – this mysterious John, the rude man on Lara's stairs, the Jeep-driving prowler in my room – but no answers.

'You see him yet?'

'No. Hoping not to. I don't know if he knows anything about this case or if it's some copycat. But April, I've heard he's not happy about the book.'

She snorts. 'Well, of course he isn't. He's a serial killer, he doesn't get to have opinions on what people say about him. There's no way he can sue.'

'I'm not worried about being sued.' I'm worried about having the blood of yet another woman on my hands. 'What if someone's holding this girl, someone working with him? What if he's directing the whole thing?'

She's silent, and I can almost hear her mind whirring. 'You know, we should get you on to do some TV.'

'No! I don't want anyone knowing I'm here.'

'Come on, they know already, or they will soon. I bet the press have spies all over that prison. The guards, they don't earn much, right? Nice to have a little extra on the side?'

She's right. It's actually a miracle the story hasn't broken yet. 'So?'

'So get out ahead of it, babe. Yes, you flew all that way because there was a possible connection between this new case and him. You're doing everything you can to help, despite all the trauma it stirs up for you.'

She's good. Even I almost believe that. 'But . . .'

'Trust me, hon, you can't avoid the attention. What you can do is direct it. Feed the narrative of Karen the survivor, working to help women. Emelia Han's there too? I saw her post from Manchester.'

So much for staying off-grid. 'Yeah. She's terrified too, I think.'

'That's perfect. She's Little Miss Victim, so if she says you're OK then the internet will believe it. You'll finally be out from under it. The curse of *she must have known*.'

It's certainly tempting, to be able to control the story in that way. 'OK. But just local TV. It won't have much interest beyond Yorkshire, I'm sure.'

She sighs. 'You do know we want it to have interest, babe? As in, we want to sell the book you're publishing next month? I know you think it's tacky, but selling books keeps the lights on, Karen.'

She is also right about that. I can't write a book about it and hope it doesn't sell. And I need the money. My bank account is getting stretched, what with flights and hotels. It's hypocritical to want both sales and anonymity. 'Alright. God, you're so persuasive.'

'You'd be worried if your agent wasn't, babe. OK g2g, I'll get on it.'

As she hangs up I can hear her asking someone for a light. April is convinced that, because she only does it now and again, she's a non-smoker. We all have our delusions.

I can't believe I am almost forty and back in my teenage single room, which still has a tide mark on the wallpaper from where I spilled a glass of Orange Tango when I was thirteen. I can't risk looking at Jen's diary again while Arlene's in the house, so I lie in bed for a while staring at the ceiling until I pass out. In the morning, I'm woken by Arlene opening the door. She stands in the doorway, hip against the frame, arms folded, cigarette burning in one hand.

'Feeling sorry for yourself?'

'No. Just – trying to figure out what to do.'

'Sandra's downstairs – you know, my mate who works at the prison. She can tell you what he's like nowadays.'

'Oh. OK.'

'Brush your hair first, maybe.'

Arlene has never been a 'get up and face the day' mother, which I suppose I should be grateful for. If even she is urging me to pull myself together, things must be bad.

Sandra is surprisingly glamorous to be working as a prison officer. False lashes, hair extensions, dressed in her uniform but with long, polished nails. She's about ten years younger than Arlene, I guess. Late forties. When I go down, she and Arlene are discussing Botox providers. 'Little bit between the eyes, Arlene, does wonders. Oh! This her?'

'Hi, I'm Karen.'

She looks me over frankly. 'The writer. I can tell.'

I don't know what this means – nothing complimentary, I imagine – so I pull awkwardly on the hem of my oversized jumper. It may not be glam but it still cost $400.

'You know what's been going on?' I ask her.

'Oh yes. I get it from him, you know. Talks about you all the time, he does.'

Of course, I have always been aware that you are alive, carrying on, ageing like everyone else, but have been able to proceed as if you are dead, locked away for ever. Now I realise you are only behind a few sets of bars, and people escape from prison all the time. It was stupid of me, to forget that. 'So he's annoyed about the book?'

'Well, he thinks he should have been consulted.'

'He kind of gave up that right when he killed all those women,' I say, hotly.

'Oh, things get written about him all the time, all manner of rubbish and lies. He accepts that. But he says you of all people should have asked him. He said you had a deal?'

'A deal?' I swallow. 'What does that mean?'

'Search me, love.' She holds her hand out to the light, examining her nails for chips. 'All I know is he was ever so angry when he heard about it. And he's calm as can be most of the time, unlike the rest of those animals. He likes his peace and quiet.'

'Do you monitor his letters, his visitors?'

'Of course. He doesn't have visitors, save the odd journalist or researcher. Always likes talking to them, to set the record straight. He doesn't like mistakes being repeated. Sloppiness.'

That sounds like you. 'His dad never went? To see him?' I know your father has been dead for a few years now, found several weeks after he passed in that isolated house, even more mad than before.

'Not once. Nor the mum. There's nobody.'

'And his letters? Has anyone been in touch?' It's definitely possible you've set this whole thing up with someone on the outside.

'Nothing so far, just a lot of proposals and more journalists.'

'Proposals?' says Arlene.

'Oh aye, he's a popular boy, our Aaron.' Right. You're Britain's Ted Bundy, with the fan club to match. Women who wouldn't have looked twice at you if you hadn't committed eight murders.

'And – he still says he didn't do it?' It seems ridiculous to maintain your innocence after being convicted of eight killings. But you are careful, and you know how to wait. You have never said anything to incriminate yourself – there was only my evidence, and Emelia's, and a few circumstantial bits that could be explained away. You might reasonably have had hopes of acquittal. And now, if there's a new crime . . . But I can't think about that.

'He's never admitted to a thing,' says Sandra.

I sigh and put my head in my hands. 'So he wants to see me?'

'He'll talk to you, he says. No one else.'

'Meaning, what? He does know something about this disappearance?'

'He won't say. Just drops hints, like.' So this could all be nonsense – Lara just a non-connected case you're using to get me to visit you, to manipulate me, and I do feel manipulated.

I've taken a dislike to Sandra. The way she talks about you is proprietary somehow, like you're a tricky genius only she can manage. I suppose she knows you better than I do now. I haven't seen you for ten years. And the way she looks at me, I can almost see her itching to give me a makeover. 'So how did you and Mum get to be friends?' It seems suspicious, her working with him and suddenly being BFFs with my mother. On the other hand, Marebridge is a small place.

'Oh, through the book club, wasn't it? I said straight off, you're the mum of that Karen, are you? I don't mince my words, see. And she said aye she was, and I said I worked with him up at the prison.'

'Weird coincidence.'

She laughs. 'Hardly, pet. Half the town works at the prison, no other jobs, are there. Anyway, he's sent you a visiting order, so just book yourself in and he'll see you.' As simple as that. Like making an appointment with the dentist. Last time I saw you it was in the dock at the Old Bailey. The time before that was in my bed. How can I face you now?

'I – I don't know if I can. Not yet.'

'Let me know and I'll be there. Everyone'll want to get a look at you. The big reunion. Aaron and Karen.' She pronounces your name so it rhymes with mine, the way people did around your trial for a time. 'Kare-Aar, that's what they used to say in the papers, isn't it?'

I scowl at her so hard I almost strain my neck muscles. 'Please don't use that name. I don't – I'm trying to move on from it. Rebuild my life.'

Arlene intervenes. 'Ta, Sandra. She'll have a think about it. Big step, after all this time.'

Sandra stands up, brushing off her uniform. 'I best be away to work. I'll tell him you're thinking about it. He'll be ever so pleased.' She looks at me critically. 'Maybe put a bit of lippy on before you go, love, you're pale as death, you are.'

I can see now why Sandra and my mother get on.

Chapter Nine

From *Becoming Bagman* by Karen Walker

For a long time after Aaron's trial, I was obsessed with reading true crime. Not for the horrible details – I'd had enough of those. No, I wanted to read about the wives, the lovers, the friends and families. Ted Bundy's girlfriend Liz, who called the police on him several times and thought he had tried to kill her once, yet still stayed in contact with him even after his arrest. Let him play with her daughter, act the family man. He came home to her on the weekend he killed two women at Lake Sammamish. She couldn't say she had never suspected him and yet it wasn't easy to stop loving him. Doubt kept her stuck, doubt and need.

Then there's Sonia Sutcliffe, the wife of the Yorkshire Ripper. She had alibied him for several of the thirteen murders he committed, never seemed to notice him burning clothes at the house or cleaning off blood. How? The Golden State Killer had a wife, and so did BTK, and the Green River Killer. These are normal-looking men we're talking about. It's not about desperate incels. I don't know what it's about. Maybe a sudden urge to violence, allowed out once then impossible put back in its box. If they aren't caught, if the police are incompetent, they must start to think they can carry on doing it. Because they enjoyed it. The fear of the woman, her pain. That feeling of power and control. I think that's why they go so far. Because we let them. But what the media doesn't realise, in the black and white of why didn't she know, why didn't they report him, is that you can believe two things at the same time. You might wonder if your partner, acting strangely, is the serial killer you're living in terror of, but a larger part of you will hope he isn't, because it's ridiculous, it's mad. He's a man you have loved, who you've seen be kind. Of course the monster isn't living in your house. Wouldn't you know?

I'm here to tell you, you would not know. Not always. Even a monster is not a monster to everyone. That's how they stay free. That's how it was for me. Sometimes I thought – maybe, God, maybe? But then I'd wake up and see the daylight and remember how he was with me and I'd dismiss those thoughts as phantoms. Gareth had killed Jen out of jealousy, and these other women were being killed by someone else. The Bagman. A ghost.

103

Desperate for something to do that isn't seeing you, I text Emelia's crime guy while I eat breakfast, some depressing low-calorie bread that's all Arlene has in. I don't even know what to say. *Hi can you help me work out if my murderous ex is behind a new crime, even though he's in prison?* I settle for *Hello it's Karen, Emelia gave me your number.* As soon as I press send I see him typing back, dweeb. He's currently in Harrogate at a true-crime convention and wonders if I would like to meet him there. There are 'many in the community with theories'. I don't know why people give such weight to theories. They don't have to be proven – they're just anyone's mad story about an event that's hard to understand. Look at 9/11. But I agree anyway. It will keep me moving, and give me the illusion that I might be helping.

The convention – CRIMAPALOOZA, I wish I was joking – is held in a surprisingly nice hotel in the centre of Harrogate that has been restored to its former Victorian splendour. On the way there I deliberately avoid the deserted roads where Emelia ran and ran from you, finding no one that could help her, until a car finally passed and she dashed into the road to stop it. The entire ballroom and downstairs conference rooms have been taken over by stalls and booths and attendees milling about in lanyards, trying to drink coffee from those squat little cups while eating a biscuit at the same time. I'm dismayed to see they aren't all twitchy weirdos either. There are lots of young women with tote bags, like the one who broke the news to me in New York. I pass a bookstall and eyes stare out at me. Ted Bundy. Peter Sutcliffe. I know you will be there too, that famous photobooth shot of you laughing. I was just to your side when that was taken, sometime in 2008 or 2009, and in the other three on the roll we are squashed together. A rare picture of you smiling, and I suppose that's why they use it. The contrast. The way Ted Bundy was supposed to be handsome, but I can't see it. There's a madness barely hidden in his eyes, I think. Sends a shudder through me. I don't have a lanyard, but no one stops me wandering about, and I find my way to where Matt said he would be, in the Diamond Room.

I find the door propped open, and a session in full swing, a man standing up in front of a projector screen and talking. A board by the door reads *Armchair Detectives: ordinary citizens solving crimes. With Matthew Cooke.* So this is Emelia's weirdo, and I'm further dismayed to see he is actually normal-looking. My type, even, with dark-framed glasses and a little stubble. He's short and trim, in a navy hoody and jeans. He's saying something about a podcast called *Teacher's Pet*, and then he looks up and spots me. I duck to the side.

'Just one more question then? Yes, lady at the front there?'

A dogmatic-looking woman in a floral dress asks, 'Would you agree that all police material should always be released to the public, so we can know what's going on in cases? We might even help solve them, like you've said.'

He thinks about it. 'Well, I'd have to say no, in fact. There are reasons they keep active cases confidential. For example, the suspect might actually be someone known to the victim, pretending to be helpful and concerned, getting involved in the investigation. Or they might be innocent and leaking their name could destroy their life. But for cold cases with no movement, then yes, it would be helpful for citizen detectives to have access to the evidence.' She seems satisfied with the answer, and I wait as he wraps up and a gaggle of women swamp him with further questions. He answers them all patiently and kindly. He's not even a weirdo. Damn.

Finally, it's my turn. He smiles. 'Sorry. Overran a bit. You're Karen Walker – or Karen Cruz. I recognise you from your book jackets.'

I'm surprised – not many people read those books. 'I don't know why I'm here. Emelia just said to talk to her "crime guy".'

He rolls his eyes at this. 'She has no concept of actual detection work. That whole trauma, resilience, influencer side of true crime – it's important, but it's not for me, I'm afraid.'

'Me either. But then I'd just prefer to never think about it again.'

'I understand. Shall we?'

We get coffees from an urn, barely warm and bitter. New York has spoiled me. I feel people watching him as we find a table to stand up by, as if he's a superstar in this world. I should have googled him first, I suppose. 'So like I said, I'm not sure why Emelia wanted us to talk. How can you help?' Fear has made me surly.

He sips his drink, makes a face. 'I know a lot about the Hughes cases. You didn't listen to my podcast?'

'Of course not. That was my actual life.'

What fun, listening to hours of breathless millennials discussing my worst nightmares.

'No. Makes sense, I guess. Sorry. But I did a pretty deep dive into it all.'

'Me as well?'

He doesn't even blush. 'Kind of hard to leave you out. The girlfriend. The one who reported him.'

'The one who alibied him, too. Allowed him to get away with – Jen.'

'That's not strictly true though, is it? He wasn't charged as a suspect in the murder of Jen Rollason. And it was his father who falsely alibied him.'

There had been talk of charging your dad for that, but even then it was clear he was so far gone he probably did think you'd been home all day.

'I confirmed he was at home when the murder took place. He wasn't.'

But Matt seems determined to think well of me. 'You just repeated what his dad told you, right? It's understandable. You were only a kid, and Hughes was your – well, he was something to you, wasn't he?'

'I was wrong though. And I sent the wrong man to prison.'

'You did what you could with the evidence you had.'

He is kind, and I want to believe that about myself, but I just can't. After all, I know myself better than he does.

'Have you spoken to Gareth?' I ask.

'I did for the podcast, yes. He was – keen to get his side across.'

'So what do you think's happening now? This new disappearance?'

He swallows coffee, and I watch the slide of his throat under his hoody. It has the *X-Files* logo on it: *I want to believe.* 'It's an interesting one. Obviously, Hughes is in prison, that's indisputable.' Though I would still like to prove it with my own eyes, if I could bear to see you at all. 'But someone with knowledge of the case has clearly taken Lara Milton.'

'You know it all, huh. That it's the real symbol?'

But is it, *is it*? The needles of doubt, suppressed once you were safely in prison, they are back. It's only my memory that proves it was the same symbol found on the bodies and in your notebooks. Can I rely on that? If it's all that's stopping a murderer walking free?

He shrugs. 'I have contacts. People talk to me.'

I stare into my grey coffee. 'I don't think it would be helpful right now to confirm to the world that someone drew Aaron's symbol in the blood of a missing girl.' So far, the police have been cagey with what they release to the press. Donetti's the only one who even believes there's a link.

He recoils, offended. 'I do think about the ethics of what I do. Especially with live cases, there are all sorts of legal issues to consider. I'm careful.'

I want to ask what's ethical about using my pain to make money, but I bite my tongue. I need his help. 'OK. You have to keep that to yourself, that it's the same. Have you ever seen the symbol?'

He shakes his head. 'That's what makes it so potent, I suppose. That hardly anyone ever saw it, and there are no pictures in circulation. Hard to believe, in this phone-saturated world, that nothing has ever leaked.'

Almost all the crime scene pictures that show the symbol were destroyed or kept in physical form under lock and key. No hackable clouds or secret WhatsApp groups back then. You went to prison in 2013, just before smartphones were everywhere. 'There must be one somewhere out there,' I say. 'People have seen it. Some people, anyway.'

'You'd have to know it well, to reproduce it,' he says. 'Like not just a brief glance at a crime scene over ten years ago.'

I shut down my doubts again. 'So who could it be then?'

He mulls it over, tapping his fingers on the table. They are long and graceful, like a pianist's. 'You've talked to the families?'

'Not yet. They mostly weren't keen to talk to me for my book.'

'I got them all for my podcast.'

That actually impresses me. 'You did? Even the Khans?'

'I flew to Pakistan. That's how I know Emelia, actually, the podcast. She really wanted to control her own narrative. Full editorial approval or she wouldn't talk.'

'She's smart. If annoying.'

I shouldn't have said that out loud, but he smiles slightly. 'There's a few people here at the convention I'd like you to meet, if you're up for it. Experts on the case – they've helped me research quite a few things in the past.'

I sigh. 'I take it you don't mean actual experts, like police officers or forensics people.'

'Amateur experts. But not doing something for a living doesn't mean you can't be good at it, you know. Like writing.'

'It's nothing like writing.' I don't know anyone who just writes for the sheer joy of it. We need our words to be read, to exist in someone else's head.

'I'm actually working on a book myself, you know.'

I roll my eyes. 'Sure you are. Maybe I'll just fire off a podcast, can't be hard.'

He laughs. 'It isn't hard. Hard to keep the listeners, however. People have almost zero tolerance for boredom in the audio space.'

I drain my horrible coffee. 'Where are these weirdos then?'

'I've booked a break-out room, if you don't mind. I thought we could sort of pool our knowledge of the case. Of course, you know the most of all.'

As we walk through the crowds, I realise that probably isn't true. I avoided much of the details of the murders at the time, and wasn't allowed in the courtroom for most of the evidence, and have done my best to forget it all for the last ten years, whereas these people are absolutely steeped in it. I mentally prepare to be corrected about my own life by some total strangers.

Matt pauses with his hand on the door. 'Eh. They call themselves the Brains Trust. But don't let that put you off, they do know their stuff.'

Three people are waiting for us in a small conference room, around a horseshoe table that could hold twenty or so. There are bottles of expensive water on the side and some curling pastries. I walk into an argument. '. . . I can't believe you would even say that, Jim, the second-man theory was widely debunked at the time . . .'

'Maybe it's time to open our minds, Janine, and . . .'

'Really quite irresponsible to peddle these old theories and . . .'

Matt raises his voice. 'I found her, everyone.'

They stop and turn to stare at me. A woman of about fifty (Janine, I presume), with scraped-back hair and a large T-shirt with a magnifying-glass logo on it. An older man in a blazer and slacks who smells strongly of cigarettes (Jim?), and another example of my absolute nemesis, a young woman with long mousey hair and thick 1980s glasses. Gen Z, the most avid true-crimers of the lot. These are Matt's experts? I shoot him a sceptical look, but he just smiles pleasantly.

'You're Karen Walker?' says Janine, accusingly (I will soon learn she says everything this way).

'Karen Cruz.'

She ignores this. 'Can't believe it's *the* Karen Walker. Thought you never came to stuff like this. Too good for true crime.'

I stare her down. 'Maybe you mean unwilling to constantly relive the most traumatic moments of my life.'

'She's right, Janine,' says the young girl. 'Conventions like this always fail to serve the needs of victims or create a safe, harassment-free space.' She gives me a shy smile. 'I'm Mercedes.'

'Jim,' the man says, sticking out a red paw and crushing my fingers to a pulp with it. 'Ex-crime reporter. Never really leaves the blood.'

'I'm a criminology student,' says Mercedes. 'And YouTuber. You might have seen my vlog – *Doing the Crime, Drinking the Wine*?'

'I haven't.' I can't think of anything worse.

Janine is still staring at me. 'You look totally different. I wouldn't have known you at all, you're so much older now.'

'And what do you do?' I ask her rudely. 'Any background in crime or law?'

She sniffs. 'I run the web's biggest forum for amateur sleuths.' She taps her ample bosom, which bears the logo I noticed before and the words *Citizens Detect*. 'We've actually solved at least three cases in the past two years.'

God, why are these people so keen on seeking out crime? Why are they drawn to the horror of it, the pain and suffering and fear? Why is it fun to them? I suppose they've never experienced it close up. 'Anyway. You have some thoughts on this latest disappearance?'

Jim indicates a legal pad full of loopy scrawls. 'We have a number of working theories. You confirmed the symbol was real?'

How does everyone know about this already? 'As far as I can tell.'

'I'd do anything to see it,' says Mercedes wistfully.

'Most people who've seen it are dead.' I am sharper than I meant to be, but she's exactly the age of a number of your victims. And you carved it into their skin.

'I've looked everywhere,' says Janine, who I assume is Extremely Online. 'Dark web, even. It's not findable. Not without access to hard-copy police records.'

'It could be one of them,' Mercedes jumps in. Young people seem to hate the police, not asking who is supposed to catch the murderers if not them. 'Institutional corruption is rife in Yorkshire. Look at the Ripper investigation.'

'I'd rather not,' I say tartly. 'But let's say that might be true for a second. It's someone in the police who has seen the archive photos, or remembers the symbol from a past case. Why now? Why Lara Milton?'

'We have some theories,' says Janine. I imagine she says this at least once an hour. 'First, she lives in the town where your ex is imprisoned.'

'He isn't my ex!' I snap. 'We were . . . friends.' The twisting of the truth, always elusive and just out of reach, like dandelion fluff. Who could say what we really were to each other? I have always maintained I was not your girlfriend. That doesn't mean I didn't want to be. Or that we never touched, never kissed, never slept together. That I didn't love you.

111

'Whatever. It's the same town, so that must be significant. And the symbol. They want us to think he's involved – or else he actually is.' That 'us' rankles with me, as these randoms have no connection to the case at all. If they did, they wouldn't find it all so enjoyable.

'How could he be involved though?' I have my own theories, of course, but want to be told it's not possible.

Jim lists them off for me. 'Any number of ways. Prison staff he's got under his thumb, ex-offenders who've got out, or he's writing to someone on the outside and pulling the strings.'

'But why this woman? Why Lara?'

'That's the big question. Is it just opportunistic or does she have some connection to the case, to him, or to someone who worked on it maybe. Now I knew everyone involved back then – reported on several of the murders. I can dig them all up, the old officers. Though in some cases I'd have to actually dig them up.' He gives a wheezy laugh and Mercedes frowns at him. Clearly, the levity of it all offends her, if not the actual murders.

'I can look into Lara's background,' she says. 'We're about the same age, I can maybe get her friends to talk to me. Was she dating anyone? Statistically, that's the most likely person to have hurt her.'

'Apparently, she had been, and it hadn't gone well. There's been no luck on finding the man, John someone, though I think that's a fake name. He was using a burner phone.'

Mercedes frowns. 'Dating apps are supposed to release any information on abuse if the police ask.'

'Wasn't from an app. They met IRL.'

She looks shocked by the very possibility of this.

Janine chips in next. 'I'll work the web. Girl that age, she'll have a footprint larger than China. If there's a connection, we'll find it.'

Matt has been nodding along all through this, eyes focussed and full of empathy. I wonder if that's his secret. The projection of giving a shit. 'And I'll do what I do – track people down. Any of the families that haven't talked, Hughes's mother perhaps.'

'She's been gone years,' I object, but he just shrugs.

'I'm good at finding people.'

I hate to say it but I need to. 'What can I do?'

Janine scowls again. 'Obvious, isn't it?'

'Is it?'

'You know him. You take that angle. Why'd he pick her, if he did. Who's he in contact with. Any reason he might be doing this now, after ten years inside.'

That's when I realise what could be the trigger for all this. Sandra said you knew about my book. That you weren't happy about it, that we'd had a deal.

What if you're doing all this, arranging Lara's abduction somehow, dispatching a proxy to hurt her, telling them how to draw the symbol, holding her somewhere or even killing her – to send a message to me? To make me come to you – and finally tell the truth about what happened all those years ago?

On my way out from the convention, still trembling at this possibility, I am stopped in my tracks. It's you. Staring out at me. My heartbeat soars and then levels out, shakily, as I realise it's a large poster of you, tacked up on a board by the door of another break-out room. A wonkily printed piece of paper reads *The truth about Bagman – new leads in the Aaron Hughes case*. Of course, everyone here will know there's a new case, one that could throw doubt on your conviction. The room is crammed, standing room only already. All of them so keen to soak up the details of what you did, and even play with the idea you didn't do it after all, that some other killer has been lurking all this time, waiting for their moment.

I have to get out of here. I turn blindly, and almost collide with someone on their way into the talk. 'Oh, sorry.' Then I blink. It's one of the young tote-bag-carrying girls, but I recognise her. It's Rosalind Rollason.

She looks shocked to see me. 'Oh! You're here.'

'What are you—?'

'Just interested. You know, the narrative around victimology.' It makes sense, I suppose, since her sister was murdered, though I've personally done my best to avoid all this stuff. And why does she look so rattled to see me? I wonder if she's somehow figured out that I took Jen's diary.

'But why that session?' I'm amazed she could listen to details of your murders without breaking down. I don't think I could.

Her response is fierce. 'What do you think it's like, having this perfect sister you never even met, because someone murdered her? When you wouldn't exist if she hadn't been killed? Of course I want to know what I can. God knows Dad won't talk about it.'

I hadn't thought of that. 'Listen, Rosalind, I—'

'I've got to go.'

Hurriedly, she shoulders her bag and pushes her way into the packed room. No one even notices her, or suspects who she is.

114

Chapter Ten

From *Becoming Bagman* by Karen Walker

The day Jen died was normal. Seven years I spent in that school, over two hundred days a year, and yet it's all a blur of meaningless information and bone-crushing boredom. English, probably. *The Tempest*. Our revels now are ended. Maths, history. I do remember it was raining that day, the floors smeared with mud and grime. It was the first day of school after Jen's party, where she had the big public row with Gareth Hale. The Sunday I'd spent alone in the cold and dreary house, texting both Jen and Aaron, neither answering. Arlene came back around six from her weekend away with Ash Rollason. She seemed sad, subdued, so I was surprised to find out later that Ash had proposed over the weekend. She didn't seem like someone who'd got engaged, and she mentioned nothing to me. I remember we watched *Bridget Jones's Diary*, Arlene smoking cigarette after cigarette down to their dregs, so I had to wash my hair in the morning to get rid of the smell.

Aaron didn't actually come to school that day, which was hardly unusual since he didn't see the point of it. Obviously I didn't see Gareth Hale. I presume he was at home, or working on the farm. I did see Jen, once, crossing the lobby, on her way to the big main staircase. Hair swinging, skirt hitched up, followed by her friend Sinead. We stopped to chat for a bit. I can't remember what about.

After school I got off the bus as usual, near the woods. It was there that I saw Gareth, sitting in his car by the steps leading down to the Dale. It was definitely him, I have no doubt of that, and anyway, the ANPR proved he'd driven by there around that time. He was looking at his phone, and didn't see me. I've already discussed what happened next, how I called round to Aaron Hughes's house and thought I saw him in bed, then went home and sat in front of *Neighbours*, disconsolately doing my homework by the electric fire. No sign of Arlene. Everything seemed leached of colour that day, one of those damp December ones where the light is dying and so is your spirit. It was unfortunate for me that no one saw me go into the house, that I spent so much time alone. It was unfortunate for Gareth that I believed Aaron's father when he told me Aaron was home, but in bed. I did not see him with my own eyes, no, but I believed, and so I gave him a false alibi.

Ash rang about seven, I think. Jen had not
come home. Was she with me? That was the first
inkling I had that anything was wrong.

◆ ◆ ◆

I've never been to a prison before. It seems ironic, when I was
so close to ending up in one myself. I'm already breathing hard
as I pull up to the gates. The officer checks my ID in silence, as
if wondering who I'm visiting and what they've done. I want
to tell him I've never come before, that I've never visited you,
unlike Sonia Sutcliffe, who kept seeing her husband. I'm only
going because you have forced my hand, despite being locked
up, despite having no power. Somehow you are still controlling
my actions.

Arlene has come with me and I'm not sure why. Something
to do, she said, shrugging, as if we're on a lovely outing to see
a serial killer. I can feel the secrets between us, the hard shapes
of things we've never said out loud. How lonely it is, to have
no one I can truly open up to. For a while, that was you, and
then after Jen we had spikes between us too, things that could
never be talked about. That was partly why I lived so long with
my suspicions, why I couldn't bring myself to say, *Hey, you're
not the Bagman, are you?* There were things I didn't want to talk
about either.

'You didn't have to come. It's nothing to do with you.'

She makes a huff of annoyance. 'You know, you took off after
it happened, after the trial, but the rest of us have to live with this
every day. I have to picture him sitting in my living room drinking
orange squash. Knowing what he did.'

I've never thought of it that way before, how she felt about the whole thing. The insinuations that her only child was somehow implicated in the murders.

'It wasn't my fault.' A teenage reply coming out of my adult mouth.

She sighs. 'I never said it was, Karen. Maybe some did, but not me.'

The prison is a single-storey building, seventies breeze block, surrounded by a barbed-wire fence. Cameras everywhere. Inside is searingly hot and stuffy, a hundred radiators stewing up the smell of cooked vegetables. A disinterested uniformed woman sits behind the desk, and she logs my fingerprints, pressing them on to a smeared pane of glass. My prints were taken when they arrested us too, rolled in ink that time. They wouldn't let me wash it off properly, and I spent the next three days rubbing at my nails and skin, driven mad by every whorl exposed.

Arlene won't come in with me. 'I'll stop out here. Don't want to go through the machine.' She settles into reception with her book-club book, something brooding and crime-ridden. Irony again. I surrender most of my possessions: lip balm, phone, headphones, bank cards. I'm patted down and given a badge to wear. Sticky. No pins, nothing sharp.

I feel fear rising in my solar plexus. This is a building of caged men, dangerous men. I feel like I'm stepping into an alternative reality, one where I went to prison at seventeen for Jen's murder. I'd be out by now, wouldn't I? I was only a kid. But still, there's no coming back from something like that. I only have to look at Gareth to know.

Sandra is waiting for me on the other side of various locking doors, heavy make-up, hair back, uniform neatly ironed. 'You made it, then.'

I just nod. I can't speak.

'Come with me. Lot of locks to go through.' It seems to take a long time, into the bowels of the prison, cream-painted corridors of cold stone, door after door of reinforced glass, the buzz of electric doors and the inappropriately jaunty jingle of Sandra's keys. I clear my throat. 'What will it be like? Will there be, you know – the phones and the glass? Like on TV?'

She laughs. 'That's America, you daftie. You'll just be in a little room, guards with you. He'll be sitting down but not cuffed. That's his human rights.'

'So – he could come at me? Touch me?'

'They'd stop him. Anyway, he knows what side his bread's buttered. He's never getting out, so he has to behave himself or things won't be very nice.'

It seems shockingly lax to me, the idea that you'll be sitting opposite me, free and unfettered. I've always been liberal, but it's amazing how quickly that changes when you're face to face with a murderer. I still can't believe I'm actually going to see you. That you are a real man of flesh and blood, not the bogeyman and monster of my dreams.

We come to another door with two guards outside it, a man and a woman, both very young and slight. What protection would they be against you? Sandra nods to them. 'Damian, Kerry, this is Karen. Take care of her, yeah?' Kerry has bad skin and heavy eye-liner, which I see when she shoots me a judgemental look. She unlocks the door and suddenly, before I am ready, we're in the same space. It's you. After all these years. After all those books and documentaries and podcasts, this is you, in the flesh, a real live man.

You look older. Of course you do. But older than I'd imagined, even. Your skin is sallow and you're not the lean boy you used to be. Puffy from prison food and likely medicated, if the yellow tinge is anything to go by. You wear a grey tracksuit, not the orange jumpsuits you see in American films. You look up and smile and it's the same, though your hair is receding instead of just shaved like it used to be. Your eyes are just the same icy blue. 'There you are, Kare-bear.' What you used to call me, pronouncing my name so that the phrase rhymed. How I loved that, once.

My body is flooded with stress, rooting me to the spot and jamming my tongue to the roof of my mouth. I'm too dry to speak for a moment. 'Um.'

'I'll get you some water,' says Sandra, disappearing down the corridor. The two guards take up positions in corners of the room, both looking totally disinterested and staring into space. The male one is picking at his nails.

You give me a little wave. 'I'm not going to bite, Kar. It's just me.'

I pull out the plastic chair with a scrape and sit down. There are no windows in here. Nothing but the table and chairs. 'Hi.'

You search my face. 'You look good. All grown up. Make-up and highlights. Botox yet? No. You don't need it.'

I just stare.

You wave a hand over your own face. 'I know, I know, prison isn't the best beauty regime.'

'Why am I here? What's going on?'

You smile. 'Straight into it? No, Kar. It doesn't work like that. First we talk.'

I swallow again. 'What's there to talk about?'

'Well, the last time I saw you, you were across the Old Bailey, telling them all kinds of things about me. A splash of blood on my shoe once. Cuts on my hands. The symbol.'

'It was all true.' I can't look at you, so I look at my own hands. The manicure I got in New York, before any of this nightmare began, is starting to chip around the edges.

'Still. A bit of a shock that it was you who called them.' And here you lean in close, so close I can feel your breath on my

120

skin, and the guards will surely not be able to hear your intimate whisper. 'I thought we had a deal, Karen. That we'd look after each other.'

I speak at normal volume. 'I don't know what you mean. What deal? What do you mean?'

You laugh. 'I know it's hard to let go of the story you've been telling yourself for ten years. But you will. You're a good storyteller, Kar, you always were. They have your books in the library here. Not bad.'

I don't know what to say to that.

'I always knew you could do it, if you found the impetus. I guess my conviction was enough.'

I'm trembling. 'I lost everything. I had to leave the country. I was getting death threats and being stalked by the press, and you were the one who . . .'

I can't speak your crimes to your face. Not without a court and judge and lawyers in between us.

'Well, you seem to be doing alright now. How big was the advance for the memoir?'

'So that's what this is about.'

You shrug. 'I'm just interested. It's a book about me, after all.'

'It's a memoir. It's about me, by definition.'

You laugh. 'You'd be nothing without me. I think we both know that. Working in some mid-level job in Leeds or Manchester, dreaming of being a writer but too afraid to try. I ripped away your safety blanket and look where you ended up. I'm proud of you, Karen. And pleased I could help you become yourself.'

I look at the corner of the room. 'Where is she? Lara Milton?'

'The missing girl? Karen, I've been in prison for ten years. What could I possibly have to do with a woman going missing last week?'

'If you don't know, why pretend?'

'Calm down, Kare-bear. I may not know for sure, but I can maybe offer some – insight.'

'But the symbol . . .'

'Lots of people have seen the Bagman symbol. And there was only your word for it that it even matched mine, wasn't there?'

'But – she's been hurt, they think.'

'Karen, there are lots of predators out there. Surely you know that. And I'm . . . well, not to brag, but I'm famous. Everyone knows about me, so it would be easy to copy the things they say I did.'

Always so careful, never actually admitting that you did anything. Smart.

'Not the symbol. It wasn't made public.'

'Anything can be leaked. You must know that as well. There are pictures, somewhere.'

I look at you again, emboldened by anger. 'Someone took a copy of my book from my hotel room. You wouldn't know anything about that?'

'Again, I'm locked in here. How could I possibly?'

'I don't know. You might have – people on the outside.'

'My dad died, and I've been in here ten years. I don't have people. I never did. Just Dad, sort of, and you. And maybe, for a short while, Jen.'

You have said her name. We never said her name, after it happened. We never even talked about it, how I sent Gareth to prison, how she died. You couldn't have been with her that day. If you had, the alibis I gave us both would have crumbled. So we never addressed it. 'I saw her dad.'

'I hear he has a new family.'

'Yeah. A daughter.' I think of Rosalind's undented teenage rage and her perfect skin and shiny hair, and I think of what you

122

did to other young women on the cusp of life, and I can hardly breathe.

'And how's your mum?' You're courteous, like any old friend catching up.

'The same. Fine, I guess.'

'It would never have worked between her and Ash, you know. You did her a favour. He's too basic for Arlene.' I purse my mouth at the suggestion I did something to end the relationship. It was Jen who did her best to stop it.

I hear myself say, 'I'm sorry about your dad.'

'Don't be. He was a nutcase, as you know.' How strange to be surrounded by people all the time, and yet so utterly alone. You have no one now. No one who would care if you died in here, except perhaps some of the staff. Sandra spoke of you with something approaching kindness.

She comes back then, with two plastic cups of water, one for me and one for you. 'Catching up?'

'It's been a long time for sure,' you say. 'Too long.'

Sandra looks between us a few times. 'Well, I suppose I'll leave you to it. Remember to stay in your seat, Aaron. Be good.'

She goes again. You smile. 'She's a hoot, Sandra. I bet her and Arlene tear the place up.' You were always strangely fond of my mother. Of anyone with fight in them.

'So why did you want to see me?' I say again. 'It can't just be to tell me some theories about Lara.' I don't entirely believe you know nothing, but as you said, how could you be involved? I can see with my own eyes you're a captive here. 'Is it the book?'

'I was hurt by that, I'll admit. That you didn't think to run it past me, like all of the other people involved. Libel laws do still cover prisoners you know. I checked.'

'I didn't libel you.'

'Well, I wouldn't know. Since you didn't send me a copy.'

'You can read it, if you really want to. Why would you want to though? It's not exactly flattering.'

'Oh, I don't know. To see if you kept our pact, maybe.'

This again. 'I don't know what you . . .'

Your eyes are intense, burning. I remember how I used to gaze into them, the fiery blue of your irises. Once I tried to paint that colour, mixing colours on a plate, but I didn't come close to the shade.

'Yes, you do, Karen. That day. What we agreed.'

'But we didn't even—'

'We didn't need to talk about it! You know and I know what we agreed. In the corridor, at the police station. The day after she died.' You mean Jen. I bow my head, unable to speak. 'You broke it when you called the police on me, but fair enough, I can see you had no choice by that point. But telling a story you *know* isn't true? That's lying, Karen. And we never lied to each other.'

It's true, in a crazy way. I never asked you if you were the Bagman. Would you have told me if I had? I actually think you might have. Because I was the only one you trusted, and I had earned that by lying to the police for you, as you had for me. Until I gave you up to them.

I'm losing the thread of the conversation. You always had this effect on me. 'So that's why I'm here then? You just wanted to mess with me?'

You speak simply. 'I wanted to see you again. That's all. Ask you why.'

'Why what?'

'Why you lied.'

'I don't know what you—'

You roll your eyes. 'The book, Karen. The record needs to be true. Not like this TV show they're making, just a pack of lies. Everything in the book needs to be exactly true, because that was our deal.' What I've said in the book is of course not what I said to police twenty years ago, the testimony that sent Gareth to prison. I've had to revise my memories of that day, explain why I got it so wrong in such a way that seems like confusion, gullibility, rather than deliberate calculation. I suppose it makes sense you want to know what story I've spun now.

'So you want me to amend it? How can you even know what I've said?'

'I want to read the book, at least, before it's published.' Your tone is so mild and reasonable.

'And then you'll tell me what you know about Lara?'

'I will tell you whatever I can deduce about this case. I didn't say I *knew* anything.' Your riddles, your games. I used to find these so thrilling. Now I just feel nauseous.

'What do you mean, deduce?'

You sit back in the chair, as relaxed as anyone could be while in a high-security prison. 'I've had a lot of time to think in here. I can bring a sort of – clear vision to a case like this. Tell you where to look, you and your policeman hunk, Officer Hot Bod.'

I glower. You could always see too much of me.

'But you'll need to earn it, Karen. I'm not just going to tell you. You're going to have to do something for me. That's how it worked, remember? We helped each other.'

I'm getting angry now. 'But what can you possibly want? Why all these games? You're not getting out of here, so why risk the life of some other woman, if you know something?'

You roll your eyes in a familiar expression of impatience. *Get there faster, Kare-bear.* 'I always said the CPS didn't have enough evidence to put me in here.' Not this again. You have hinted on and off over the years that you didn't do one, some, or all of the murders you were convicted of. I've come to believe it's just more games, keeping us on our toes even as you sit behind bars. 'I want you to look at the Bagman cases again. Look for inconsistencies. See what the police got wrong.'

'Alright. So you want to play instead of just telling me. Instead of finding Lara before it's too late.'

'Why not? I don't have much else to amuse me in here. And I'm fairly sure that whoever has Lara won't kill her. Not yet, anyway.' I don't ask how you know. You know because you are a killer, one who never kept his prey alive to play with. Not your style. You seemed to pride yourself on the cleanness of it. Anonymous, a need satisfied. 'Also, the key to Lara's case might lie with one of the past murders too. One of the ones I didn't do. Whoever did this has seen the symbol, so ask yourself who has a copy?'

'One of the families, you mean?'

'It's quite likely, isn't it?' What does that mean? One of the families has a copy of the symbol, which found its way to whoever took Lara? 'So, what – you want me to clear your name, or something?' I'm lost in the maze of your hints and half-truths.

You shrug. That half-smile I used to love, that now terrifies me. 'You tell me, Karen. If there's a chance I'm not the Bagman, wouldn't you want to know?'

There's no chance of that. There can't be. But you are not wrong, all the same.

'Alright,' I hear myself say.

'You accept?'

'What choice do I have?'

You smile, sitting forward. 'I'm pleased. OK, here's something to start you off. Lara will have been taken by someone she knows.'

'Because she opened the door to them?' I have worked out as much by myself.

You hold up a finger, just like when we were seventeen and you were lecturing me on ancient Egyptian funerary rites. 'Because they knew where to find everything. The bags, the layout. They will have been in her flat before.'

'How do you know about the bags?'

You shrug. 'People talk.'

'OK.' I resist saying thank you. I will pass it on to Chris Donetti, say we need to look even more at Lara's friends and family, her exes, if any. Right now I need to get out of here, because I can feel it has gripped me again, your dark current, the magnetism you always held for me. It took everything I had to run from it last time, and I'm not sure I can do it again.

'I'm going now.' I catch the male guard's eye, and he slowly reacts, pressing a buzzer on the wall.

'Well, it was nice to see you, Kare-bear. You'll come back again.' It's not a question. You already know you have me.

Arlene gives me space on the way home, after I snap 'I don't want to *talk* about it' to her mild question about how it went. Thirty-six going on thirteen. We sit in silence for the drive over the moors, her smell of hairspray and cigarettes filling up the car until I roll down the window, gasping in damp air tanged with soil.

Out of nowhere I say, 'He looks older.'

'We all do, I'm sure.'

'He's not the same. Put on weight, lost his hair.'

'That's what happens.'

'But he is the same. The – intelligence. The games.'

'Mm. You know you don't have to see him if you don't want to.'

I scowl out the window. 'I've no choice. If we want to find this girl.'

'There's always a choice. What makes you think he even knows anything about it?'

'I don't know.' I feel as if I'm being guided by the hand down a dark path, powerless to resist. It's comforting in a way, for someone else to be in control once more. 'It's OK. I can handle it.'

Arlene makes a 'hmm' sound that enrages me. What does she know about me, my capacity for pain, my strength? She hasn't seen me in ten years. She has no idea what I'm really capable of. No one does – except, perhaps, you.

Chapter Eleven

From *Becoming Bagman* by Karen Walker

My first question when Ash rang about Jen was whether her car was gone. He said no, the little pink Mini was still on the drive, but she hadn't come home yet. I could hear a flicker of alarm in his voice, but Ash was protective, and it didn't worry me. Jen didn't drive to school every day, depending on what plans she had after. I had last seen her heading off to an early bus. I told Ash I didn't know where she was, sick of covering for her. Where was Arlene? Working at the pub. The police checked her out too. She was well-alibied, seen by at least ten people pouring pints and flirting. I was alone with no one to alibi me. It was dark by then, of course, early December. Ash rang again at eight, and nine, and ten. There was no answer at the Hughes house when I called. Aaron's dad was likely out rabbiting, using one of those guns with lights on, trapping the prey in the beam, terrified and helpless. The police were called at eleven, and they said they'd come in the morning. Jen was almost eighteen, she was likely with a boy. Gareth Hale had no alibi between 4 and 7 p.m., after which he'd been seen in a pub in town, drunk and belligerent. His mum woke him up to take Ash's call that night – no, he hadn't seen Jen since Saturday. He appeared angry and unhelpful, Ash would say at his trial. His mum said he'd put his clothes in the wash that evening.

None of us slept much that night. Where was she? Where was Aaron? I even tried his dad again, to receive an earful and a hang-up. No, he weren't bloody there, stop calling. The next morning, around six, Ash was at our door. Someone had found a body down by the river.

I can't settle to anything after I see you, turning over in my mind the terrible bargain you offered me. You'll give me clues, and in return I'll try to, what – clear your name of the eight murders you were convicted of? It's absurd, and there's no way you'll succeed. Is there? I spend the rest of the day going over all the information I amassed when I wrote the book, though I focussed mostly on my own experiences. And I read all of Jen's diary, her loopy teenage writing. I don't glean much in between the complaints about school, Arlene, and Gareth. The odd moan about me. She gets coy in the days before her murder, but I think she was planning to dump Gareth, which makes sense given what happened at the party. No mention of you. But something has been torn out, so who knows?

At least I have a plan now – the 'Brains Trust' are all off on their missions too, eager to dive into the case. I didn't get the impression Jim or Janine had much else on, though she did ask about 'expenses'. Matthew just laughed and said that if there's a podcast out of this, he will of course split profits. In the meantime, Donetti is taking me to view the archive pictures in Sheffield. And before that, we have another interview.

I'm terribly nervous about seeing Andy Dickinson, DCI retired. He made his name off convicting Gareth Hale, and was even called in to work on the Bagman cases when it became clear there was a serial killer. He coordinated the investigations between the different forces where the murders took place, only to retire early when it came out he'd entirely missed the connection, even interviewed the killer right at the start of his career and let him go. Surely he must blame me for that, another life I have ruined. But Donetti is driving me now to see him, so I have to go through with it.

He keeps glancing over at me as I fidget, picking at my peeling manicure. 'He's a good bloke, Andy. It'll be OK.'

'Is he? Maybe not when you're a scared teenage girl.'

He inclines his head slightly. 'Maybe. But give him a chance. The landscape has – shifted since then.'

'It's all mad, this. Isn't it? The idea he might – not have done it.'

I need Donetti to tell me it's never going to happen.

He just thinks about it, in his annoying considered way. 'It's true there wasn't much evidence at the time. One or two of the cases might be shaky, I suppose.'

'So what – the wrong man's in prison?'

Donetti shakes his head. 'I highly doubt that. He had no alibis for any of the murders, and there was *some* evidence. Just not a lot. Anyway, if we got the wrong person, does that mean this other guy's done nothing for ten years before suddenly grabbing a girl out of her flat, something he never did before? No. I'm only checking so that *he* can't claim we got it wrong.' The only 'he' there is, for me.

'But he won't get out.'

131

'It's very unlikely.'

Not unlikely enough to suit me, and soon I have picked off most of my remaining gel polish, exposing the weak, scuffed nails beneath.

He says, 'I'm sorry I didn't come with you. He said he'd only talk to you alone.'

'It's OK.' I think of your comment, *Officer Hot Bod*, and I find my gaze drifting sideways, his strong thighs on the seat, his hand moving as he shifts gears. He catches me looking and I blush. 'It's so weird, you know. In part of my brain he's still Aaron, my best friend.'

'Your boyfriend?'

'Not exactly. I never knew what to call him.' I risk: 'What about you, any dodgy exes in your past? Nice wife at home?'

'I'm single,' he says shortly. The thought pleases me, which I find annoying. I can't have a crush on a police officer, especially not one who's running this case.

Dickinson lives in a nice bungalow edging on to the moors. His wife is in the kitchen listening to Radio 4, and he's tending to marrows in the garden. Idyllic. The front hall is hung with family pictures, and I remember he had a daughter about my age, Jen's age too. There's her wedding photo, those are her kids, I presume. I might have had this life, if I hadn't done what I did. And Jen never got to have it at all.

In my head he was old back then, but when he straightens up I can see he's barely into his sixties even now, healthy and fit despite clutching his lower back. 'Shouldn't kneel. Chris, lad.' He shakes Donetti's hand and looks at me. 'Miss Walker.'

'It's Cruz now. Ms Cruz.' I don't know why I say this. As if I'm trying to show I'm not the same person now.

'Aye.' He doesn't shake my hand. 'Well, you'll come in?' He slips off his shoes at the door and calls to his wife in the kitchen. 'Love, will you put t'kettle on?'

She calls back, 'Aye, Andy, just finishing my programme.'

'Obsessed with *The Archers*,' he informs us. 'That Alexa's like a magician. Our Stacey bought us it.' That must be the daughter, the one he referenced at the press conference about Jen's murder. *As a father myself* . . . As if you have to be a parent, or related to a woman, to feel sympathy when someone chokes the life from one.

I sit down on a very firm striped sofa. The wallpaper is pure nineties, with glossy strips, the over-vacuumed carpet is an eye-watering green, and the furniture is fussy, with curved legs and doilies. Still, it's a nice house. I bet Stacey Dickinson had a nice childhood, normal. Chris does the talking. 'Andy, we're here about this Milton case, you're following it?'

'Course. Terrible thing.'

'You know there was – something drawn on the wall?'

'I heard rumours. But it can't be . . . that, can it?'

'It is,' I say. 'He brought me over to identify it and it's real.'

Donetti says, 'We're headed over Sheffield way, double-check against the Bagman photos, but we think it's the same, yeah.'

Dickinson's eyes rest on me for a moment, inscrutable. 'And how could that be?'

I scowl. 'You tell us. Your lot have the only photos of it.'

Donetti smooths it over. 'We're hoping you might have some insight, Andy. Could it be someone from one of the investigations, or one of the families?'

He shakes his head. 'Most of the families didn't see it. Didn't want to look, you know. And we made sure it never got in the press.' Scarred by the Yorkshire Ripper case, where three more women died while they were looking for someone with a Sunderland accent after a tape was sent by a hoaxer, the Bagman team ran a very tight ship.

'But people must have seen it. Officers, CSIs, all of that?' I say.

He narrows his eyes. 'You're suggesting one of my officers did this?'

133

'No . . .' I don't see why it's not a possibility, given the recent revelations about police corruption, but I try to bite my tongue. 'They could have described it to someone though. Or secretly kept a photo?'

'We didn't allow any photos save for a few official ones. And I'll tell you, I saw that symbol dozens of times, in the flesh so to speak, and in pictures, and I still couldn't draw it to save me life. Wasn't that the whole point? That it was complicated?'

He's right. You designed it on purpose to be exclusionary, something only you could draw. Even I have never successfully managed it.

I say, 'So . . . if you're sure about that, then I have to ask – could it have been . . . someone else?'

He narrows his eyes at me. 'What?'

I swallow hard. I can't believe I'm even going to say this out loud. 'There were no copies of the Bagman symbol ever found in Aaron's possession. Right?'

'No. He was careful.'

'It was just me who identified it. And I didn't have a copy either, no one did.' Not that we could find at the time anyway.

He sits forward, watching me closely, and suddenly I'm back in that interview room with no windows and the smell of his BO and I can't breathe. 'You're saying you made a mistake. That he's not the Bagman.'

'I don't know.'

'Another mistake. So what, you wrongly accused *two* people of murder?'

Not exactly fair, since I never directly accused Gareth of killing Jen.

'I don't know! I never knew for sure. Also, there was no symbol when Jen died. She wasn't – cut. No bags used. Maybe the same person didn't even do all of the murders.'

He thinks about it for a moment. 'A jury found him guilty of Jennifer's murder.'

'And one found Gareth Hale guilty, too.'

He glares at me. 'On your evidence.'

'Not just that.'

Donetti says, 'I know it's a long shot, Andy. But now that it's surfaced again, we think it's worth going over all the old cases. Has to be done on the quiet though. There's enough crazies out there think Hughes is innocent.'

'He's not innocent. The case held water, even if it wasn't . . . the strongest. Unanimous verdict.'

'But we have to check.' My voice is wavering, and the look he gives me is so full of hate I can't stand it. I want to scream that it wasn't my fault, that I was seventeen and I loved you and I could not have known what you were.

He looks at Donetti. 'Does your gaffer know you're looking into this, lad?'

'Eh. Not entirely. Karen's keen to help, so I thought why not. It's my own time.'

'Well, on your own head be it.'

The wife comes in then with mugs of tea. Logos of Sheffield Wednesday, Jorvik Viking Centre. So normal it makes me want to cry. She's holding a half-open packet of KitKats under her arm. 'All we had, sorry. We do that keto now, don't keep sugar in the house much.'

'That's lovely, thank you, Barbara.' Dickinson smiles at her.

Her eyes flash over me and I realise she must know it all, how my best friend was murdered and I made it through three days and nights of questioning without even flinching. How I alibied a monster and sent the wrong man to prison. Dickinson must have gone home during that time twenty years ago and said, *I've almost got her, love, I can see in her eyes she's lying.* But then you and I stuck

135

by each other and it swung the other way and I got to live my life, and Gareth went to prison, and Jen was dead, unavenged for ten years. And you went on to kill and kill and kill.

Didn't you?

When the wife leaves, Donetti starts up again. 'So what we'd like to do is definitively rule out anyone from the old investigations who might have seen the symbol, or have access to the photos that exist. And as I said, we plan to look into all the old cases again.'

'It's not right,' he says sharply. 'Stirring all that up.'

'I saw him,' I say, eyes fixed on the carpet, with its hoover marks. 'He hinted he knows something about Lara Milton being missing. And he'll tell me if I – do this for him.'

Dickinson huffs. 'He wants you to prove he's innocent?'

'He wants me to look over the cases. Maybe there's one that doesn't fit?' Like Jen. Jen didn't fit. 'Even if it's rubbish, if it gets him to help us – it's worth it, no?'

Even Donetti quails at the glare Dickinson is throwing my way. 'I know it's unconventional, sir, but we've hardly any leads, and we're getting worried for Lara.'

'Sounds to me like a criminal waste of police time, chasing about doing the bidding of a serial killer.'

'Karen has kindly offered to visit the families, see if they'll talk to her.' We've decided it's best that way, not an official police investigation, no publicity or fuss.

Dickinson makes an incredulous noise in his throat, and I don't blame him. There's a good chance none of them will see me. 'I hope you know what you're doing, Chris lad.'

'I made a list of everyone who had access to the pictures or the crime scenes, if you'd take a look?' He passes over a printout of the same list he sent me, and Dickinson scans it.

'I can check this, see if you've missed anyone. But I'm telling you now, you'd need a copy of it on hand to draw it. And there aren't any copies.'

'OK. I hate to ask, Andy, but were there any doubts around his conviction for the Jennifer Rollason murder?'

'You know there were, son. Not much actual evidence, after ten years had gone by. But what are the chances that he's a serial killer, and he knows her well, and it's not him? It's someone else we've never thought of? Nah.'

I want to believe that's true, that the conviction is watertight, so I gather my strength. 'It wasn't my fault, DCI Dickinson. I didn't know what he was any more than you did when you questioned him.'

He makes a face. 'Seems unlikely not to notice a thing, and you two so close.'

'I could say the same about you, and you a supposedly experienced detective.'

At that point Donetti wisely stands up, takes my mug from my hand and sets it down. 'We'll be off now. Thank you very much for your help.'

I can't resist one more parting comment, though there's no way this man will ever think well of me, no matter what I do. 'I didn't send Gareth Hale to prison. You did that. I wasn't the only one who made a mistake back then.'

But he continues to glare at me as Donetti drags me away, and I know that neither of us is truly convinced.

Back in the car, I feel sheepish. 'Sorry. It just – brought it all back.'

He shakes his head. 'I just don't get why we're making so little progress with the case. She can't just vanish, she's a full-grown woman.'

137

'What about all the leads – this John guy, my break-in? The man on Lara's stairs?'

'He didn't show up on ANPR, whoever was in your room. We don't know that it's even the same person who took Lara. We don't know anything about this John guy, or if that's his real name. We're trawling through pubs they might have met in, but guess what, there's kind of a lot in the area.'

'I know. My mum's probably worked in most of them. I'll talk to the families anyway.'

He sighs again. 'It shouldn't be like this. Relying on trauma-tised victims to go round and interview people, based on some vague hints from a serial killer. We're cut to the bone on this. Even a missing white girl can't drum up the resources for a proper investigation.'

I don't normally get described as a victim, but I'm too agitated to enjoy it.

'You said your dad was on the force back then – does he have any thoughts?'

Donetti says, 'My dad's dead. Three years back.'

'Oh. I'm sorry.'

'Heart attack. We go young, police officers.' I think about his fitness routine, the fact he never seems to stop working, his deter-mination to find Lara. I'm not the only one who needs this case solved fast.

The rest of the day leaves me flattened with exhaustion, as if I've flown to Australia and back. Getting into the archive in Sheffield is as hard as I'd been told, with ID scrutinised, fingerprints taken again, and bags, phones, all personal items left behind in a plastic tray. I start to get jittery again as a young female officer, wearing white gloves, takes us into a windowless room lined with filing cabinets, a table in the middle. I wonder what horrors these bland metal cabinets hold that can't be released to the public. 'The box is out for you, Sergeant,' she says to Donetti, flicking him the same kind of look as the fingerprint officer did in Marebridge. Popular guy, Donetti.

The files are on the table. Boring manila ones, stuffed full of all the documents for eight murders. I cast a fearful look at Donetti as the other officer retreats to the door, watching us closely. It's her job to log every item in and out, so I can see why they're all so sure nothing leaked from here. It's not impossible, but it's very unlikely. And now I have to look at pictures of dead bodies. 'Ready?'

'I can't see – her. Jen.'

'That's OK. There was no symbol there anyway.' But the file is here all the same, and I imagine what's inside it. Notes of interviews with me. My prints, records of DNA samples, scrapings from under my nails.

Donetti flips open a file. 'Just look at this. It's from the wall at the Annie Andersen crime scene. There's no body pictured.' Annie. Your third-last victim. Found dead in an alley in Manchester, with a bag over her head. I take a deep breath and look. A nondescript brick wall. A symbol drawn in blood. Even though it's messy, I can tell this is the same one found at Lara Milton's flat.

I nod. 'It's the one.' I search my mind for proof that this is *your* symbol, the one I saw in your notebook and several other times back in 2004. I was sure, once. But doubt is like a knife slipped between the ribs. Once you let it in, you can no longer trust yourself, not entirely. I wish I could be certain. I wish the case was as watertight as a glass jug, as a diving bell. But it isn't. It never was.

He shuts the file. 'I thought so too but I couldn't be sure. I don't think we need you to look at the bodies. Let's get you home.'

As he drives me back over the moors, I can't bear the idea of going home to sit in my teenage bedroom, so I unlock my phone and message Emelia. *Are you around for a drink?* Emelia is a much-publicised 'sober girl', but she's the only one who might come close to understanding what I'm feeling right now.

To my surprise, she replies right away. *Ugh yes. Going to lose my mind if I don't get out.* Of course she wants me to go to her, but I don't care, as central Manchester will be nicer than Marebridge. I turn to Donetti. 'Would you drop me at a train station, please? I'm going into Manchester instead.'

He can probably guess I'm going to see Emelia. 'If you're sure?'

'I'm sure.'

And maybe I can get her onside. After all, there's a much better chance the families will talk to Little Miss Perfect Victim than they'll talk to me, Karen Walker. The one who should have known.

Emelia is in the bar at her new hotel, the kind of place where a cocktail is £18. She's drinking what looks like water, but I realise is neat vodka. She sees my look. 'What? It's the cleanest spirit.'

For clean read low calorie.

'So no need to ask how you're doing?' Emelia makes a huge deal of her choice not to drink, not because she has a problem of course, but just because it goes with her 5 a.m. club, rise and grind lifestyle.

'Being back here is just . . .' She shivers. 'I never come to the north. Not if I can help it. It feels like he's everywhere. Like he's watching me, every dark alley, every street corner.'

I know what she means. It's something about the landscape, the shadows that lengthen from 3 p.m. The valleys and peaks of people's accents. I never got this in London or the south. No one had time to recognise me there, but here the past is a millstone round my ankle. 'So I met your crime guy. And the "Brains Trust".'

She rolls her eyes. 'Those freaks. But Matt really knows his stuff, he'll help you.'

'I need your help too,' I say, straight up. She wrinkles her microbladed eyebrows. She's wearing another tracksuit, baby pink, but her nails are perfect and her make-up heavy. 'I have to go and see all the families. But not all of them will want to talk to me. There's a few who think I – should have known. Figured it out sooner.'

She frowns. 'Why do you have to?'

'He wants me to. Says that if I look into the old cases, he'll help find Lara. And that maybe one of the families has a copy of the symbol.'

'So you saw him then.'

'I didn't have a choice.'

She taps her pointy nails on the glass. 'He still saying he didn't do it then?'

'Of course. He's never admitted it.'

Her expression is impassive. 'So what, you want me to go with you?'

'Since you're not really doing anything.'

'Uh, I'm always doing something. Content never stops.'

'Please, Emelia.'

'Why would we try to clear his name?'

'To save Lara.'

'You really think he knows something?'

'He's smart. He did a degree the last few years, in criminal psychology. And he has a lot of time on his hands. Even if he's not behind it, he might have figured it out.' I'm struck by how odd it is, that I knew you for so long as just Aaron, someone I loved even, and she only knows you as the monster who came out of the dark

141

and stuck a knife in her. It must be strange for her when I speak of you normally. Not a monster, just a man who went to school and university and existed in the world.

'Urgh. Fine. If it helps find her. But I'm not seeing him, OK? No way. I don't know how you can stand it.'

'Of course not. I wouldn't ask.' You are a bogeyman to her, someone she saw for only a few minutes who then tried to kill her. Then across a courtroom, restrained and caged. 'Let's make a list, anyway.' I take out the notebook I've been filling in, to try and get some semblance of control. 'The weirdos are scouring the web and talking to Lara's friends, also some ex-crime journos.'

The waiter comes over, and I order something with bourbon and 'smoke'. I enjoy the pretention of it all, the little bowl of nuts, the white napkins. The world outside is dark and blood-soaked, so why not carve out a square of light, however stupid? Maybe that's what Emelia is trying to do with her social media. She takes my notebook without asking and reads it. 'God, your writing sucks. Who's Chris?'

'The detective.' I try to keep my voice casual. She glares at me as if she knows.

'I can't be seen to support cops. Police reform is very hot right now.'

'Well, we don't have much choice. And wasn't it the police who rescued you that night?' She had flagged down a car and demanded to be driven to the nearest station.

She frowns. 'I rescued myself.'

'Fine. Anyway, here's the list of families. I can drive us.'

She passes back the notebook. 'Oh, I already hired a driver for as long as I'm here. That'll be easier, then we can work on the way.'

I roll my eyes slightly and wonder how much money she's making from being online. Maybe I should actually listen to April's pleas for me to get on there, and that reminds me I need to talk to her as well.

I stick to one cocktail, as I'm too scared to lose control, but it makes me feel better. Something about Emelia, her inherent shallowness, makes the world seem less dark. Or maybe it's the fact that she's the only other one who understands. The only one who saw what lurked inside you, and lived to tell the tale. She slew the beast, instead of taming it like I did, or thought I did. Really, it was just toying with me while I was useful.

In my notebook is a list of your victims. The names are arranged in order of how you destroyed their lives. At the start there's Jen. The first girl.

Then Catherine.

Alison.

Nita.

Roshana.

Annie.

Victoria.

Julia.

And Emelia. The last girl, the one who lived.

Arlene is out when I get home – it's book-club night, maybe, or she's working. Back in my old room, listening to the sound of someone else's TV next door, I run my fingers over the names of your victims, scored into paper. Gone, but still haunting the world.

Chapter Twelve

From *Becoming Bagman* by Karen Walker

When a bad thing takes place, it unfolds in several grim stages. First there was the night Jen didn't come home, when part of me knew something had happened, but I did not let myself know it. A small tick of panic at the base of my skull. When Ash came round the next morning I was up and in the kitchen, having barely slept at all. It was freezing and I had my dressing gown on, looking out over the misty fields as I drank my tea. My mother had not come home or rung. Ash was the colour of his namesake, as if he were going to be sick. I opened the door to him.

'There's a body,' he blurted. 'The police called. In the woods.'

'Where in the woods?'

'By the river.'

Where Aaron and I always hung out. I refused to let myself feel it. It could be anyone.

'Did they say anything else?'

'They told me to come to the station. Is your mum here?'

'No, she's . . . she stayed over at work. Busy night.'

He looked confused, and I wondered in that moment if he even knew her at all. 'I tried the pub but there was no answer.'

My mother refused to have a mobile phone, preferring to spend money on cigarettes rather than credit. 'She's probably on her way back. Can you let me get dressed? We can both go.'

He was nodding hard. 'Yes. Yes, thank you, love, but be quick.'

I went upstairs and pulled on a jumper. Together, Ash and I drove to the police station. There was a sense of going slow, delaying stepping into the new world we were fast approaching.

He said, 'It might not be her.'

'No. We don't know yet.' That was stupid. They would not have called him in if they didn't think this was Jen. But we let ourselves hold on to hope for as long as possible.

'Mr Rollason?' A detective was waiting for us in the old, shabby lobby of the station, which had lino floors and tiled walls like my school. A paunchy middle-aged man in a suit. DS Andy Dickinson. I would come to know him very well over the next few days. He glanced at me, confused.

'Um, this is Karen, she's Jennifer – my daughter's best friend. My fiancée's daughter, also.'

Fiancée? My head whirled – my mother hadn't mentioned this the night before. Was it true? He'd proposed over the weekend? I stared the detective in the face, looking for clues as to what to feel.

'You'll have to wait here, Miss, OK?' Dickinson motioned me to a plastic seat in a corridor, and led Ash away. He was gone for some time. It seemed to stretch on for ever. I read the notices about domestic violence and video piracy and waited. It was almost nine, I would be late for school. I still thought I was going to school.

When Ash came back I could tell from how he stumbled that something was very wrong. Even then, it didn't have to be true until he said it. 'Oh, Karen.' He fell down on his knees as if he were going to put his head in my lap, but he didn't. 'My little girl. My Jenny.'

I met the detective's eyes, and saw no sympathy there. 'I don't understand.'

'Miss, I'm sorry but we've found your friend's body.'

'No.'

'Yes, I'm afraid so.'

'No. It can't be, because . . .' Why couldn't it? Because Jen was Jen, a princess, an angel, queen bee? She couldn't just be . . . dead.

Ash was weeping. I had to raise my voice to speak over him. 'What happened?'

'She's been killed.'

'You mean like an accident, a fall or something? A car crash?' A girl in the year above had died that way the year before.

He gave me an impassive glance. They must have already suspected me even then. 'She's been murdered, Miss. Someone has strangled her.'

◆ ◆ ◆

I'd hoped to sleep in a bit the next day, exhausted from wading through pain and fear, but Arlene wakes me by dint of opening the door and shouting, 'Oi, you awake?'

'I am now,' I grumble, pushing aside the duvet in its cheap polyester cover. It's a world away from my king-size Egyptian cotton nest in New York, slept in only by me and Jane Pawsten, when she feels friendly about once a month.

'Went out to get milk. Saw the paper.'

'So?' I mumble.

'Karen, will you wake up and look at this?' Her exasperated tone rouses me, and she chucks a tabloid on to the bed. There, on the front cover of the paper, is a picture of me. Sunglasses on, head bowed, like a celebrity or a criminal. Walking across the car park at the prison, with my expensive bag hanging from one hand. I look very New York. That will not play well locally. The headline is: BAGMAN'S LOVER IN PRISON TRYST. Tryst? I went to try and save a girl's life. God, April was right. If I don't take control of the narrative it will wipe me out, along with all the work I've put into rehabilitating myself for the past ten years.

'This – isn't good.'

'It's not. And that Gareth's been mouthing off too.' I turn the pages, getting newsprint on the sheets, and there's a big picture of him. EXONEREE SAYS: BAGMAN COULD STILL BE

147

OUT THERE. My eyes bounce off the article. Serious misgivings. Insufficient evidence. Symbol in missing girl's flat matches Bagman's. Jen maybe killed by someone else, or all the victims. So it's all out now. I swear softly, raising Arlene's eyebrows.

At the same time I hear my phone buzz in my bag and guess correctly that April has seen this too, likely through the Google Alerts she has set up for all of her clients. I realise I'll have to do what she wanted and agree to a TV interview, because if I don't, I'm going to be vilified all over again.

The lights in the TV studio are blinding me. I can't see anything beyond this halo of brightness – anyone at all could be out there in the shadows and I wouldn't know. The semi-famous local news anchor, Marina Delby, is having her face powdered with a giant puff. She sits across from me on an identical armchair, a coffee table between us with flowers and water glasses. Cosy. It's going to be confessional, tell-all. As if I haven't spent my entire life trying not to tell all. Less than two hours have gone by since the story broke – April, and TV news, works fast.

Up close, Marina is pushing sixty, but her mask-like make-up and Botox do their job on camera, and she looks glossy, trim in her body-con dress and giant heels, her hair enormous and bouncy. I refused wardrobe and make-up, even though they tell me I will look 'washed out'. I'm wearing my usual boots, jeans, leather jacket, though I've had to take that off as it's a thousand degrees in here, even without accounting for nervous sweat. Marina speaks in low tones to her team, a sort of confidential code, and I could not feel more out of place if I tried. There's no trace of the warmth she's famous for, and indeed she barely looks at me, flipping through her notes, rolling her shoulders back and forth like a boxer going into the ring. Maybe that's how she sees it. That she's going to take me down. I spot that there is a copy of my book under her notes. April will have sent that, probably, a little plug for what we're trying to sell. I was proud of the book before all this, but now it makes me feel dirty. The other women are dead and I'm here, making money out of it.

'One minute,' says a skinny young man with a radio mic. Finally, Marina looks at me.

'You're ready?'

'Um. I suppose. What are you going to . . . ?'

'Oh, just a few questions about the current case, the past, all that. People are very interested in him, you know.'

In you. Not in me. 'OK.' I wipe sweat from my brow, and a make-up person darts forward with a brush. It smells of stale powder.

We watch the cameras blink into life, and so does Marina, with a warm smile and a louder, more expansive voice. 'Welcome, viewers. Now, we have a really special interview for you tonight – if you can believe it, this is actually a world exclusive, right here on *North Today* with me, Marina Delby. Karen Walker is a name that many of you will know. As a young woman she called the police on her own boyfriend, who went on to be convicted of a string of murders. Aaron Hughes is better known as the Bagman, and he's been in prison here in South Yorkshire for over ten years, after Karen testified against him.' I don't know how she's managing to make me sound bad, when it was me who put you in prison. 'Karen, first thing everyone's going to want me to ask is, did you know?'

This is why I never do interviews. My mouth is dry and for a panicked second I can't speak. 'Um. Of course I didn't. It's very easy in hindsight to say I should have, but who would really think that a man they knew – loved – was a heartless killer? We lived in different

149

cities, we weren't together much. I wouldn't even have called him my boyfriend, to be honest. So no, I didn't know. Of course not.'

She doesn't look convinced. 'But he was a suspect in a murder back when you were at school, isn't that right? The murder of your best friend?' A picture of Jen flashes up on the monitor behind us. The party one, where she's dressed as an angel, her nipples clearly visible under the tight white top.

'No, he wasn't a suspect.' Not entirely true. 'Or rather, he was cleared by police.'

'After you gave evidence against another man.' Pictures flash. Jen. Gareth. So it's going to be this kind of interview. I take a deep breath and sit up straighter.

'Marina, I don't think there's any point in raking over the past. No one knew what happened back then, including me, and I just told the police what I saw, which was Gareth Hale near the scene of the crime that day, and the bruises he'd left on Jen before. That's all true and backed up by other sources. But I'm here today because another young woman is currently missing.'

She looks a bit put out, but we turn to stare at the next picture, which is of Lara Milton, arms round her sweet old granny on her eightieth birthday. She could not look nicer. 'Lara Milton, as most of our viewers will know, has been missing from her home in Marebridge for over a week now. Tell us why you're involved, Karen?'

'There were some – signs at her flat, that suggested a link to the older cases.'

'The Bagman ones.'

I want to shout at her not to use that name, which I've always hated. 'The Aaron Hughes killings.'

'What signs?'

'Um – plastic bags strewn about the place. As you know that's how he – that's what he used. And also the – there was a symbol on the wall.'

No picture this time. Marina explains to viewers, 'The Bagman was famous for leaving a mysterious symbol at crime scenes. Sometimes daubed on the wall in blood, sometimes carved right into the flesh of the victims.' I wince at that. 'And it was the same symbol?'

Everyone knows it now, no point in hiding it. 'It was the same.' I can hardly explain to her the sliver of doubt that has crept into my certainty. These are the same but are they *your* symbol? And if not, what does that mean?

'And you are one of the few people who know that, as police were very careful never to release pictures of it during the investigation, and hardly anyone has ever seen it?'

'That's right.' Is it just me, or has she made it sound like I might be guilty myself? Even though I was in another country when Lara was taken?

She shivers dramatically. 'So it must be something to do with him. Hughes.'

'Not necessarily – a few people do have access to the pictures of it. People who worked on the cases back then, or who knew Aaron when he was young. Maybe some of the families saw it.'

'You're saying a *family member* might be connected to this?'

'No! No, that's not what I . . . Look, we just don't know is the answer.'

'But it's true you've been visiting Aaron Hughes in prison?'

'The police asked me to talk to him in connection with this case. It's the first time I've ever visited him.'

She leans forward, cosier now. 'And how was it, seeing him after all those years?'

'Um – it was weird. Scary.'

She leans in more, so close I can see the pores under her thick make-up. My lips are so dry, I can't stop licking them. 'Do you still have feelings for Aaron Hughes, Karen?'

I think of how it was, feeling the heat of your skin across the table, as if volts had been pumped through my body. How my eye followed the curve of your brow and mouth. 'Of course not.' My voice is shaking. 'My feelings ended as soon as I knew what he did to those women.'

'And you really had no suspicions, ever?' She clasps a hand over one knee, and I see the grain of her tights digging into her leg.

'I . . .'

'Just a whisper of – maybe it's him? It would nearly be strange not to. All those appeals saying is the Bagman in your bed, asking women to turn their partners in if they had any doubts, any at all? And he'd talked about murder in the past, hadn't he?'

'He was interested in true crime. A lot of people are, that doesn't make them killers.'

'But come on, Karen. It must have crossed your mind. Especially after your friend was killed! It's too big a coincidence, surely.'

'I – maybe, but . . .'

I see a flash in her eyes that lets me know I've said the wrong thing. 'So you did suspect him.'

'Not suspect! I just – maybe I wondered once or twice, that's all.'

'But you didn't call the police.'

'I – like you said, every woman in the north of England probably suspected the men she knew. The police told me lots of women had reported their own partners. I didn't know enough to ring them. It was just – vague worries.'

'But if you'd called them when you first had these worries, some of these women might still be alive?'

'I don't know . . .'

'Which ones? Nita? Roshana? She was only seventeen when she died. Annie? Victoria? Julia? He was only stopped after he attacked

152

Emelia Han, brave final victim of the Bagman, who fought and survived.' There's a nice shot of Emelia, well lit, sympathetic.

I think of myself in the university common room, watching the news report about Alison Johnson, feeling cold all over. Writing the police number down in my notebook. 'I don't know! Don't you think I would have reported it, if I'd actually thought he was capable of that?'

'You tell us, Karen. Seems weird he could kill eight women including your best friend, and you, his girlfriend, never suspected a thing.'

'You've never been in that situation. You don't know what it's like.' Should I say again I wasn't your girlfriend? That we never lived in the same city, even, after school?

'Tell me, Karen. Can you honestly live with yourself, face the parents of those girls, knowing you might have stopped it?'

Tears are filling my eyes, and my throat is closing up. I choke out, 'I have to. What choice do I have? I have to live with it or die myself.' I get up, pulling the mic out from my waistband. 'That's all I have to say.' And I run offstage. I lean against the wall in the corridor, breathing hard, shaking, trying not to burst into sobs. That was a disaster. I've just undone years of work trying to convince people I am not responsible for your crimes. Maybe this is what you wanted all along.

When I finally stop shaking enough to pull my phone out, I remember I turned it off for the interview. When I switch it back on there are several missed calls and messages from Donetti, from Emelia, from April, even from my mother. I delete all of them and switch off my phone again.

◆ ◆ ◆

The Brains Trust are gathering in a café in a garden centre between Marebridge and Sheffield. I debate not going, wanting only to lie in bed for the rest of the day with the covers over my head, but I'm soon driven out by Arlene's loud pop music and the drifting stench of her cigarettes. When I arrive, Jim is giving out about the cost of the scone half-crumbled on his plate. He smells strongly of cigarettes too. Janine is working her way methodically through a Full English, while Mercedes is hunched over a cup of green tea. No sign of Matt, and I groan internally at the thought of having to deal with them by myself.

Jim greets me. 'Don't get anything to eat, unless you want to take out a second mortgage.'

'I don't have a first mortgage, I live in New York.'

He sniffs. 'Won't seem expensive to you here then.'

'Oh, quit whinging, Jim,' says Janine, wiping bean juice off her chin. 'Matt's off down south, he says, chasing some lead, so it's just us.' She squints at me. 'Saw you having your fifteen minutes of fame. Lot of traffic on the socials about it. People saying he's not even Bagman.'

'People have always said that.' I don't know why. The lack of evidence, perhaps, or the spice of a potentially unsolved mystery. But it is solved. Of course it is.

'Well, we'll see. You visited him then, did you?' *Him* once again being you.

'I had to.'

'I can't believe you actually saw him. What was he like?' Janine looks temporarily star-struck, the least grumpy I've seen her.

'Well, he's changed. Put on weight, gone bald. He wouldn't tell me anything useful.'

'But he told you something?' Mercedes jumps in, pushing up her big glasses.

'Just riddles. Stupid stuff.'

They are all gazing at me avidly. The riddles are what they want, I realise. The mystery, the intrigue. And you probably know that too. 'He said Lara knew her abductor. That she opened the door to them, and that seems borne out by what the neighbour said too, about hearing a car that night but no shouting or screaming.' I have to tell them the rest, though it's going to be like dropping a lit match into a barrel of gunpowder. 'He also wants me to – re-examine all the evidence against him. And he said one of the families may have a copy of the symbol. So he wants me to go and talk to all them again.'

'You didn't say yes?' The last from Mercedes, her thick eyebrows disappearing into her thin hair.

'I didn't feel I had a choice. They deserve to be kept updated in any case, and God knows the police don't have time.'

That deflects her, as I thought it would. 'Too busy crushing innocent protests and covering up their own crimes.'

Janine says, 'So he's saying he didn't do it? Any of them?'

'He's always said that. Doesn't mean anything.'

'But there must be something to find, if he's sending you out.'

'I don't agree. He always liked to play games.' I cast about for a lifeline. 'Jim, you covered the cases. Did anyone seriously believe he wasn't the Bagman?'

Jim is practically rubbing his hands in excitement. 'Evidence was thinner than Kate Moss, love. But at that time, police just needed a scalp and he fit. And the murders did stop after.'

'Until now,' says Janine, her eyes slitted with fascination. I can practically see her writing the blog post in her head – *Is the Bagman still out there?*

'Lara isn't dead,' I say crisply, hoping that's true. 'I think it's all just a head-fuck, but I'm doing what he asked, because I want to find her. So what did the rest of you learn?'

Jim goes first, talking over the women in a way that seems entirely natural to him, the habit of a lifetime. He has also drawn a blank, despite talking to every contact he still has in every northern police force, and every crime journalist too. 'Most of them had never seen it. The symbol. The pictures are locked away.'

'And – at the time of the murders, were there any other suspects? Anyone else on police radar?'

'They looked at hundreds of fellas, love, but they'd no decent leads of any kind.'

'None of the murders seemed – out of place? Like maybe it didn't fit?'

'Well, he did vary his methods. Nita Chowdry, he went into her house. The two girls, that was the first time he did a double.'

'Anything you thought was weird at the time?'

Jim scratches his head. 'They cleared the husband very fast, let's just say.'

'Nita's husband, you mean?'

'Aye. You know he was a copper?'

'I didn't.' That's very interesting. Nita Chowdry's husband was on the force. How closely would police have checked his alibi? 'Thanks, Jim. That might be useful.'

'I went down every rabbit hole I could find on the internet,' says Janine, cutting in. 'Even asked my dark-web guy.' Of course she has a dark-web guy. 'The symbol never found its way on there. But I did see one thing.' She takes out a piece of paper, which I note has a smear of tomato sauce on it. It's a printout from a bulletin board about true crime, posted in the 'murderabilia' section, where people buy and sell souvenirs from serial killers. 'I searched under his name, loads came up. People are selling his old clothes; the leather coat went for fifty grand last year.' I scan down the list she has printed, marvelling that I have seen some of these things in real life, your shoes, your calligraphy pens, a poster from your

156

room. And now strangers will pay thousands of pounds just to touch them. I wonder what became of all your books, the collection on the occult and true crime that you pored over. At the time it just seemed a bit alternative, not ominous.

'Where did this all come from?' Your belongings would have ended up at your dad's, probably. Did no one think to get them back when he died, to stop them ending up for sale to sickos?

She shrugs. 'Police sometimes sell things on, make a few quid. Or the family. Anyone who knew him. House clearance firms too. You'd be surprised what people let go when someone dies.'

'It's disgusting, these websites,' says Mercedes, and for once I agree. I wonder about your mum, wherever she is. Might she have sold her own son's possessions for money? They even have items from the victims, I see, a stray shoe, a scarf. How horrible for the families. I destroyed everything I had that you'd ever touched, though it would be worth quite a bit on here.

Janine is getting impatient. 'Point is, look at this ad someone posted.' I peer at it. LOOKING FOR PICTURES OF THE BAGMAN SYMBOL, ANY LEADS ON THIS? WILL PAY. The name of the poster is a meaningless string of numbers, but I see it was put up barely a month ago. Just weeks before Lara was taken. Below it is a series of answers, all deriding the poster for even asking, because 'as everyone knows', there aren't any pictures of it in circulation. 'There's no way to find out who posted this?'

'Nah, I tried. VPN routed.'

I sigh. 'OK. Mercedes, did you find out anything?'

Mercedes opens a notebook full of neat writing. 'I've been through all Lara's social media. I found a comment on a board about stalking, posted with her email as username. She asks what to do if an ex is bothering you.'

I think about this mysterious John again. Could it have been him who posted the message about the symbol, looking to buy a copy of it? 'Anything else?'

'Well, after I saw that I made contact with Melissa and we're having a coffee next week.'

'How did you get her to agree?'

She shrugs. 'She does yoga at the local gym every Tuesday, always posts about it on Insta. I went along and got chatting. She was happy to talk about it – seemed to really want to, actually.'

'She was?' I'm used to people avoiding talking to me, so I can't believe Mercedes has had so much success.

'Yeah. I just said I'd seen her on the news and how hard it must be, offered to chat it through if she wanted. She was keen. All of Lara's friends are so confused and upset, and the police aren't telling them anything. She's in bits actually.'

I'm stunned she's got this far with just the internet and a sympathetic attitude. In fact, weird as they are, all of the gang have come through for me. 'Well – good. That's good.'

They're all looking at me avidly, enjoying the hunt, not feeling the horror I do. As I drink my tea, they launch into an enthusiastic discussion of which of the murders didn't fit the pattern. 'Well, with Annie he didn't cut her, but not Jen Rollason either . . .' The names just names to them, not real people. I can hardly blame them. The sections in my book that deal with the dead ones are like this too. Clinical, stark, veering from sentimental cliché to brutality. My editor tactfully called this *some variations in tone*. The truth is I don't know how to write about what happened. The dead women were ordinary until they weren't. Catherine was a normal girl, anxious and not that popular, who would likely have ended up teaching history in a normal secondary, probably marrying eventually and having a kid or two, like most people do. Instead, someone came out of the dark and suffocated her, left her desperately sucking on air, the taste of plastic filling her mouth, the fear rising up in her throat like sludge. Roshana was only a kid, in a strange country. Annie was struggling with addiction, trying to survive. Nita, Julia, Victoria, Alison, they were all smart, determined, confident, on course for a brilliant future, until someone snuffed it out. Someone took their lives and everything they might have been away.

Not someone. You.

Had I met any of the dead women, I'm not sure we would have had much in common. I made it out alive. The rest of them didn't. Neither did Jen. I could say they haunt me, that they all do, and that would be trite but it's also true. I hear Jen's voice all the time. In everything I do I'm conscious of how she would have done it better, had she been allowed to live. But apart from Emelia, there's just me, the unelected spokesperson for the dead, the women that you killed. And I can't always hear what they're whispering in my ear.

Chapter Thirteen

From *Becoming Bagman* by Karen Walker

I left Marebridge when I was eighteen years old, six months after my best friend had been found dead in the woods, and I had been questioned over her murder, cleared, and ultimately helped convict her boyfriend, Gareth Hale, of the crime. Of course, we now know that wasn't true, that she was killed, as with so many others, by Aaron Hughes. He murdered Jen when he was only eighteen. I was seventeen, and so was Jen. Just kids.

Less than a year later, Aaron would kill again. This time he was at university in Lancaster, studying classics. It was a boon for our school to get a working-class boy like him on to the course, rubbing shoulders with the public-school kids called Portia and Toby. I know they asked him to be in the school brochure and he refused. He'd hated the place.

Catherine Collins was a quiet student in her first year of a history degree at Lancaster University. She was bright, but had almost failed her A levels due to extreme nerves, having been bullied all through secondary school. She was the middle child of three, with an older brother, Rick, who'd gone into the Army, and a younger, Sam, who was smart and popular. Catherine was just . . . quiet. Studious. She hoped to become a teacher or historian in a National Trust property. She liked those Philippa Gregory books about the Tudors, and fat biographies of dead people. She had a poster of *Friends* on her wall and one of *Sex and the City.*

Towards the end of her first term at university, on a cold and damp night in the last week of November, Catherine told her friend Laura, who was in her tutorial group, that she was going to the library to finish her essay about the causes of the First World War. Laura was going drinking at the student union, and wanted Catherine to come too, but she said no. She was worried she couldn't keep up with the course, and wanted to make a good impression before term ended.

Students do not share rooms at most British universities, and although most had mobile phones in 2005, they were only used for basic texting. So no one noticed when Catherine didn't come back from the library that night. Early the next morning, her body was found behind the building, near the bins, by a cleaner taking out the rubbish. She had a plastic bag over her head, a thin Tesco one, her hands clawing at her neck. She had suffocated. She was fully clothed, no evidence of sexual assault, and had a thin layer of frost over her body. But she was dead. And worse still – a symbol had been carved into the flesh of her stomach, her jumper and T-shirt pushed up to reach it. A mysterious symbol no one had ever seen before.

But that wasn't true. I had seen it. In a leather-bound notebook on a boring day in maths class, and then again several times throughout my final year at school. But of course I didn't know it was the same one. They didn't publicise it, and I was doing my best to forget Marebridge, after all that, and I wasn't following the news. I was trying to settle into my own university in York, and make my own life. Grappling with my own Portias and Tobys. The resident geese honked all night long and it was impossible to cross campus without stepping in their poo, but I felt like I could breathe. The last year of school had been intolerable, what with losing Jen and the police and all eyes on me every time I walked down the corridor. I didn't know. How could I have known?

I remember the moment quite clearly. I had gone into the common room at the bottom of our halls of residence, where there was a TV and a ratty sofa. Several people were sitting around chatting, waiting for *Neighbours* to come on after the news. Something about it caught me. I didn't normally socialise with these people, or with any-one much, afraid that it would all come out about my past.

The newsreader said, *The body of a student was found in the grounds of Lancaster University last night . . .*

'Turn it up,' said someone. Not me. I stood rooted in the doorway. A picture came up on screen. Catherine Collins. A normal girl, who looked like anyone I might have been studying with.

The other girls were exclaiming over it, enjoying their safe proximity to danger.

'Oh my God, that's just like here. It's what, eighty miles off? Oh my God.'

I wanted to shush them so I could hear the details. Instead I went straight to the computer room and swiped my student card to get in, entered my log-in and called up the BBC site. She had been found suffocated, was all it said, and a murder inquiry had been launched. She was described as a history student from Walsall. That was all they had to say about her, not knowing she had entered into the annals of the famous. The victims, the dead girls. Though of course we remember the names of their killers first.

Emelia and I have decided it's best now to work through the families in order, if only because it might be somewhat less raw for them the more time has gone by. Deep down I know that isn't true, that it never gets less raw. Certainly it hasn't for me, but I need to begin somewhere. And so we start with Catherine.

When I was writing the book, at April's urging I made a big show of contacting all the families, telling them what I was doing. Emelia was furious, having her own TV project in the works. With the rest I had to be careful. Sensationalism is very much out in the true-crime world now, it's all about sensitivity, focussing on those who died, their lives. Bringing dead girls to life, their breathing reality and how that was taken from them. Not all of them responded. Not all of them were happy to hear from me.

Emelia's driver is completely silent, the inside of the car warm and leather-scented, spotlessly clean. There are phone chargers and bottles of water in the back pockets. I could get used to this. Emelia spends the entire time stabbing at her phone with her pointy nails, one earbud occasionally leaking tinny music as she scrolls through social media. 'You're all over the internet. I've seen ten TikToks about your TV appearance today alone.'

'How nice for me.'

'They're saying maybe he didn't do it.'

'Do you think it was him?'

You had covered your face with a scarf – not strange on a cold night – so she only saw your eyes in the dark, heard your voice, which we know from previous cases you were good at disguising, affecting an accent from somewhere else in the north.

'Yes. Of course.' But her voice wavers, and I know she's having the same creeping doubts as me. Can you trust your eyes, your own memory? This is exactly what you wanted, I think. To throw us all into confusion again.

I ask, 'What's the plan then? Just walk up to the door? I don't know if they'll let me in.'

'They're expecting me. They're more than happy to talk about Catherine.'

'But not to me.'

'I didn't say you were here. But I think if we tell them what's going on, you know, with the symbol and all, they'll talk to you. It's too important not to.' She's convincing and I start to hope she might actually be right. Because it would make me feel better, that forgiveness. Absolution, from the guilt that never leaves me.

As we drive I obsessively google you, the women, trying and failing to avoid mentions of myself. I sometimes don't even recognise my own picture in these articles. They get things wrong – my dad isn't dead, for example. Just dead useless. And Jen didn't have a sister, though she does now. A sister she never knew. Pictures come up of me that I've never even seen, other people's memories from university, paparazzi shots of me walking to the court for your trial, even some in New York. It's a very odd feeling, like my identity is not my own. A composite of photofit impressions. I search for *Aaron Hughes symbol*. No images. Lots of discussion about why so few have ever seen it.

While Emelia calls out facts from Wikipedia, I run through the evidence that connected you to Catherine Collins. You were at the same university, and you had no alibi for the attack, though it would have been hard to remember by the time you were finally arrested. The police dug up some former student who said they'd seen you limping that night, washing soiled clothes in the laundry room. So flimsy. There was no DNA recovered from her body, no prints, no hairs. Just the symbol. The one I identified.

Mary and Paul Collins live in the Midlands, about a two-hour drive away. They politely acknowledged my letter and did not dispute my right to publish the book, but they didn't want to be involved. They've never been the most vocal of the parents. Just melted away with their grief, as some people do. It must be a heavy burden, to know that no one remembers your daughter for anything other than being murdered by a famous killer. You took that from Catherine too. It's not the violence you enacted on her body, hopefully already dead by then, it's the worst kind of theft imaginable.

I tell myself things. That you are of course, in prison, so you can't hurt me now. (That isn't true. You can hurt me in many ways, just not physical, which I've come to believe is one of the easier types of pain to bear. The body heals, the mind doesn't.)

I take a deep breath, standing on the suburban street, the trees wet from a sudden rainfall. The driver and I wait, engine running, while Emelia goes into the house. I try to engage him in some small talk about where he's from, but he isn't keen and he's so softly spoken I can barely hear him. I bite on a hangnail. God, what are they saying about me even as I sit here? After about ten minutes, Emelia bangs on the window of the car and I open the door. 'Come on. Quick, before they change their minds.'

There are flowers in pots around the door, a garden gnome fishing into nothing. Imagine, you're just a normal person, gardening and reading the paper and then your daughter is murdered and you can never be normal again. People treat you differently, like someone under a curse. They want to be part of your story. *I went to school with Catherine, you know. I taught her speech and drama. I sat behind her on the bus.*

I suck in all the air I can. Breathing no longer seems as effortless as it did. Someone is coming to the door. A woman of around sixty, grey-haired, wearing a cardigan and leggings. She has her reading glasses on and I can hear *This Morning* in the background.

'Hi, Mrs Collins? My name is Karen. Karen – Walker. It's – you've seen there's a girl missing in Marebridge?'

'I don't watch the news any more.'

I can understand that. Every time you think you're making progress with your grief, another woman gets killed or raped. Another man gets away with it.

'There's a young woman missing. And they think, the police think, that maybe it could be linked to – Catherine.'

She just gapes at me, like I've plunged her right back into her nightmare.

She calls out. 'Paul. Paul!' A man comes around the side, holding a trowel. He's in gardening gloves and an M&S checked shirt. 'There's . . .' She gestures to me and Emelia. 'It's about that missing girl again.'

'What's it got to do with us?' says Paul Collins. He's still holding the trowel, dropping soil on the path. 'They told us about the symbol but – we didn't see how it could mean anything.'

Emelia nods empathetically. 'We don't know that it is connected, but we have to check. Please, can we come in?'

They exchange a long look, then stand back. 'Take your shoes off, please.' Her voice is rough. He removes his garden shoes and gloves and she makes tea, brings biscuits on a tray. In the living room are about twelve framed pictures of Catherine at all ages, with her brothers and her parents but also alone. I wonder how the brothers feel. Still being alive.

'Lovely pictures,' I say, just for something to fill the silence.

Her mother reaches for one, wipes dust from it with her sleeve. 'She was a lovely girl. Before him.'

'I remember you,' says the father. 'From the trial.'

'That's right. I gave evidence on the last day, then I was in court for sentencing.'

As a sequestered witness, I had missed most of the grisly content, for which I was grateful. The weeping parents and experts discussing how long a human can go without air. But I want them to know I'm on their side, even if I loved you once.

She hands me tea, with bad grace. Manners fighting rage. I take a foil-wrapped chocolate biscuit. 'Thank you.'

'So what are these similarities?' says Paul. He's holding her hand now, beside her on the sofa, protecting her.

I swallow a thick paste of chocolate. 'The symbol. It was – on the wall. Of this girl's flat. Where she went missing from.'

Mary sucks in a scream. I don't tell them it was written in her blood. They can probably figure that out for themselves.

'How can you be sure?'

'I saw it.'

They sit for a moment in mute horror. 'But anyone could have done that.'

Emelia jumps in. 'Right. But not that many people have ever seen it, so we need to check with everyone who might have, anyone who knew . . . anything really.'

'We never saw it,' Mary says, worrying at the rings on her hands. 'We asked not to. When we – identified her. Just her face. She was under a kind of sheet. Up to the chin.' She would have had ligature marks around her neck. Her face would have bloomed with petechiae, the small red dots of burst blood vessels. It's what happens when you're strangled or suffocated. The rest of her was intact, except for the wound on her stomach. The blood would have stopped flowing by then, and dried. I'm glad they didn't see it.

I have to press them. 'And you were never shown a picture or anything?'

'No. They described it a bit but – we didn't want to know. It wasn't her. Not part of her.'

'I understand.'

'You don't understand,' says Mary, and looks away. He rubs her arm. 'She does, but not you.' *She* being Emelia. The good victim. Also marked by your knife.

'I'm sorry. I was horrified when I found out the truth about him. I could never have imagined it, really I couldn't.'

'How could you not know? He was a monster. And you – helped him go free. For killing your friend!'

I want to tell her that monsters look the same as everyone, but the truth is I find that question a difficult one. Because in some ways, I did know what you were. Of course I did. I knew you better than anyone, and we saw the true monstrousness of each other's hearts, because that's what real love is. 'I told the police everything I knew back then. There seemed to be an obvious suspect for Jen's murder.'

She stares at me then, her eyes red and accusing. 'That's not what the officer told us. The one who dealt with your friend's death.' Dickinson. She must mean Dickinson.

'I'm sorry, I don't know what you—'

'He said you framed that boy on purpose, to save your own skin. That you were a liar, and our Catherine would still be alive if you'd told the truth back then.'

On the way back to Marebridge we stop to get petrol and go to the loo. I find myself drifting to the McDonald's counter, buying a cheeseburger, stuffing it into my mouth, filling up the emptiness with cheese and pickle and meat, hunched over so Emelia won't see if she walks past. I never eat like this in New York. Only salads or homecooked soups or stews. Now I just need it, the blare of salt and fat in my mouth. My hands smell nasty from the bun and I feel sick. But also better. Unlike Catherine Collins and Jen, I am alive, and can stuff down a greasy burger in the middle of the afternoon in a service station should I so choose. I am alive.

There are six more families, not counting Jen's. Can I really do this six more times? I know that I have to. On my way out, I catch

169

sight of a giant TV playing the news on mute. There's Gareth Hale again, standing outside his parents' farmhouse, silently mouthing off. I don't stop to read what the subtitles are saying. I already know.

Emelia wrinkles her nose when I climb back in the car. 'Ew, what did you eat in there?'

'I was hungry.'

She squints at me. 'What was all that about back there? Saying you lied?'

'I have no idea. That policeman always had it in for me. Just trying to blame his mistakes on a young woman, I guess.'

It's the kind of inspiring thing she would say on her reels, but she doesn't seem convinced. The words seem to echo in my ears. *You're a liar, Karen.*

What I said in my book about the death of Catherine Collins, it's true but it's not the whole truth. Here's what I left out.

It was late 2005 by then. I had been doing my best not to go home for Christmas. Ash, distraught, had broken things off with my mother right after Jen died, and I couldn't face Arlene. I didn't know what I felt about you and I going to different universities. On the one hand, it was like wrenching one of my organs out of my body, but on the other it felt like a great weight had lifted off my chest. When you are questioned in a murder inquiry, you are never the same again.

It's true that I heard about Catherine on the TV in the common room, and I felt as if a bolus of terror had lodged in my solar plexus. It was just a coincidence, I told myself. Girls did get killed all the time, and the shots of the campus on the news had shown it was big and green, with paths criss-crossing main roads. Easy to

170

grab someone walking or jogging along them. This was nothing to do with me. And yet. You had gone to Lancaster University. Could it really be a coincidence, two murders in such a short space of time? I hadn't told anyone at York I was *that* Karen Walker, the friend of poor dead Jen Rollason, who had been questioned over her murder. It's probably why I have no friends from that time in my life. Why you were my only one.

In the computer room, I opened my university email and typed your address with shaking hands. *Someone was killed on your campus? What the hell?* I was really saying, *Please tell me it wasn't you.* Later that night, I would get a call on the payphone at the end of our corridor, mobiles costing too much to ring at that stage from landlines. You didn't own a mobile yourself, something that would look weird now, in 2023, but back then just seemed a tiny bit behind the times.

Some boy knocked on my door. His red eyes suggested he was stoned. 'Eh, there's like, someone on the phone for you.' I went to take it, locking my room up carefully as I went. Other girls were always losing their keys and getting locked out, but I never did.

I thought it might be my mother at first. Maybe she was ill. 'Hello?'

'Hi.' The sound of your breath down the line.

'What's going on?' You had never called me before. I'd sent you the number optimistically, knowing you never used the phone. We would email instead, long and rambling screeds, like old-fashioned letter writers.

'Just calling. Your message.'

'Yeah? Did you – know her?'

'The girl? No, not at all. It's a big place, you know. Different course, different halls and everything.'

'It's so awful.'

'Yeah, people are really upset. I just didn't want you to worry.'
I digested what that might mean. Worry that you were sad? Worry about something else?

I broached it. I remind myself of this sometimes, when the guilt comes to suffocate me. I did try. 'It does seem strange. After. You know. Do they have any idea who . . . ?'

'Don't think so. Some weirdo, I guess.'

The silence stretched on. How could I ask my best friend, *Did you do this?* Did you kill a girl? I had already told the world you didn't kill Jen, that Gareth Hale did it, and he was in prison. I shuddered. 'Awful.'

'It's why I used to walk you home. Lot of mad people about. How are you otherwise, Kare-bear? Going home for Christmas?'

'Not if I can help it.'

'Know what you mean. How about I could drive over and get you, see your uni, take you back home? Put in an appearance at least, spend a few days.'

'You have a car?' And why did that make me feel panicky somehow?

'Saved up all the Mum guilt-cash and bought one. Breaks down every twenty miles or so but it does the job.'

What could I say? 'Sounds great.' Time with you, a road trip together, several uninterrupted days. Maybe you'd even sleep in my bed. I could set that against ruining our friendship for ever, by speaking whatever vague worries were on my mind. Of course you weren't a killer. This was all just some terrible coincidence.

After a few weeks, the Catherine Collins story died away and was forgotten. The truth about the symbol carved into her was never released to the public, only some vague references to 'mutilations' to the stomach, which drew speculative links to Jack the Ripper. I spent a lot of time reading news articles about it, in the computer room that smelled of hot dust and always hummed with static electricity. The bag over her head, that was somewhat similar, though Jen had been strangled with someone's bare hands. But mutilations, no. Stomach injuries, no. Nothing that needed to keep me awake at night.

And yet it did.

Chapter Fourteen

From *Becoming Bagman* by Karen Walker

Alison Johnson. A normal English name, a normal English girl. Like Catherine, she was a student. Like Jen, she had a pony. Like Julia, she had red hair. Like Annie she was twenty-one. But none of it means anything. Aaron Hughes didn't pick the women for any particular reason. It was all just blind bad luck.

It was over a year after Catherine Collins had been found, over two since Jen's death and me sending Gareth to prison. No one had whispered the words yet. *Serial killer.* Jen's murder had been solved, why would we link it to the death of a girl miles away in Lancaster? Alison was at university in Durham. I don't know if he did that on purpose, changed his location, or if he didn't even try to not get caught, just assumed the police were too stupid to catch him. Alison was more outgoing than Catherine. She had been head of the student union in her second year, shouting loudly about rape alarms and lighting on campus. Some thought that's why he chose her. But I think she was just unlucky.

There was a day when Ted Bundy went to a public meeting, spoke to several women, asking them to come out to the car park with him. Some said no, escaping through some instinct or chance. One girl was chatting to him when her older brother drove up, saving her. Everyone imagines the danger lurks in the shadows, outside. No one could have imagined the monster would walk into the bright, and smile and say, *Come with me*. That's what happened to Alison. She was hosting a meeting about campus safety, and was pleased to see one or two men had turned up. This was the mid-2000s, the time of *FHM* and *Loaded*, when it was acceptable for boys to have naked pictures of Jordan Blu-Tacked to their college room walls. Alison stayed to put the chairs away and lock up, and one of the male students helped her. Several of the women at the meeting remembered him but none could describe him clearly. Brown hair, tallish. Just kind of nice. He said his name was Simon and that he was studying maths, though none of them could remember seeing him around campus before. No one mentioned long hair, which Aaron still had at that point.

Alison had a year of her degree to go, having deferred one to lead the student union. Next she planned to intern for an MP and make her way into politics. Maybe be prime minister one day. Instead, the last anyone – anyone else – saw of her was as the door shut on the small meeting hall, laughing at something 'Simon' had said. Since it was before widespread social media and camera phones, no one took a picture of him at the meeting. There was CCTV attached to the hall, but it caught only the back of his head as he walked away with her, hair hidden by a hat. She was carrying a backpack stuffed with leaflets. His hands were empty, folded behind his back. He wore a long black coat, but no one said if it was leather or not. He had said little during the meeting, nodding along supportively. He had a northern accent. Yorkshire, one of them thought. The other said maybe Lancashire.

Alison was found the next morning by some students out jogging. One of them was in her economics lectures, and recognised her right away, her face intact, though frozen and blue. The front of her white T-shirt was soaked through in blood, sodden. Police found the torn handles of a plastic bag around her neck, pulled so tight they could hardly be cut off. He'd taken the rest with him, but had left no prints. Her fingertips had deep grooves in them, as if she'd tried to pull the bag off, gasping for air. Her stomach bore the same wound as Catherine Collins. That was when everyone realised. There was more of this to come.

I found out about this one from girls chattering in the kitchen of the halls I had moved to for my second year. 'Did you hear? They think there's a serial killer. My mum's sending me a rape alarm in the post.'

People sometimes ask me when I knew. I always say, right before I called the police, of course. But the truth is, I knew in that moment, boiling the kettle to make my Pot Noodle. I knew but I didn't let myself know. I even went back to my room and looked up the number for the police tipline, wrote it down in my diary. On the outside nothing had changed, but inside everything was falling apart, devastated. The only thing that kept me going was denial, a shred of hope. Durham was miles from Lancaster and from Marebridge. Why would Aaron go there? Maybe this meant it was someone else who had killed Catherine Collins too. Maybe it was all fine. And so five more women would die.

I am watching Emelia be killed. Emelia – or rather the actress playing her, who is actually Chinese and can't quite get the mid-Atlantic accent right – runs down a lane, panting and terrified. She's followed by a cameraman on a track, and the night scene is lit by blazing lamps. It's six in the morning, in reality, not the time Emelia was attacked, which was around nine at night. We're also nowhere near where it happened – instead of Harrogate we're in Salford, near the BBC studios there. The show is called *Survivor: The Emelia Han Story.* It's trendy now to find a different way into true crime, to focus on the victims, or ideally the survivors, instead of the killers. Waiting in Make-up is the actor playing you, a blanket round his shoulders and script on his lap. He doesn't look anything like you, which I'm glad of. He's at least ten years too old and has a full head of hair, which will soon be hidden by an unconvincing bald cap to portray your close-shaved skull. I wonder how he feels, embodying someone who murdered so many people. Channelling even a fraction of that. Does it seep into you, does it change you?

The film apparently focuses on Emelia, her life up to that point, the night she spent running and hiding from you, her survival and recovery. The deaths of the other girls are dealt with in passing, and then your arrest and trial, Emelia bravely giving evidence. Some manufactured suspense around whether or not you will be convicted. I'm not in this film. Since I'm still alive and not a convicted criminal, it was easier to leave me out than wrangle with 'life rights'. Instead, you are caught by a doughty police officer, and for this they have fleshed out the role of the female detective I eventually spoke to, the one who coaxed me into giving you up. She never even met Emelia. I wonder how Dickinson will feel about that, being totally erased. No mention of Gareth either – I can only assume he's working on his own drama about being wrongfully convicted. They'll likely leave out the part where he once half-strangled Jen himself in a jealous rage. The truth doesn't make such a good story.

I wonder about the ethics of this, sometimes, of dramatising real events, making them seem more exciting or clear-cut than they were. Distorting the facts. Because the facts are important. Without that strict adherence, there is room for manoeuvre. To say, maybe he didn't do it after all, or at least not all of it. Water freezing in a crack in rock, forcing it apart. And then, a new appeal, a new trial, a door opening up on someone who should be sealed away for all eternity. Maybe you're right to say it must be the absolute truth. It's all stupid anyway. Without me, without my existence, this would have been a very different story.

The director calls 'Action' and actress Emelia runs down a darkened lane, her breath almost a scream. She only runs a few paces before the scene cuts. 'It gets looped,' says Emelia, who's sitting beside me in a folding chair with her name on the back, which I have to admit I'm kind of jealous of. 'No way could they track her

178

as far as I actually ran.' Six miles, she has always claimed. She just kept going, across moors and fields, she would not let you take her. Her stomach bleeding from your knife. The actress has been made up so it leaks through her thin white top.

'You weren't actually wearing that, were you?'

Real Emelia rolls her eyes. 'Of course not. It was freezing. I had my coat on, my jogging gear, a hat.'

The actress has long flowing hair, not tied back, and doesn't seem to be wearing a bra. Of course the director is a man.

'Doesn't it bother you? That it's not the exact truth?'

She shrugs. 'It gets the message out, that's what matters.'

'Which is what exactly?'

'To fight against male violence in all its forms. To not be caught by "nice girl" norms.' Emelia had stopped to talk to you on her run, taking out her earbuds. To be polite, to answer your enquiry about a lost dog. She had gone to help you look, only to be cornered in the bushes, your knife suddenly flashing from its hiding place strapped to your leg, through a hole you'd cut in your trousers. You had slashed her before she even knew what was happening. But then she ran. She kicked and clawed and slipped from your grasp and ran. And didn't stop running. She didn't see one person who could help during her six-mile sprint, and several cars that passed did not stop. If she had fallen or slipped at any point, if she hadn't been in training, if you hadn't hurt your ankle running after her, she would be dead and you might still be out there. You still had the limp when you were arrested.

I am suddenly cold all over, and it's not from the dawn air. 'You ready to go soon?' We have six more families to see. Six more homes utterly devastated by loss.

'I'll just tell the director I'm off.'

I've had offers for my film rights, of course. But I could never bring myself to let it happen, someone playing you and someone playing me. A scripted version of our most intimate moments. Once there was a script, with lots of kinky sex in it, and I couldn't explain that it wasn't like that between us, so I tanked the contract, to April's chagrin. Some things cannot be made into a story, locked down in words or facts.

Soon we are in the quiet, cushioned car again, speeding away in the morning light. Emelia's face is wreathed in the steam from the mint tea she got from Catering – *fresh leaves only, please*. I have a coffee that I wish I hadn't bothered with. In any case, my stomach is aching, nauseous. So much death still to face.

The Johnsons, David and Susan, have gone in a different direction to the Collinses. They want to say Alison's name as often as possible. They're the first to sign up to any documentary going, and they have established a political internship in her name, campaigned for new laws on data protection, so police in different forces can share information more easily. Rent-a-quote, my mother once said snidely, and even though I scolded her, I knew she said it to support me. Because the one person the Johnsons won't talk to is me. They're convinced I knew, when Jen died and when Catherine died, and that if I had taken action, their daughter would still be alive and possibly prime minister.

Who knows? They might be right.

The Johnsons live off a country lane, in a red-brick house that backs on to fields. Trees in the garden, a summerhouse. She grew up well-off, Alison. Another house hung with photos of the dead. That same shadow as I step inside, despite the scented candles and wax-polished furniture. A haunting. Emelia has already been in touch with the parents, so when the door's opened I follow her to the back of the house, to a conservatory (though they'd probably call it an orangery, conservatories being terribly middle class), where a scowling seventyish couple sit over tea and biscuits. No cup for me and none is offered.

'This is Karen.'

'We know who she is,' says the father, in a sonorous voice. He was a barrister, I know. 'We saw you on television also. You may as well sit, I suppose.'

The furniture is made of wicker, and creaks under me. 'Thank you for talking to me. Emelia explained what's been going on? The symbol?'

'We never saw it.' The mother is twisting her hands, looking down to the floor. She has ash-blonde hair, tinting into grey in spots. They both wear gilets and slacks. 'They told us what it – looked like. Her stomach. But we didn't see.'

'Of course we didn't,' says the father gruffly. 'We aren't ghouls. We wanted to remember her as she was, before that beast got to her.'

'Her face was perfect,' trembles the mother. 'So still and pale. Like an English rose.'

What can I say? 'I'm so sorry for your loss. I hate to ask – but was there ever any doubt in your mind that it was him?' The evidence so thin again. Alison's friends asked to ID you, after years had gone by. The fact you owned a long black coat.

The father shoots me a fierce look. 'You've got a lot of nerve.'

'I'm sorry. We just want to find Lara Milton. We just need to know there's no doubt, none at all, that the right man's in prison.'

He sits back, letting out a nasty little laugh. 'Wasn't it you who sent him there? And now look – setting yourself up as some kind of victim too. This book of yours.'

'I – sir, I assure you I called the police as soon as I had any inkling. They're good at hiding, these men. The Yorkshire Ripper was married. The Golden State Killer too, the Green River Killer, um, Maxine Carr with Ian Huntley . . . You can't always tell.'

'I can't accept that. You knew him for years. He killed your friend.'

'He lied to me. And I – I was just a kid then. I was vulnerable, no dad, single mum. He took advantage.' Even as I say these words I can imagine you shaking your head at me, and the ghost of Jen rolling her eyes. *That's not how it was, and you know it.* But I can't explain how it was. I let my voice break. 'He – he hurt me too, you know. Not in the same way, but – he did.'

I feel Emelia shoot me a look, but ignore it. The mother softens into tears. 'He's a psychopath. Deceived everyone. Carried her bag for her, even. Everyone said he was so pleasant, this "Simon" like he claimed he was. Of course it was him. Are you saying it wasn't?'

'No, no, I'm not saying that. We're just – making sure.' Emelia raises her eyebrows at me and I know what she's thinking – why have we come here, throwing doubt on the one thing that gives them any comfort, the fact that their daughter's killer is at least behind bars? What am I hoping to achieve, by finding Lara Milton? Forgiveness? A tipping of the scales?

I stand up. 'I'm sorry to have bothered you. I'll never forgive myself for not spotting what he was sooner. Never.'

When I say it out loud like this, I can see they believe me, and for a moment I even believe it myself.

The doors in the prison make an aggressive buzzing noise, like a swarm of trapped bees. I couldn't live with the racket in here, distant calling voices, squeaking shoes on lino, slamming doors. Sandra seems unaffected by it though, leading me along with her ponytail swinging. She moves aside a burly inmate who's washing the glass of the internal doors. 'Budge up there, Barry.' He could snap her in half, but she has no fear. She tells me, 'Aaron was ever so pleased you came last time. Cheered him up for days after. Here we are.'

182

The same room with the barred door, and through it I can see you waiting. Your posture is alert, as if you're really looking forward to seeing me. Wouldn't I have given anything for this, before? Just – before.

'You came back!' A real and genuine smile.

I slump into the same plastic chair. 'I don't have much choice. No sign of Lara still.' I search your face for a flicker of knowledge, but there's nothing.

'Tell me what you've been doing. Apart from causing a TV sensation.'

I wince. 'My agent convinced me. It was a mistake. I'm all over the internet.'

You make a dismissive gesture. 'They'll say anything to get views, Kare-bear. Ignore them. What have you found out?'

I recount my visits to the families. 'I haven't seen them all yet. But there's nothing so far. No evidence of anything.'

'Not much evidence linking me though either, right?'

'There never was much.' Except what I gave them.

You're nodding along as if all this has nothing to do with you. 'And who've you been going with, Karen? Who set this up? I can't imagine the families all want to talk to you.'

'Um – Emelia Han.'

How weird to say her name to you, the woman you tried to murder.

'Ah, Emelia. Always good value. Always something to say. Who else are you talking to?'

'Well, this guy who did a podcast about – it.'

You nod. 'Matt Cooke, I assume. He's thorough, I'll give him that. Tried to get on to my visitor list several times. But even he missed the anomaly. Have you figured it out yet?'

'I don't know. I'm thinking – well, Annie Andersen was an odd one out. But lots of them have differences. Roshana, Nita too.' Jen.

183

Your face gives nothing away. 'So you haven't. Figured it out.'

'Not yet. I don't know what there is to figure.'

You stare into my eyes. 'One of them is wrong. You should be able to see which. In fact, you've always known, I believe. You mentioned it to me, back when it – happened.'

'Did I?' Sometimes I did use to bring the murders up with you, when I felt brave. Your nonchalance about them relieved me. These could not be *your* murders, that you discussed with such ease, though you always said you didn't follow the news or know any of the details.

'Never mind, Karen. I can see you're trying, so I'm going to give you something about poor Lara.'

I sit forward, my hands on the table just inches from yours. 'Please. Please, tell me what you know.'

You smile. 'I don't *know* anything, like I keep saying. But I can guess. Now, this crime, it was planned. It wasn't a last-minute loss of control. There had to be organisation, to get the symbol, to remove her with no one watching. So what does that mean?'

I hate this Hannibal–Clarice bullshit, but I have to play along. 'He was careful.'

'Right. But also, he's an amateur. He hasn't done this before.'

'How do you know?' I can hardly bear to ask.

'It's showy. Messy. So, ergo, he will have made a mistake. Left something behind at the scene.'

'But the police have been—'

'Something the police missed. It does happen, you know. We both know.' You say it mildly, but I know what you're referring to and my stomach grips into a tight knot.

'So I should tell them, what? Look again?'

'Ask him to show you everything from the scene. Your nice cop. Ask him to walk through it again. The whole building. He'll find something.'

184

I scowl.

'I mean, just guessing. Don't be so cross, Karen. I haven't seen you in ten years, you could at least smile at me now and again.'

'It's all dead ends though. She met a guy in a pub, but he was using a burner phone, and we only have a first name to go off, which might not even be real.'

'It won't be.'

'How do you know?'

'Men like him, they don't use their real names if they can avoid it. All the more reason to meet women IRL. The apps leave a trace.'

Hopelessness rolls over me. 'So how can we find him then? And Lara?' Assuming she is alive. She has been missing now for over a week. The odds aren't good.

You shift in your seat, resting your hands on the table. 'You need to think like him. Why would he take her? Figure out what he wants from her. How does he want to feel? That's how you'll find him. And her.'

I turn it over in my mind. 'They were dating and she turned him down, blocked his number. We know a man left her flat angry, a few weeks ago. He wants – her validation?'

'Good, Karen. He wants to feel like a big man, because she made him feel small. Rejected him.'

'So he wants – power?'

'Most people want power. Once she's dead, she can no longer reflect that back to him. The source would be . . . run out.' As you say it, so casually, I wonder why you never abducted women, to keep them and play with them. Maybe you wanted different things. Or maybe you simply never had a place to take them, no house with a soundproofed basement, no backyard dungeon. I wonder briefly if that's why there are more serial killers in America – more space for cellars.

'But how do I find him?' I can't shake the feeling that you know, but how could you unless you're involved? Is any of this even true, or is it you behind it, not this mysterious John at all?

'You already know his name, I think.'

'What? How?'

You shake your head, a faint smile on your lips. 'That would be too easy, Karen. You need to play my game to the end, and you'll find it all makes sense.'

'But, please! Aaron, come on.' The first time I've said your name.

'You come on, Karen. The most sordid everyday story you can imagine and still you're spinning about in circles, you and Hot Cop?'

'I'm trying!' My voice rises in frustration. 'Please, tell me what you know.'

You laugh. 'That's all you're getting for today. I still don't have a copy of that book of yours, remember.'

'Don't you?' I risk. 'Because someone took the one I brought with me.'

'You can get another. You're the author.'

I'll have to ask Sandra if I'm allowed to bring it in. But what happens when you read what I said about Jen? What does that mean for me, for you? 'It's all things you know.'

'I'd still like to see how you remember it. I find it fascinating how much memories can differ.' It's grotesque how you're enjoying this. I suppose it's all you have left, the power to compel me to come in here and see you, when I swore I would pretend you had never existed.

'If I get you a copy, will you tell me who did this to Lara?'

'You think I know?'

'I think you have a good idea, yes.'

'Well, we'll see about that.' You wave in the direction of the surly guard. 'Time to go, please. I'm tired.'

You stand up and just for a moment, as the guard is gathering himself, you lunge towards me. I feel the tip of your fingers brush mine, just for a second, but it's as if I've been burned. 'Be careful, Karen,' you whisper to me. 'There's more going on here than you know.'

Chapter Fifteen

From *Becoming Bagman* by Karen Walker

I've never been able to account for the three-year gap between the killing of Alison Johnson and that of the next woman. Maybe he was trying to change, to halt the runaway train he was on after killing Jen, and Catherine, and Alison. He had finished university in 2008, but instead of looking for work had moved back in with his dad in Marebridge, seemingly content to do nothing, hunt rabbits, watch TV all day. Myself, I had clawed together some funding for a masters and was still in York doing that. Probably I felt I could relax again. But in 2010 it all started up again.

Nita Chowdry. Indian heritage, working as a solicitor in Sheffield, married to a white man, who she was separated from. Last seen leaving her office at around 7 p.m., captured on CCTV buying a ready meal at her local Tesco. Didn't turn up for work the next day despite having several important meetings. Didn't answer her phone. Found the day after that in her own terraced house. She had been strangled, not with a bag but with a pair of tights. There was a plastic bag lying on the floor with Nita's prints on it, as if her killer had tried that method and for some reason abandoned it. This time he had both carved the symbol into her flesh and also daubed it on to the wall in blood. Messy, almost impossible to make out what it was, the liquid having dripped and run. Neighbours heard nothing, no struggle, no screams. It took a while for police to connect the case with Catherine or Alison, since it had been three years by that point, and most serial killers stay within their own ethnicity. Though the Yorkshire Ripper didn't – he attacked black and Asian women as well as white. If we think we can predict what these men will do, we're lying to ourselves.

Family and friends were also bewildered as to how Nita's killer got into the house – did he come home with her, invited, even though she was safety-conscious? Did he break in and hide, wait till she got home, her food eaten, the leftovers on the side? Did he ring the bell and somehow talk his way in, a tradesman, a neighbour, some-one from the council about a gas leak? No way to know, and Aaron never gave any details of his crimes, not even after multiple life sentences. But police did know now that there was a man, a man who strangled and cut and left a weird symbol behind, and that the same man had killed three women. It was four, of course, but at that point no one knew Jen's case was connected.

Three murders are enough to officially qualify you as a serial killer. In fact, the vast majority of British serial killers have only murdered three or four people. I say only. We don't rack up the dozens of victims of Ted Bundy or a Golden State Killer. But we are a small country, and three was enough to engender panic. A nickname began to emerge. The Bagman. The plastic bags, did that suggest auto-erotica? Had Nita willingly indulged in a dangerous sex game? Her family had to go on TV after that and beg the press to stop speculating whether their daughter had taken part in her own murder.

Like every time, there were no prints, no forensic traces, not even fibres or footmarks, despite the fact that he had actually gone inside a woman's house this time. So brazen, so daring, and still no way to catch him. The Bagman knew how to clean up after himself. And so a bogeyman was born. Because these killers are just men, violent damaged men, until fear makes them immortal.

The next victim was also a woman of colour. Roshana Khan, aged seventeen, the youngest to die. It's possible he didn't spot how young she was, although of course Jen was also seventeen when she was killed. Roshana had gone to a street party in Leeds with her cousins, to celebrate the royal wedding of Prince William and Kate, in 2011 this was, but she had become separated from them, not knowing her way around the city. She was found in a tangle of undergrowth between the train line and the backs of houses. The bag was still over her head this time. It was a Sainsbury's Bag for Life and the investigation got bogged down for a long time trying to trace who might have paid for it that day, examining CCTV from every branch in the city, although there was no way to know what day it had been acquired on. It had been very public, lots of CCTV around, though none of it seemed to capture a young girl in a hijab walking away with a white man. Why did she go with him? She was shy, with a conservative upbringing, not used to being alone with men. Maybe he pretended to be a police officer, told her she was breaking some rule. She wouldn't have known any different. Maybe she was upset about getting lost and he seemed kind, helpful. Maybe he used the same dog trick he tried on Emelia. He has never said, and of course Roshana, like the other women, cannot tell us.

All the victims were different – two students, a teenager from a conservative country, a young professional woman. Different ethnicities, different cities. But the symbol showed it was him. The Bagman.

Back in the car the next day, Emelia says, 'So, we can Facetime the sister, she said. It's late afternoon there.' Roshana Khan was killed in 2011, but she was from Pakistan, staying with family in Leeds, so it's not going to be easy to talk to her family. Emelia has managed to find her older sister's Instagram and they are corresponding across thousands of miles.

'You're sure she – wants to talk about it?'

Emelia throws me a look. 'This was your idea, remember.'

'I know. But could they really know anything, realistically?'

'We have to check out all the cases. You said so yourself, and Matt agrees.'

'Oh, well, if *Matt* agrees.'

I can feel her rolling her eyes. 'What is the matter with you? You think I want to be here, in this freezing-cold country where apparently even an hour of proper light a day is too much to ask for? My melatonin is so all over the place, I'm gonna need to buy a SAD lamp.'

'I'm sorry. This is just all really hard. I feel – churned up.' Seeing you, seeing the families – my usual defences are down and I'm flooded with guilt and fear.

'How do you think I feel? I've spent the past week watching someone act out the moment I thought I was going to die.' Her hands rest on her stomach, unconsciously perhaps. The plastic surgeons did a good job, but Emelia will always carry your marks. Unlike mine, hers are visible, etched into her skin, long lines of scar tissue like braided rope. She's done some videos where she shows them, to 'reduce stigma'. Since you didn't finish with her, the symbol cannot be reconstructed from her stomach.

I look out the window while Facetime dials. I'm hoping it won't connect, but it does, and there we are, talking to a woman in Karachi. She sits in a nondescript room that could be anywhere in the world. Her shiny hair slips out from the richly patterned scarf round her head. 'Ashira? Hi, I'm Emelia.'

Roshana's older sister. Twenty when her sister died, so she must now be in her thirties. She looks just like Roshana, or at least the

192

pictures I've seen of her. Huge dark eyes, pretty. 'Hello Emelia. Can you hear me?' Her voice is tinny but audible.

'Yes, yes. I'm here with Karen. You know who Karen is?'

'Yes.' No tone to that word. Does she blame me, like so many of the others? I got no response from the Khans to my approach about the book.

'Ashira, we don't want to make you relive any trauma. Believe me, I get it. We just need to check some things with you super-quick, is that OK?'

'Yes, it's fine. You can ask me whatever you need.' Such a colourless voice. I wonder what pain lies beneath it.

'Thank you. Your dad came over to identify Roshana, is that right?'

'Yes. He saw her body. It broke him, I think. He had a stroke the year after, passed away.' Another for your death toll. It wasn't just the women you murdered with your own hands. You ruined other lives too.

'I'm so sorry to hear that. Do you know if he ever saw the symbol?' Emelia's tone is soft, but matter-of-fact.

On screen, the woman shakes her head, so that more lustrous hair slips out. 'He asked not to see anything but her face. He had to make sure she was – prepared in the right way. It was already too long past the time for burial, when they released her body.' Of course. Muslims bury their dead within a day or two, but that didn't work with a murder inquiry, where a body might be held for weeks, the scene of a violent crime. At least, people said, you had not interfered with the women. At least.

'That must have been so tough, I'm sorry.'

'My father never spoke her name again. Even now, we never do. She would be thirty next year, you know. My uncle never forgave himself either. He was supposed to be caring for her. This kind of thing – you just never get over it.' I realise with a jolt that her eyes have shifted to me. Just looking, not saying anything, but I feel a hot wave of shame swamp me. If I had called that tipline number after Alison Johnson died, or told someone of my suspicions after Catherine Collins, this woman's sister would still be alive, maybe with children, a partner, a career. A life. All that taken from her.

'Um – I'm so sorry for your loss, Ashira.' She just nods and I can't bear it, I gasp for air in the overheated car, staring out at the moors, overhung with grey fog. I didn't do this. It wasn't me who killed anyone, and yet I will never manage to serve my time. Like you, my sentence is for life. 'I have to ask – did you have any doubts around the time of the trial? That Roshana's death maybe – didn't fit?'

She says nothing for a moment. 'Sorry, what do you mean?'

'I just mean – you were sure that Hughes did it?' It's strange to call you that.

Her tone is incredulous. 'The court convicted him. And the bag and the – symbol, surely it had to be – the Bagman, as you call him.'

But there wasn't much evidence to connect the Bagman to you. The police found a train ticket you'd bought to go to Leeds that day, but you often went there, looking in record stores and Army-surplus shops. No prints on the bag, no forensics, nothing useful on CCTV once again. No witnesses from the hundreds who must have seen you.

The night of Nita's murder, you came to see me. A planned trip, but you were so late, hours late, and when you came in you put your arms around me and held me tight, something you so rarely did, and I could feel your heart fluttering in your thin chest, like a small trapped bird. Did you kill a woman just hours before? During Roshana's murder, I was reluctantly in the pub with work colleagues, enjoying the Bank Holiday for the royal wedding if not the wedding itself. I'd asked you to come and avoid it with me but you had made some weak excuse about seeing your father. I could not alibi you for either death.

Emelia says, 'Right. I'm sorry. Thank you for talking to us.' Ashira vanishes, leaving a rectangle of black behind.

We drive on in silence after that, heading to Sheffield to meet the family of Nita Chowdry, who died aged twenty-eight and was found in her own home. Going into a house is a major escalation from killing women outside, a shift in method that signifies getting bolder, getting arrogant. Making mistakes, sometimes. Losing control. Going inside means you can get trapped, leave fingerprints, leave fibres or DNA or hair. But you left nothing. Like a ghost.

Emelia's driver leaves us outside a terraced house, melting away, so we don't even need to think about parking or juggling coins and apps. Emelia has found a way to smooth the edges of the world, and I'm envious. I could do this too. I don't need to always take the hard option, but I hear Arlene's voice in my head. *A driver? Bloody hell, what's wrong with the train? You got some fancy ideas in that New York, our Karen.*

Inside we are hit by warmth, and noise, and cooking smells that make my stomach growl despite my nervousness. I got up early and haven't eaten yet, sick with guilt. Again, Emelia seems to know what to do. She makes a hands-in-prayer gesture to the man who opened the door, who's about forty and has a squirming child in his arms. Nita's brother, perhaps, one of them? She was the second child of four, I know. 'Hello, I'm Emelia, this is Karen, thank you for seeing us.'

He has a Yorkshire accent, similar to yours in fact. 'Jihan Chowdry. Mum and Dad are in here, come through.' He leads us through a chaotic steaming kitchen, various women crowded by the cooker, and out to a rickety conservatory, where an older couple are seated. He's wearing slippers and she has hearing aids in, thick glasses. Jihan raises his voice. 'Mum, Dad, they're here. Sorry,

Mum's pretty deaf these days and Dad never spoke a lot of English. I can translate.' He passes off the toddler to a woman, perhaps his wife, who stares at us frankly. I've never felt so out of place in my life as we sit down on the conservatory sofa, which is covered in a cheap blanket with a tiger print.

Emelia adopts the same expression of sad efficiency she used at the Johnsons'. 'Thank you for seeing us in your home, Mr and Mrs Chowdry. I'm Emelia Han, the last woman attacked by Aaron Hughes. This is Karen Walker. She was – well, she knew him when they were young. He killed her best friend. Karen helped put him behind bars.' I flash her a grateful look for that intro, and try to copy her sorrowful expression, hide the guilt that is seeping from every pore.

The father says something and Jihan translates. 'He's happy to talk to you, but isn't sure why – is it for a book, a documentary?'

'No, nothing like that.' The Chowdrys did actually give me permission to write about Nita, and even sent some childhood photos for my book, but I didn't speak to them directly. Miles away in New York, it seemed like an OK thing to do, write a book about you and me and them, the dead women. Now, I'm not so sure. 'You've been following the news? You know there's a girl missing in Marebridge?'

'We know,' says Jihan. 'The police told us about the symbol, all that.'

'It is the same one,' I say, clearing my throat. 'We don't know how or why, but we wanted to speak to all the families, so you know what's going on, and also . . .' I stall, and Emelia takes over.

'The thing is, hardly anyone ever saw the symbol. There are, like, no pictures of it in circulation, even. So the only people who'd know what it looks like are the police at the time, and – the families.'

They exchange a look, then the father says something else. Jihan nods. 'I've seen it.'

'You have?'

The first positive response.

'The police wanted someone to look round her house to see was anything missing, or for anything that shouldn't have been there. Clues, like. So I saw it, on the wall. But it was really sloppy. You know, it could have been anything.' It was your first attempt at drawing it on a wall and maybe you didn't know how. Maybe blood is a difficult material to work with.

Or maybe it wasn't you. Again, no evidence. Your car was spotted in Sheffield, but you lived only twenty miles away and went there often, and anyway the reg was obscured so all the police had was the colour and make.

'Anyone else in the family see it?'

'No. Just me, and the police and that, I guess. But I honestly couldn't tell you what it was like.'

Emelia is sympathetic, head tilted to the side. 'I'm so sorry you had to see that, it must have been awful.'

I cut in with a blurted question. 'Where's Nita's husband?' Everyone stares at me. 'I mean – are you still in touch with him?' Mark Ackley was thirty-four at the time of Nita's murder, living apart from her in a rented flat.

Is it just my imagination, or does a slight coldness come over them? Even the parents, who don't speak much English, supposedly? 'Oh, we don't really know where he ended up. Think he re-married. We lost touch after she died.'

My mouth is so dry. 'I'm sorry to ask this, but was Nita – was she afraid of him?'

The brother looks at me. 'She didn't say if she was. But she'd left him, yeah. I didn't know why. None of us did. Mum and Dad weren't too pleased, truth be told. Thought she should work at it.'

'Did you like him?' I ask baldly.

He hesitates. 'Not much, no.'

'But his alibi checked out.'

'It seemed pretty rock-solid, yeah. He was miles away, playing golf. Just because I didn't like him doesn't mean he killed her.' He looks at me, brow furrowed. 'You aren't saying maybe they got the wrong man? Hughes? I've seen stuff online, but I thought . . .'

'I'm not saying that.' I don't know what I'm doing. Why even listen to your half-hints and evasions, the suggestion that maybe you didn't do all – or any – of the crimes? Isn't this just you kicking at a locked door, hoping it might open? Trying to throw doubt, trying to confuse things. 'Thank you for your help, anyway.'

Emelia gets up, and I follow her example. 'Thank you so much for seeing us, and I'm sorry for the intrusion.'

Jihan says to me, 'Your book's coming out soon, yeah?'

'Yeah. Well, it was meant to. I don't know what's going to happen now.' I'm ready with my excuses, that I'm allowed to write about something that happened to me, that my book has value and isn't just another sensationalist memoir, but he doesn't challenge me. Instead, his mother says something, gesturing to Emelia.

'What is she . . . ?'

Jihan winces. 'She's saying you're the girl who survived him.'

'Yeah. I am.'

'She wants to know – was there anything Nita could have done? Could she have got away, if she fought harder?'

I freeze. Emelia thinks carefully about her answer. 'Nita was in her own home, right? I was out running in the dark, I was on high alert. Even then he had me fooled, so no, I don't think she could have got away. He was very strong, very cunning. I was just lucky. He tripped, and I saw my chance and ran and kept on running. It was only luck a car eventually stopped.'

That seems to have been the right thing to say, because the mother nods as Jihan translates what Emelia said. Comfort, maybe, in knowing that Nita never stood a chance, that she did nothing wrong. She wasn't even out after dark, not that this should ever matter. She was in her own home, eating a microwave meal. Then her mother says something else. Jihan responds, his tone argumentative. She says it again and he rolls his eyes. 'I'm so sorry, but she wants to know if she can – see your scar. So she can picture it. What he did. You can say no, of course.'

The father remonstrates with the mother, and Emelia looks to me, shocked out of her usual calm. Then, she slowly raises the hem of her jumper, showing her flat, honed abs, which no matter how many crunches she does will always have that twisted scar on them, the half of the symbol you carved into her while she was still alive. Nita's mother stretches out a hand, and very gently traces its curves. Emelia lets her. Then she sits back, nodding. 'Thank you,' she says, her accent strong.

She says something else in Hindi, and Jihan tells us, 'She says she's glad you survived, that you were strong. She's glad he was stopped. That you stopped him. That you lived.'

Emelia smiles her thanks, and makes it all the way out and into the car before bursting into tears.

When Emelia's driver drops me home after that grinding day of trauma, feeling old and worn out but still like I've been kicked in the guts, Arlene is out working, so I get into bed and pad myself around with synthetic throws and obsessively google the cases some more, looking for a loophole. Catherine, that had to be you. Your room was in the building she was found outside, and it was amazing police didn't figure out that you'd been questioned over another murder barely a year before. Alison – the women at the meeting identified you, after you were caught. Roshana? She doesn't fit your MO in various ways – might it have been a random hate crime? Why the bag, though? And the symbol – that had to be you. Nita. Being killed in her own home also didn't fit your MO, or at least not at that point. I'd been sure, when it happened, that it was her estranged husband. Not wanting it to be you, because that was the same night you had mysteriously disappeared, not shown up to meet me as planned. I google the husband, find him on Facebook with a wedding shot as his profile picture, a second wife. The occasional link to an Ironman sponsorship or petition against potholes. Nothing to indicate that his first wife was murdered by a serial killer. Maybe you didn't have an MO. Maybe you were too sophisticated for such things. Annie? A sex worker was also different. Her life must have been dangerous, and she could have been killed by any number of people, and that night you almost had an alibi – me. You had slept in my living room, though police concluded you had gone out and come back again before I woke up. Victoria, Julia – there actually was evidence in this case, a boot print that matched one you owned, though your defence said it was a make widely sold in Army-surplus stores throughout the country.

Hating myself, I fall into a rabbit hole of scrolling reels and videos, searching the hashtag of my own name. Young girls with dewy skin discussing what I knew, why I lied about Gareth, reviewing all the Bagman evidence in the same way I've been doing. Taking it one step further, speculating that you're innocent, even. After the fourth video saying I must have known, I shut it down in a hurry.

It's late, too late to call, but all the same I find myself punching in Donetti's number. He picks up on the second ring. 'Not asleep?'

'Not exactly relaxing, the day I've had.' I fill him in on what we learned from the families – not much – and what you hinted at in prison. We are so close, and yet nowhere near.

He sighs. 'Dead ends. Nothing but dead ends. And now the true-crime lot have latched on to it. They're calling the station every two minutes, swamping our Facebook page. We've had to put officers on the door of Lara's building again because they're bloody breaking in to take pictures.' It's what I feared. Lara, the young and pretty lost girl, makes the perfect victim and the circus has come to town.

'What about the CCTV from my hotel?'

He sounds defeated. 'Have you any idea how many Jeep owners there are in South Yorkshire? It would take weeks to get out to them all, and a stolen book isn't exactly a priority.' And CCTV doesn't always help. If someone covers their face with a cap or scarf, it's not much use. 'No, there's nothing.'

His slump is starting to affect me too. Days of investigation, all the clues we've found, and still we're stumped. For all we know, Lara's been dead this whole time and we're just looking for her body. It's turned so cold outside as well. How will she survive if she's locked in some outbuilding or shed?

I rub my hands over my face. 'I could go and see him again, I suppose. Though I don't have any answers for him. He won't like that.'

I hear his silence down the phone, the rhythm of his breathing. 'No clue at all, from any of the family visits?'

'Well . . . The night Nita Chowdry died, that was the one that really alarmed me back then, because Aaron was supposed to come and visit me, but he was really late. Like he didn't show up until two in the morning. Said he had car trouble. His shoes were dirty, I remember. Could have had blood on them. After the trial, I thought he must have gone and killed Nita first, then come to me. But the timeline, it was very tight.'

'Right. So – were there any other suspects in that case? The husband had an alibi, yeah?'

201

'Well, I was wondering about that. Did anyone actually check it out? You know, Aaron's dad alibied him for Jen's murder, said he never left the house that day, but it wasn't true. Someone could slip out without being noticed, or a friend could lie even, thinking it was just helping a mate, innocent, like. Also – the husband was a police officer, did you know that?'

'Yeah.' I can hear him turning pages. 'Hmm.'

'What?'

'Nothing.'

'Chris! Tell me.' It's the first time I've used his name.

He sighs deeply. 'Looks like the golfing mates, who gave the alibi, were all cops too. Some of them actually got called in to work on the investigation.'

'Jesus Christ.'

'This doesn't mean anything in itself.'

'Could he have accessed pictures of the symbol?' I have to be careful. Donetti is triggered by the whole police-corruption angle.

'Maybe. I'll look into his alibi, but it seemed pretty solid from what I recall.'

'Yeah.' I sigh too. 'What are you up to?' It's a weird question, I realise as I ask. Unprofessional.

'Eh, not much. Watching the darts.'

'The darts?'

'It's very soothing. Puts me right to sleep.'

'I should try it. None of this is especially restful, I must say.' For a moment I hesitate, almost say something dumb like *are you alone* or *maybe we should watch it together*. But that would be mad. 'OK. Night.'

'Sleep well.' I make myself hang up. This whole thing is ridiculous. If you've killed seven women, why would you care about being accused of one more? It's been a long time since we played this kind of game and I don't have the stomach for it. But it might just save Lara Milton. I'm scared. Am I crazy, or is there a chance that pulling on these threads might lead to the whole case against you collapsing? Take away Emelia's testimony, discredit me – wouldn't be hard – and what is left?

Chapter Sixteen

From *Becoming Bagman* by Karen Walker

Annie. I've noticed that when the murders come up in America, where they aren't so widely known about, people will first ask if the dead women were sex workers. Of course they don't say sex workers, they say *prostitutes*. In Annie's case, she was doing sex work, and it was as if he chose her to mess with the narrative yet again, create a story where there wasn't one. Like people think the Yorkshire Ripper killed 'prostitutes', and he did, but also a student, a lawyer, many other women. No woman was safe from him because no woman out after dark could be truly 'pure' in his twisted logic, and in the end he just wanted to kill and anyone nearby would do. These men don't have a reason for it, not really.

Annie Andersen was found dead in an alley in Manchester, beside the bins, an avalanche of rotting food and empty drinks cans on top of her body. This was later in 2011, a speeding-up, an escalation, to kill two in one year, Roshana and then Annie. The symbol, daubed on the wall again. The bare bricks of the alley. Suffocated again, but the bag taken away this time. Perhaps it offered too much of a clue. The press made much of what she was wearing, the tight red pleather dress, no coat in the December weather, the over-the-knee boots. No one said the phrase *asking for it*, but it hovered about like a bad smell. As with Nita, he left no fingerprints when he drew the symbol, must have used gloves. He never seemed to leave hair or fibres. Did I make the connection to Aaron's recently shaved head, the Army-surplus leather coat I had teased him about in school? I have to believe I didn't. There was talk on the news of the Bagman drawing an 'occult symbol' on or near the bodies. Moral panic about computer games and violent horror films and Satanic worship in our universities, all of it just a distraction. 'Occult symbol' made me think of pentagrams, not whatever it was I had seen doodled in Aaron Hughes's notebook back in 2004. Again, I have to believe this.

Here's a thought to chill your blood and haunt your dreams. Prisons are not as secure as we think. There are more than two thousand escapes every year in the US, for example. Ted Bundy managed to escape twice. Peter Sutcliffe had a well-developed plan to flee from Broadmoor by smuggling in a hacksaw. The more understaffed and underfunded prisons are, the more likely this is to happen. So I can't sleep easy while I'm in the same country as you, let alone just a few miles down the road. I keep getting up and checking Arlene's front door, testing the lock and the Ring camera. There's a way to hack them, isn't there, to open doors automatically?

Lying in bed, thoughts keep coming. What if you get out, come here? Hurt my mother? Hurt someone else? If the bargains I'm making with you lead to your freedom? I ask myself, what do you really want? Is it possible you still hope to clear your name? Or just get out? What ends am I being put to?

I don't sleep much that night, and when I wake up, groggy and dry-eyed, there's a message from Emelia saying she's been 'called on to set' and can't make today. I text back *But this is urgent!* She replies right away. *Yes thanks am aware. Sending Matt instead. Annie's family all briefed and ready to talk. They love him anyway.*

Huh. I'm being passed over to Dad for the day, clearly. When I get up, Arlene's room door is still open, her bed neatly made. Did she actually come in last night – I didn't hear her if so? She's downstairs, however, brewing up coffee that smells surprisingly good, in a glass cafetière. 'That new?' I ask.

'Borrowed it off San.' She looks me over with a critical eye. 'Well, you look like warmed-up poop.'

'Thanks.'

'I mean it, don't upset yourself going round all these families. Did anyone say owt to you?'

I shrug, taking the cup she hands me. 'Not really. Not exactly warm, though.' Not like with Sainted Emelia, the Girl Who Lived.

'You going out again?'

'Yeah, but not with Emelia, she's sending—'

Just then the doorbell goes, and I see the jaunty shape of Matt beyond it. I didn't realise he was actually going to call for me, but before I can stop Arlene she's off to the door, greeting him warmly.

'Oh hello! You're that podcast fella, aren't you, saw you on the news last year. Coffee? Tea?'

'Oh, thank you, we best be off though. Lots to do. Mrs Walker, is it?'

She laughs merrily. 'Mrs would be a fine chance. Call me Arlene, love. Must say I never knew our Karen to get anywhere near this many gentleman callers when she lived here. Scared them all away, she did, with her grumpy face and Goth clothes!'

Matt comes through to the kitchen, in a nice grey jumper and jeans, a silver watch round his wrist. Arlene is giving me significant looks again, so I drain the coffee, even though it burns my mouth. 'Right. Let's go.'

Matt's car is tatty, the cup-holders and side pockets filled with rubbish, the back seat rattling with books about true crime. Matt is the kind of visual thinker who likes to illustrate his thoughts, so when I settle into the passenger seat he passes me a large sketchpad, its sheets scrawled over with notes. 'You're missing a trick not having bits of string connecting them,' I remark. He has even printed off photos of the victims and stuck them on, though they are from the internet and smudgy, the faces blurring into one. Dead girls all have the same expression, as if they knew what was going to happen to them, that they were walking into the wrong kind of story.

'Ha. Things are getting spicy online, did you see?'

'I saw.'

'Apparently they're making TikToks in the police-station car park.' He sounds scathing. 'Honestly, it does more harm than good when these absolute amateurs get involved. They go into crime scenes, they destroy evidence, they openly libel people and they don't even realise.'

How different is he, though? 'All the more reason to get on with this,' I say pointedly.

'So I've been going over the MOs of each murder, to see if any were different.'

'And?'

'The most obvious one to me is this.' He taps the pad without taking his eyes off the road. Roshana. 'She was so young, and taken off a busy street, not from some isolated spot.'

I'm not convinced. 'He changed his tactics. He wouldn't have wanted to be pigeon-holed.' You had scorned the very idea that people's behaviour could be predicted. At least the behaviour of someone as smart as you. An apex predator. 'What about Nita, or the two girls? It was different every time.'

'Well, which one stands out to you? Were there any you didn't think he could have done?'

It's a good question. I run my hands over the pictures of faces, stopping at one. 'Her. It was one reason I didn't call the police for so long – he was with me that night. He slept on my sofa.' That was after I'd moved to Manchester, and was renting a tiny flat, working in an office job I hated, trying to write a novel. 'The police decided he slipped out while I was asleep. He didn't sleep well; I'd often wake up to find him gone. But it seemed so unlikely, and it was ten miles from my flat.'

He glances at the picture I'm indicating, recognising her right away. Like me, he is so familiar with the cases he can use a kind of shorthand. 'Annie. The only sex worker.'

I like him for saying that, not *prostitute* or even *hooker*, terms I still hear people use so casually. 'Right. She never really fit the pattern, as she would have gone to the alley with him willingly. That didn't suit his – aesthetic, I suppose you could call it. I think he liked being the lone stalker at night. The fear of it. Your keys in your hand, your phone with 999 ready dialled in. And a sex worker. He would have thought that was a cliché, perhaps. Too Yorkshire Ripper for his taste.'

'No chance he'll just tell you?'

'I don't think so.'

'I could come in with you next time?' I hear the hope in his voice, casually disguised.

'He'll only talk to me.' Not that I expect much. Maybe you will reward me for my efforts, the rounds of atonement I'm making by visiting the families. The blame I'm accepting, that I don't even know is mine. I did ask April to send a copy of the book to the prison, but I'm not sure it will make any difference.

After a moment Matt says, 'I've been thinking. If he's really not guilty of one, would he not have said off the bat, when he was arrested – I didn't do that one in particular?'

'No. He never admitted to any of them, so he could hardly say *especially not her*.' I've been trying to understand it. When you were imprisoned, when it was too late, why would you not have said something then, if it mattered to you not to take the fall for someone else's murder? I suppose because you were hoping for an appeal. You could get a new trial, and maybe, just maybe, you might win that one. And Lara? Maybe it's as simple as you don't know or even care about her. She's just a convenient lever to get me back here.

I sigh heavily. 'He's playing me. After all these years, he never stopped.' A true chess player, only you are ten years of moves ahead, and I never had a chance.

'He's certainly smart,' says Matt, with more than a hint of admiration. 'I mean, he had to be, to evade capture for so long.'

'That's not true at all,' I say, crossly. 'They don't have to be smart. The rest of us just have to be stupid.'

Matt drives fast, running the steering wheel lightly through his hands. Not like the overly correct driving style of DS Chris Donetti. 'So you think Annie's the one? We'll get some proof today?'

'I don't know. How do you explain the symbol being there if so?'

You were with me that night, sitting at my kitchen table reading a book about Ted Bundy when I woke up in the morning, with no sign of any injuries from Annie's scratching nails, or that you had left my flat that night. We never shared a bed when you came over, though I suggested it often. Instead you would take the sofa, saying you didn't want to keep me awake with your insomnia. When you were arrested police looked for CCTV from my building, to see if you could have left that night, killed Annie, and made it back again, but it had already been wiped. It was just a rough edge on a nice neat case by then, one no one wanted to poke at. But can it be true? Are you actually innocent? 'What will it mean?' I say, agitated, as Matt changes lane so rapidly I clutch the side of the car. 'If we find out he didn't do one of them. Will he be able to launch a new appeal? Get all the cases reopened?'

'Maybe. But Karen, he didn't protest his innocence at the time.'

'He never admitted guilt either! You know they were rough with him, the police. He tried to sue them a few years ago.' And there was little forensic evidence, because you had been so very careful. It was just my testimony, and Emelia's identification, but it was dark and she was terrified. A good lawyer could argue she was wrong. Oh God, this is like those nightmares I used to have, where you would turn up in my living room and tell me, *It was all a mistake, Karen. I didn't do any of it. You called the police on me. I protected you, and you didn't protect me.*

Matt tries for a reassuring tone. 'It's highly, highly unlikely.'

'Not impossible though.' What a terrible thing to hope, that a woman was brutally murdered by a serial killer. Rather than, what, a normal man? A normal murderer? There are hundreds of women killed every year by normal men, their husbands and ex-boyfriends, their sons and brothers. Why is it killers like you we find so very chilling, when so many of us live with another type in our homes and beds?

As if feeling the urgency, Matt drives very fast the rest of the way, quite probably breaking the speed limit. I imagine how we'll explain it to the police, to Donetti, if we get pulled over. I have to stop thinking about Donetti. Annie's family – another large and sprawling one – meets us in an overheated terraced house that smells strongly of smoke and dogs. Several shaggy beasts wander about, and when I stand up from the sofa afterwards I have hair all over my jeans. It's interesting to watch Matt at work. He has a cajoling tone, a piercing sympathetic gaze, and his body language radiates sadness and understanding. No wonder people don't warm to me, stiff and defensive. Soon we have cups of tea and Club bars and two small children are climbing all over Matt, giving me a wide berth.

Annie's mother is startlingly young for a woman whose daughter would be in her thirties had she lived. She heaves a big sigh. 'I always knew something bad would happen once she went on the game. The drugs, you see. Got into her. And then she just wasn't herself.'

'I'm so, so sorry, Deirdre.' She has already asked Matt to call her this. Annie's father is long gone, identity unknown, but Deirdre is now married to a man called Colin, who seems to be the father or grandfather of some of the kids running about the place. It's amazing to me that families can be like this, big and chaotic. It was always just me and Arlene, and sometimes even that seemed like too much. It was so easy for me to slip all bonds and leave the country, after one best friend was dead and the other in prison for her murder.

I ask, 'Do you think Annie would have been less cautious, from the drugs – like she might have gone willingly into the alley?'

Deirdre lights a cigarette, in a gesture that reminds me of Arlene. 'Most likely, love. When she was on that stuff she hadn't any sense.'

'And – she'd have asked to be paid in advance?' Police had found a twenty-pound note clutched in her dead hand, which had seemed like a promising lead for a while, before petering out. It had been withdrawn in Manchester Piccadilly station, which I knew you had passed through the day before to come and visit me. Just another coincidence, I told myself.

'Aye, she wanted the cash for drugs, that's all she cared about.'

I let Matt take over. 'When you heard she had died, did you think someone specific had hurt her? Was there anyone in her life she was scared of, a boyfriend or anyone like that?'

'I thought it were a punter. Happens all the time, to working girls. Then they said it was him. Bagman. That he'd – put that symbol.'

'And you believed that?'

Like the other families, she looks bewildered by the question. 'Who else could it be, love?'

'I don't know.'

'But he didn't cut her and I was pleased about that. Wouldn't like to think of her cut up.' Annie had a head wound instead of a symbol on her stomach, from where she'd been smashed against the wall. Another difference in MO.

'Did you see the symbol?' I ask, leaning forward. 'A picture of it or anything?'

She shakes her head. 'No, love. I've no idea what it looks like.'

Just like everyone else. We drink our tea and speak some platitudes and Matt affects an interest in Man United and then we leave. Another dead end.

When I get back that night, the lights are on and I can see the TV flickering and it gives me an odd sense of warmth. However fast I might have run from it, this is my home. However deep our differences, Arlene is my mother, and when it comes down to it, she'll take my side. I'm not sure I realised that before, so desperate to flee

212

first from Marebridge and then the UK. But when I open the door I see Arlene is in front of the TV smoking a cigarette, and that she has company. Rosalind Rollason is sitting there with her, watching some reality show where people have to lie to win. It's very Arlene not to have turned the TV off for a guest. 'Got a visitor,' she says, side-eyeing Rosalind. It must be strange for her, to see this girl and imagine what her life could have been. I wonder if Rosalind knows her father was supposed to marry my mother, meaning she would never have been born. She would not exist if not for her sister's murder.

'Rosalind. This is a surprise.'

She's bundled up in a heavy down coat, the shape of her body entirely obscured. It's different from when we were young, when Jen would take any opportunity to wear clothes that were tight, revealing, low-cut. 'I wanted to talk to you. About the other day.'

'Well, OK, shall we go into the kitchen?' Arlene's eyes follow us as we leave.

There's nowhere to sit in the tiny room, so I put the kettle on to boil and lean against the cupboards. 'You OK?'

She shrugs. 'I wanted to explain why I was there. At the conference.'

'You don't have to explain to me.'

'It's just no one will *tell* me anything,' she bursts out. 'About Jen, about what happened. What she was like.' I think of the diary upstairs, hidden under my old bed. Does she know I took it? 'And people are saying Aaron Hughes didn't even kill her, that someone else did. Or that he didn't do any of them. It's all over TikTok.'

'I know. But you can't believe everything you see on there.'

She glares at me, her eyes just like Jen's. Same shade. 'You think he did it. That he's the Bagman.'

'In the end, yes. I did and I do.'

'Even her?'

213

'I – what are the odds, that she knew someone who went on to kill so many women, but she was murdered by some other random person?' I'm using Dickinson's argument.

'But did she know him? Wasn't he *your* boyfriend?'

'Not exactly. We all knew each other.' How much, I have never been exactly sure. 'Do you want a cup of tea, Rosalind?'

'Ew, no. I want to know about my sister.'

I can't face this now, after the day I've had, but she deserves to know. 'OK, well how about this. I can look out some old photos of her and me, and we could get a coffee sometime – in your café maybe – and I'll show you them. Tell you what I remember. All the Jen things.' And what would that be? Lip gloss. Film stars. Boys. Shiny hair, devious mind. Almost thirteen years of seeing each other every day. Best friend. Enemy.

She nods. 'OK. But I need to know – how did you get it so wrong? You told the police it was her boyfriend who did it. Gareth.'

'I said I saw Gareth's car near the woods, and that he hurt her in the past. That's all true, you know.'

'But you said you saw Aaron Hughes at home that day. That was a lie?'

'I – I did go to his house. His dad said he was sick in bed, and when I looked past him, I thought I saw Aaron through the bedroom door. He'd been off school, after all. Then his dad told the police he'd been home all day, so I just – corroborated that.' As I say it I can hear how it sounds. Poor Karen, a victim swept up in events. Not responsible for the terrible things that happened.

She looks at me shrewdly. 'I thought you said you'd talked to him, spent a while at the house with him. So he wouldn't have had time to kill Jen.'

'I was confused. It's a lot, you know, being questioned over a murder. And my best friend was dead.' And I had loved you. At

214

times I honestly didn't know if I was saving you or saving myself. Or if that was the same thing.

'But he said he saw you too. You hung out. And that was your alibi as well.'

'I suppose. I didn't know what he'd told the police. They lied to us a lot. Trying to get us to say things.'

'You didn't have another one. Alibi.'

'My mother worked a lot. The neighbours were in and out. No one saw me come back here.' A lifetime of slipping by unnoticed had come back to haunt me that day.

'OK,' she says. 'I guess that makes sense.'

It doesn't, not at all, but I want nothing more than to stop these questions. 'Sure you don't want tea?' That's my way of saying, *You can go now*. 'Or a lift home?'

'I have my own car.' Of course, she is almost eighteen. Same age Jen was when she died. It's natural she'd want to ask questions and I should be more sympathetic.

'Well, take care then.'

When the door shuts, Arlene comes and stands in the doorway.

'Pretty little thing. Sulky though. Not like Princess Jen.' No love was ever lost between Jen and Arlene, even before she took up with Ash. Bitch recognised bitch.

'She's had a rough time of it.'

Arlene takes a drag. 'Haven't we all?'

I go upstairs, rooting around for the diary again, scanning over its pages of loopy writing looking for a clue. What has been torn out, and by who? Did Jen remove something herself, and if so why? It's just lists of what she ate, TV shows she liked, boys she fancied, complaints about Gareth, her dad, and sometimes me. Did she rip it out to hide something? Or could the page have been removed by whoever killed her?

Chapter Seventeen

From *Becoming Bagman* by Karen Walker

I'm almost at the end now of the litany of victims, and yet there are still two more women to list. Such a heavy toll, all their names. I remember that feeling that it would never end, the terror of it just going on and on. *There's been another one? How? How is he getting away with this?* When most British serial killers barely break three victims, how did he kill eight women and not get caught? It wasn't the eighties, with all the misogyny and bloody-mindedness of the police then, the deadly conviction that the Yorkshire Ripper was from Wearside. There were computers, systems to make sure information was shared. What if the man had already been questioned and let go, like both Peter Sutcliffe (nine times!) and Ted Bundy, who was even charged twice and allowed to escape all the same?

Who was he? What was his name? We waited, in terror, for the blank of his features to settle into a name, a face. A real person, not a monster.

Victoria.

Julia.

It was May now, 2012. I remember we only walked in pairs during that winter, that our work-places offered to subsidise taxis, provide us with rape alarms. We made ghoulish jokes. *Don't go off alone, or you'll get Bagmanned.* Was I afraid? Or did I know, deep down, that I had been alone with Bagman hundreds of times? Let him touch me – no, begged him to touch me? Slept by his side, totally trusting? No, I didn't know any of this. Of course I didn't. If I did, what kind of person would it make me?

Victoria Lewis and Julia Dixon were best friends at the University of Preston, studying sports science and physiotherapy. Victoria was black, Julia white. They'd been inseparable since they were five and they would stay that way, dying within half an hour of each other. He kept Julia alive longer. Sometimes, the word *audacious* is used about what he did to these women. No one knows how exactly, but he got access to the university flat they shared with two other students, who were away for the weekend. Those girls must think about this all the time, the chances of them still being there, had he chosen any other day. Maybe Victoria and Julia let him in, charmed by him. Maybe he spun some story like he did to Emelia, about missing his last bus or losing his wallet. Or maybe he just broke in, took them by surprise while they were watching *Pitch Perfect*, their favourite post-night-out activity. Pictures were leaked of their flat, pink cushions and inflatable chairs and big mugs of hot chocolate, one splashed over the wall like blood. You could see the edge of the symbol in one. Was that enough to recognise it? For me, who had seen it before? No, I have to believe it was not.

Both girls were dead in their beds, bags over heads, left in place this time, hooded like criminals for execution. Both girls mutilated. The knife used was from their own kitchen, left in the middle of the floor. A messy scene. A footprint left behind this time, in blood. Maybe he struggled to control two at once. The print was from an Army boot, a size eleven. Aaron had always liked to buy clothes from Army stores, maybe some link to his ex-soldier father, despite his avowed hatred of the military. But why would I think of him in connection to this horror? He was my friend, sometimes more than that.

After Victoria and Julia, it was all-out terror. This man could abduct and subdue two young women at once, strong and healthy women – Victoria competed for the university in running, Julia was a swimmer. Who was it? Women were asked – do you have a boyfriend, a son, a father, who might be doing this? Call this number in confidence, or more women will die. I still had not used the one I'd jotted down several years before, when Alison Johnson died. And it would be another eight months before he was caught, and during that time we would just wait. And wait. And wait.

Wait for him to do it again.

It ended. I have to cling on to that. However long those years seemed, it did stop and no one else would die, thanks to Emelia if not thanks to me, and he's in prison and it's over now. It's tempting to look for answers in childhood. What was done to him to make him like this? Yes, Aaron's mum had left, and his dad was a mentally ill ex-soldier who liked to shoot small animals and skin them in the house. That was traumatic. But it doesn't explain it. Nothing does. Some people just go haywire, and do the things we aren't supposed to, press a knife to another person's skin or wrap their hands around a throat or fire a gun or hit over and over and over. There is no way to know why. We can only lock them up so they stop.

'How did you get on with Matt?' Emelia is examining her pointy nails too as her driver takes us further north, towards Newcastle. They've been redone in a slightly different shade of nude; I still hate them.

'He's good at what he does. Puts people at ease.'

'You think he's cute?' Her voice is deceptively casual. I can't tell if she likes him or she's trying to set me up.

'I'm not exactly thinking about that right now. You know, the first boy I loved turned out to be a serial killer, that whole thing. Tends to put you off.'

'But you were married, right?' I wonder how she knows this.

'For a bit. Green card thing.' Which does a disservice to Santiago, but I will never stop feeling bad when I think about our marriage and divorce, the yawning abyss I found when I tried to step into a normal life. When I realised no other man was like you.

'Listen, he's just one bad guy. A very bad guy. You shouldn't let it put you off for life.'

'I thought you were single too.'

She shrugs. 'I'm only thirty-two. Don't want to settle, and I travel a lot.' She pauses. 'Also hard to date with a giant carving in your stomach. I also have to explain I'm *that* girl, and the whole thing just gets – messy.'

'I know what you mean.' Your malign influence, going on and on still. I've always been anti the death penalty, but maybe all of us who remain will only feel safe once you're no longer breathing.

The families of Victoria and Julia are meeting us at the same time, and I wonder how they feel about that, being lumped together for all eternity because their daughters died that way. I remember the disbelief in the press at the time. How could one person do this, kill two healthy young women? Maybe you used restraints, or you threatened to hurt the other girl if one made a noise. You managed to slip in and out of the block of flats with no one seeing or hearing a thing. Would you not have been covered in blood? Did you wear an outer layer each time then take it off? Police never found any blood on any of your things, though there was evidence that clothes had been burned out the back of your dad's house. None of it quite enough proof. And me? I heard it on the news at the gym, and put my headphones in, switched to *Hollyoaks*. I was practised by then in tamping down my doubts. When it happened I was on a date, some guy I can barely remember now, who wasn't you.

It's already starting to feel familiar as we go in. A pleasant semi, two families broken and cracked. Julia's parents split up after she died, which is common when you lose a child. More cups of tea, biscuits from M&S this time. Victoria's parents hold hands, Julia's sit across the room from each other in bleak sorrow. We are told tales of prizes won, kind deeds, achievements met. We are shown pictures of two young women always smiling, faces pressed together as they grow up from five to twenty. This could have been Jen and me. I wonder if their friendship too was complicated by patches of cold, dark currents, dangerous undertows. Our pictures would only have shown smiles too.

Emelia nods through it all. I notice she doesn't drink her tea and I wonder if she hasn't previously. She's a semi-vegan, I know from social media – she eats lean, organic meat and free-range eggs, but not dairy. 'We're so sorry to make you relive it all. We just need to know about the symbol, if you or anyone you know might have seen it.'

Then, to my surprise, Victoria's mother, Carole, sighs and says, 'We didn't answer them, you know. We'd never do that.'

Emelia and I exchange a quick look. 'I'm sorry?'

'The person who asked if we had the symbol. We sent them packing, of course. Ghouls.'

'It's disgusting,' agrees Julia's dad, Brian.

I let myself speak now, panic beating under my ribs. 'I'm sorry, are you saying someone *else* got in touch to ask if you had a copy of it?'

'Of course. We hear from a lot of people, you know. Journalists. People making documentaries and writing books.' Carole gives me a sharp look at that and I stare at the patterned carpet. They never replied to my letter.

'I always say no too,' says Barbara, mother of Julia. She casts a bitter look at her ex-husband. 'Brian does them sometimes.'

'I think it keeps her memory alive,' says Brian stiffly. This is clearly a point of contention.

Victoria's father, Carlton, a former bus driver, has said nothing so far. He just holds his wife's hand, so tightly it's as if he needs to tether himself down.

'And – do you actually have a copy?' I've never heard this before. I assumed the only versions of the symbol were left on walls, photographed and cleaned off, or carved into the skin of young women. This unsettles me, the idea that there might be things about the cases I don't know. That I missed while I was sitting in that room at the court, waiting to testify.

They all exchange a look, and it's Carole who speaks. 'He drew it on a piece of paper in their room. Victoria's essay that she was writing. In pen. Like a doodle, kind of. Not – like the one on the wall.' That had been done in a mixture of their blood, likely after both girls were dead in their beds. 'I don't know if the police ever spotted it, to be honest. We got it back with her stuff after the trial and we just – kept it, I suppose. I'm not sure why. It was hers. Not something else for him to ruin.'

I'm stunned by this. 'But – why would he do that?' Why would you risk leaving such a clue at a crime scene? Your actual handwriting?

'How would we know?' Brian is fierce. 'You tell us. You knew him.'

But I can't think of any reason you would stop, mid murder, to doodle on some paper. Maybe they let you in willingly, maybe you waited and chatted for a bit, sat at Victoria's desk and scribbled on her essay. Maybe you said you'd missed your last bus, had to wait for a lift or a taxi. Got them to trust you. Maybe you had even met them before that day, hung about campus pretending to be a student, as you had when you killed Alison. Increasing the risk, increasing the thrill. Maybe you forgot about your drawing, made a mistake for once. You're just a human man. Of course you made mistakes. God, there is so much I still want to ask you, but how can

I? How can I bear to sit there and hear you gloat over your crimes, the ones you committed and then came back to me, sometimes? But you are the only one who knows the answers.

Emelia glances at me and leans forward to put down her cup. 'Thank you, all of you. We didn't know there was another copy in existence. It's all safely locked away, I assume? A lot of people would like to get hold of it, you know.'

'We're well aware of that,' says Carole, bitter. 'No one's seen it. No one needs to.'

'And do you have the details of the person who contacted you? This most recent person?'

'It was an email. Just some string of numbers, "John Smith" or something like that. I can send it on to you, Emelia, I have your details.'

'Thanks so much, Carole.' She's basically on first-name terms with all the families. I think in her they see their dead daughters, maybe indulge a brief fantasy that they too managed to fight you off, and run, and run, and survive. But me, I remind them of other things. Of the parallel world where I sent you to prison for killing Jen back in 2004, and all of their girls are still alive, going about their business, and no one has even heard the name the Bagman.

Once back in the car, I get my phone out to call Donetti. He sounds harassed, the noises of the police station behind him as I explain someone has been trying to buy copies of the symbol, likely the same person who advertised on the forum Janine found. 'Well, I'll follow up, but the IP address was VPN routed, untraceable.'

'You didn't know the family had a copy of it?'

'It wasn't in the files.' He's short with me – sensitive to suggestions the police aren't competent. So what you hinted at was true – one of the families does have a copy. Does that mean it's also true you didn't do one, or even all, of the murders? But if

223

this drawing is locked away, then how was someone able to daub it on to Lara Milton's wall?

'Any news your end?'

His sigh tells me all I need to know. 'Several dozen more sightings of Lara, all useless. Meanwhile I've got two new sexual assaults and an attempted murder on my books. It never stops.' She's slipping off the agenda, the longer she stays missing. Even the true-crime mob will soon move on to other stories, other crimes. 'And yes, we searched her flat again. There's nothing. You?'

'I don't know. All the evidence was shaky, but nothing really sticks out.'

Just then, Emelia, who's also on her phone, waves a hand in front of my face. *Matt*, she mouths. 'Oh really? Um, that's . . . OK, we're on it.' She hangs up. 'Mercedes got something. Let me talk to your hot fed.'

'He's not my—'

'FFS, Karen!'

I pass over the phone and she flips her hair aside, holds it to her ear. 'Hi, this is Emelia Han. I have some important information you're gonna want to follow up on. Lara's friend, Melissa O'Donald. Do you have eyes on her?'

I snort at her turn of phrase before I process what she said. 'Melissa?'

She waves a hand to shush me. 'I'm going to send you over something. You should bring her in and we'll all meet at the station.'

I can just imagine how Donetti will respond to being ordered about like this. She hangs up without giving him back to me.

'What was all that about?'

Emelia is already getting back into the car. 'The friend. Melissa. She's been lying all along.'

◆ ◆ ◆

As we pull up to the police station, I see them. Cars parked all along the road, spilling out from the parking area, almost blocking our progress. And people. People line the street, standing in knots in the car park, a hubbub of voices. Officers in yellow coats are trying to herd them to the edges so we can drive up.

'What is this?' There must be forty, fifty people here.

Emelia doesn't look up from her phone. 'True-crimers. Have you not seen all the posts? They want to find Lara.'

'Well, she's not here.'

'They're – calling on the cops to do more. I don't know.' She takes sunglasses from her bag and puts them on, despite the gloom of the day. 'Cover your face if you don't want to be all over the internet looking like that.'

I take umbrage at this, but heed her words and find my own sunglasses, rolling my beanie hat low over my forehead. All the same, as we step from the car they see us and the snap of camera phones is all around. It's just like the trial. *Karen. Karen! Emelia!* I feel her grip on my arm. 'Just keep walking.' When the automatic doors close behind us I gasp in air. There are more high-vis officers on the door, but they nod us through, recognising me, I suppose. Then I see Janine, Jim, and Mercedes waiting, along with Matt, all self-important with their stick-on visitor badges.

Matt is excited, bouncing on his toes. 'Crazy, isn't it? All this interest in the Bagman. And they don't even know about Melissa yet, they took her in the back.'

'None of this will help, you know,' I say. 'Where's Donetti? What's going on?'

The Brains Trust talk over each other as usual.

'. . . knew there was something shifty when I saw her on the news, I mean the guilty ones always try to get involved in the investigation . . .'

225

'It was me got her to talk,' Mercedes gloats. 'Admit she went into Lara's flat with her that night.' I wonder how we didn't suspect it before. The neighbour's comment about heavy feet on the stairs, Lara maybe being on the phone – it was two girls going up, not one. And Melissa lied about that. Maybe she lied about everything, and there was no John after all, or not one Lara was scared of. We only have her word for it.

Then Donetti pushes open the door, looking harassed. 'Right. You're going to have to keep the noise down. It isn't a public meeting, it's a police station.'

Matt has almost crushed his coffee cup with glee. 'This is a huge development, right, Chris?'

'It's Sergeant. And we don't know yet.' He eyeballs Matt. 'Whatever happens today better not end up on a podcast, OK? It's an active investigation and you're only here at all out of courtesy, because you helped with this new development.'

'*I* helped,' insists Mercedes. 'She feels comfortable with me, you know, so maybe I should—'

'No way,' says Donetti firmly. 'You can all wait here, if you quieten down. Visitors' badges on at all times.' His icy gaze turns to me. 'Karen can come in.'

Emelia makes a tutting noise. 'Whatever, I'm needed on set anyway,' and she walks towards the door, tapping at her phone, as the Brains Trust raise a storm of complaint. Donetti simply ignores them, swiping his ID to get into the back of the station, then holding the door for me to duck under. As I do I can't help but breathe in his smell, cologne and fresh sweat. Not unpleasant at all. The last thing I see is Matt's forlorn face, locked out of the action.

Donetti strides ahead. 'This is a bloody shambles. There was a reason we didn't want it getting out about the symbol. I was explicitly told to focus on other leads, and now every idiot with a ring light is descending on Marebridge. Your mates out there aren't much better.'

'They're not my mates.' I trot after him down the carpeted corridor.

'Can't stand that Cooke guy. He's got an anti-police agenda and he's always pushing it. And as for Ms Han – can't trust her not to put things on TikTok. Not to mention the Scooby Doo gang out there. Anyway, I need you.' Why does that give me a little thrill? Pathetic. 'You're the only one Hughes will talk to, so I need you across all developments.'

'You really think Melissa's involved? Aaron did say it was someone she knew.'

'Melissa's prints were on the door, but it's hardly evidence of wrongdoing. They were best friends.' Like Jen and me. All of this is horribly familiar, in fact. A young woman in a police station, suspected of harming her best friend. Terrified. And maybe guilty. Pointing the finger at a boyfriend instead.

'She could hardly have done it, could she? I mean, she'd never be able to drag a body.' Melissa is not exactly tiny, but not strong enough to lift an unconscious or dead woman down two flights of stairs without being noticed.

Unless she had help.

We've reached the interview suite now and he holds another door for me. 'I don't know. It seems unlikely, given she was in her taxi ten minutes later, but stranger things have happened. I've sent an officer to re-interview the driver, but no, I don't like her for it.' So why then did she lie?

Through an ajar door, Melissa sits at a bare table alone, hunched over. She's wearing a hoody and tracksuit bottoms, her hair in a bun, as if she's been dragged unsuspecting from her home. Her face is streaked in tears.

Donetti sighs. 'OK. She's not under arrest yet, but she's scared out of her wits right now. I'm going to do something I wouldn't normally do, which obviously will be off the record. I want you to talk to her. Think of yourself as, like – an appropriate adult or something. An advocate. She's lied about something, obviously. I want to know why, so we can rule her out and get on with finding the actual abductor.'

That seems surprisingly thoughtful, a kindness that was not afforded to me in the same situation all those years ago. 'Why are you doing this?'

He shrugs. 'We're not all total bastards.'

'Hey, Melissa.' She bursts into tears as soon as I open the door, but I try not to judge her. I never cried even once when I was being questioned over Jen. It might have helped me if I had.

'Look, I can explain everything, if you'll just give me a chance!'

'That's why I'm here. Obviously, I'm not police, so none of this is being recorded. Tell me why you lied.'

'I – hardly lied. Yeah, I went into the flat with her, just for a minute. She were going to lend me a book, that's all. A guidebook for Spain.'

'And what happened?'

Melissa takes a wet breath. 'She had another letter from him. It were – slipped under the door this time. As in, he'd come round her place. He usually just sent flowers and gifts and that.'

'Him? John?'

'Yeah. That fella.'

'So why didn't you tell the police? That could be really significant.'

'Because! We had – a row about it. Just a little one. I swear, I didn't hurt her!' There's no way this girl removed Lara's body by herself. But she could have lashed out at her, hit her, stabbed her even. I do believe that. I know how it can take you over, a rage so blind and swirling, all your love for your friend suddenly inverted into pure hate.

'What was it over?'

'I said something like – well, at least you've got a guy who likes you. First-world problems, you know? Like he's *too* romantic?'

'Sounds like he was stalking her, Melissa.'

'That's what she said. I don't know, I were just – you know, she had so much. Her own flat, she got promoted over me at work, and fellas always liked her better too.'

'She had the flat because she was an orphan.' I sound severe, and I can imagine Donetti outside, getting impatient, shifting from foot to foot.

'I know! But sometimes people can have a bad thing happen and still get all the luck. The rest of their life is great, like. But everyone just feels sorry for them.' Like Jen, after her mother died.

'So Lara didn't like what you said?'

She shakes her head, tears rolling down her face and plopping from her nose, unchecked. 'She went off at me. Said I didn't under-stand, that I were so jealous of her I couldn't see that she was scared, really scared of this guy. And she kind of – threw the letter at me and told me I'd better just go. So I got my taxi, like I said. She were fine when I left. Cross, but fine. I swear on my life.'

'And where is the letter now?' It wasn't at the flat, I'm sure.

'I threw it in the bin outside. It's probably gone by now, I'm sorry.'

I sigh. 'Melissa, if you'd said this right away, we could have retrieved it. We could have found out who he was, this John.' Maybe he left fingerprints or DNA on the note. And the hand-delivering suggests he was in the area that night, so likely caught on CCTV somewhere.

'So you don't think it were me that hurt her?' She sniffs.

'I don't. Can't speak for the police.'

'I'm sorry. I were just – scared, you know.'

I do know. All too well. 'She was really frightened of this John guy, huh?'

'Terrified.' Melissa hiccups. 'I feel so bad I didn't realise. Horrible. Like I could die.'

I know that feeling too. 'Alright. Let me talk to the sergeant.'

As I tell him, Donetti starts to run stressed fingers over his forehead. 'Bloody Gen Z,' he mutters. 'There's no way that bin'll be full still. Evidence is long gone.'

Something occurs to me. Melissa saying: he was always sending things, flowers and gifts. Someone complaining about parcels . . . 'The downstairs neighbour. The sales guy – he said he was always taking packages for Lara. Did you check if he was holding any for her when she went missing?'

He freezes. 'Surely he'd have told us if so.'

'That guy? You think?'

Donetti swears and starts to move off. I call after him, 'Can you send someone in with tissues? Your interview room's gonna be covered in snot.'

Chapter Eighteen

From *Becoming Bagman* by Karen Walker

Jen Rollason, my best friend, was found dead in the woods outside Marebridge in the dawn hours of Tuesday, 14th December, 2004. Several hours later I was being questioned by the police over it. When Meredith Kercher was murdered in Italy in 2007, it all came back to me. Aaron and I in the police station, those endless days without sleep, the over-salted microwave food eaten in our cells. The lies the police told. *He's talking, you know. It's time for you to talk too, Karen. Save yourself.* It could have been Aaron and me sentenced to more than twenty years, if they hadn't believed us. If there'd been a scrap more evidence. If Gareth Hale was not so belligerent, if he hadn't pushed Jen about. The marks of his paws on her pale neck, which she showed off like love-bites. Passion. A grown-up world of kink. We were just lucky. Amanda Knox, had she ever heard my name, could have learned from me and all the things I did wrong.

I went with Ash to the police station early in the morning of 14th December. I wasn't allowed to leave for another three days. I was still wearing my pyjama bottoms and hadn't showered or brushed my teeth. I kept imagining what Jen would say about that, how she would mock me. But Jen was dead, they were saying. It took a long time for me to believe it. A police station is like a place out of time, no windows, time running differently. First they asked me questions. So many questions. When did I last see Jen, what did she say to me. Had she messaged me at all over the last few days. What happened at the party on the Saturday. They'd heard I was upset, that I'd stormed out. What did I do after school on the Monday, where did I go. Could anyone prove I was at home like I said.

It was me who first gave them Gareth's name. He really had stormed out of the party that weekend, and his relationship with Jen had been 'volatile'. That was the word I used. They exchanged looks and said they knew all about that, in a way that made me think they didn't. Gareth was popular. Maybe no one had wanted to drop him in it, unlike weirdo outcast me.

Then it stopped for a while, and I went to my cell, which had a high barred window. I could tell from the light and my stomach it was around lunchtime. A normal day at school seemed like another life. They brought me food. I think it was mac and cheese from a microwave packet. I ate it because I was so hungry, ravenous, but also sick. I

wished I could wash my hands but I was in what I
know now is a 'dry cell', i.e. one with no running
water, so you can't clean away evidence.

After some time Dickinson came in, hitching
up his trousers, almost jovial. 'Well, Karen. He's
talked. So you better do the same.'

I paused. 'Who?' I thought they meant
Gareth at first, and was confused.

'Don't play the fool. Your little boyfriend.
Hughes.'

◆ ◆ ◆

I have felt many times this week like the past is repeating itself.
Almost shouting *Jen!* at Rosalind in the coffee shop. Sleeping in my
old bedroom. Seeing you, hearing you call me *Kare-bear.* Being at
the police station. This impression is only increased when, a very
short amount of time later, Donetti comes out of his office waving
a piece of paper and saying, 'Gareth Hale'. I refused to go home,
so I've been sitting in the relatives' room on an uncomfortable sofa,
googling things over and over as if they might reveal hitherto hidden answers. I drink glass after glass of tepid water from a plastic
cup, until I've crushed it and water spills on to my jeans. Officers
and support staff walk by outside, glance in at me, no doubt wish-
ing I'd leave. But I need to know what's going to happen. Emelia
has already done a post about the case, urging people not to inter-
fere and managing to plug her own book at the same time. Melissa
has been sent home, lucky not to be charged with wasting police
time.

'What?' I don't understand at first.

'The downstairs neighbour, the arsey one – Kremer. He did
have a package for Lara. Never thought to mention it. It was

flowers – rotting by now, amazed he didn't smell it. No name on them but the delivery firm were most helpful in tracing the credit card used. Gareth Hale. He's our "John".'

'*Gareth* sent Lara the flowers? He was John?' I can't believe it. And yet of course I can. He always was a violent bastard. And appearing on TV, talking to the press – that's classic offender behaviour, inserting himself close to a crime. And Lara not telling her best friend about him – maybe she was ashamed of having dated him, once she learned who he really was, maybe that's why she ended it. I should have seen it.

I'm running over all the evidence in my head. 'But he had an alibi! Didn't he?'

'He did. That's why we need to talk to him.'

My skin crawls. 'And he broke into my room? And Emelia's?' Arlene had a burglary a while back also, didn't she say? If Gareth was looking for copies of the symbol, it would make sense to go there. 'But how did he know what the symbol looked like? None of us actually had a copy in the end.' Unless he somehow found the one Jen claimed to have.

'Someone must have. Why did he do all this, though? That's what I'm wondering.' That's what I don't understand either. I can imagine Gareth stalking a woman, attacking her for sure, but why would he try to link it up to you? You're in prison. Not exactly a convenient fall guy.

Then I realise. Gareth has been hinting that someone else killed Jen. It was your conviction for the crime that got him out of prison, so he'd have gone along with it then. But if he thinks justice was never done, then maybe he's set all this up to bring me back.

Maybe he wanted to get me here so he can punish me for what I did to him twenty years ago, and the thought of that sends me to my feet, terrified. 'You're going to arrest him?'

'Right now.'

'Please. Please, I need to be there. It's a big farm, I've been there before. I could tell you where he might be hiding Lara.'

'It's really not safe.'

'Please. I promise I'll stay well back. I just – I can't wait here. I might be able to spot some clues.'

He sighs deeply. 'If you promise to do exactly what I say and stay well away from the scene.'

'I promise.'

For a moment he rests his hands on my shoulders and looks down at me. 'This is our breakthrough, Karen. After a while you learn to smell it. This is our guy, despite his alibi.'

Then why do I feel even more frightened than before?

I'm sent in a different car, with the ponytailed officer who took my prints the first day. Charlene, her name is, apparently, and I deduce from this she must have been born around the launch of *Neighbours* in 1986. The outskirts of Marebridge flash by as we climb to the moor, darkness falling around us. I message Arlene to update her, but she doesn't reply. It all seems to fit. Gareth's been holding Lara on that vast family farm of his, of course he has. But why then does he have an alibi?

'Any word?' I ask Charlene.

She shakes her ponytail. 'Nothing on the radio.'

Soon we've reached the gates of Gareth's family farm, a gloomy out-of-the-way spot. So many acres and outbuildings, so many spaces to hold a woman. Donetti is standing in the driveway, tooled up in a stab vest, and he flags us over. Charlene rolls down the window.

He shakes his head. 'He's gone already. Run.'

'What? How could he know you were coming?'

'Heard the cars and took off over the moors. His mother won't tell us anything. Still protecting her precious boy.' I can hear the bitterness in his tone, and I think of all the women who lie for the men they love. Including me.

I get out anyway, shivering in the chill that rolls off the moors. 'Did you search the whole place? Is Lara here?'

'We're looking – it's a huge property. The mother won't talk. We're going to take her in for questioning, see if we can break her.'

'She might not know anything,' I remind him.

'She'll know.' He holds out an evidence bag, a piece of paper inside it, illuminated in the headlights. I freeze because that is the symbol. That is your symbol, without a shadow of doubt, drawn on one of your sheets of paper, thick and creamy, with your own special calligraphy ink. 'Where did you get this?'

'Gareth's room. In among the car magazines and protein supplements.' He flips it over and I see what's on the front. A drawing. A self-portrait, it must be. Of you. It's vulnerable, naked. Above it is written: *Happy Birthday Mum* and I know what this is. I had one from you too several times. A home-made birthday card. I had no idea you sent your mother those, but that's not what matters, which is, how the hell did Gareth get hold of this?

'Must have been him posting on the dark web trying to buy a copy. The mother must have sold him it.' His voice is dark with rage, at Gareth for taking a woman, at your mother for maybe profiting off your crimes. But not as full of rage as I am. How could she? Abandon you all these years, and then still make money from the fact you became a serial killer?

'You're going to interview her?'

He sighs. 'Look. If you're there, it could disrupt any investigation and conviction we may pursue.'

'She's not actually committed an offence, has she? What would it be? Profiting from crime or something?'

236

'That isn't illegal in this context. Sadly.'

'OK then. She might know something. She might talk to me.' Though no one else has really wanted to so far, and I've never even met your mother. But I need to look her in the eyes and try to understand. For my own sake.

'Fine then. But I'm leaving right now, it's a two-hour drive. Aren't you tired?' I feel like I could never sleep again. Things are happening so rapidly now, I know the end is near. If Gareth did this, if he got a copy of your symbol, if he took Lara, then this is nothing to do with you. You were just taking a chance to throw doubt on your convictions. Maybe, like you said, you just wanted to see me one more time.

Yolanda Merrion, formerly Hughes, has been living only a hundred miles away all this time, and yet she could never be bothered to so much as see her son after the divorce when you were ten. You'd told me she had replacement kids, a new family, a do-over. She lives near Nottingham, where she works as a classroom assistant, though she must be in her sixties now.

The journey is strained. I can tell Donetti is stressed about the lack of results. 'Still no sign of anyone on the farm. Lara's been missing two weeks now. It's not looking good.'

'I'm sorry.'

'Not your fault,' he says, shortly. 'You've been a great help, and I'm aware you're giving up a lot of time for this.'

'Well, I can't exactly publish a book about the killings when they're sort of . . . in doubt.'

He shoots me a look, before moving his eyes back to the road, ever punctilious. 'You really think there's doubt? This Gareth thing, it at least means there's been no other Bagman suspect out there all this time.' He hasn't yet offered a theory for why Gareth has copied your MO, but he must have at least guessed it's something to do with me.

'Honestly, I have no idea. They were always shaky, right? The convictions?'

'The evidence wasn't strong, no.'

'And he never admitted to any of them.'

'They often don't. Killers.'

'But be honest, is there a chance, even a small one, that his case could still be reopened? If it turns out he didn't do one of the murders?'

He hesitates. 'There's a chance.'

'Christ.'

'I know. Let's just hope she can tell us something useful.'

Yolanda. Your mother. The woman who birthed you into this world. I'll admit I am fascinated, agog, to meet her when she comes to greet us at the door. She's prettier than I expected, with long fair hair greying at the roots, her body slim and toned. She's rubbing her hands together in great agitation, doesn't even offer us the traditional tea. The house is nice, a four-bed Victorian with neatly kept front and back gardens. I think of the dank cottage where you lived with your crazy dad, rabbit skins on the back of chairs, coins of blood on the kitchen floor.

Right away she says, 'It wasn't me who sold it. I didn't even remember I had a copy. I've never been able to look at it since.'

'Who was it then?' says Donetti. I hang back, trying not to get in the way.

'Jasper. My son. My – other son.' One of the replacement kids. She says, in a rush, 'He's only twenty-one, you know, he didn't get it. Wanted some cash to go travelling. It's not illegal, is it? What he did?'

'It's not illegal, but it certainly has hampered our investigation.' I like Stern Donetti. 'I'd go as far as to say he's put the missing young woman's life in danger.'

Yolanda bites her lip, staring down at her hands, heavy with rings. She's wearing leggings and a long cardigan, and her accent is cultured. *I remember your mad dad, and am surprised they were ever together long enough to produce you.* 'I can't believe this is happening again,' she says, in a murmur.

'What's that?' Donetti is impatient.

'A child of mine. Hurting people.' *It's hardly in the same league, but I have definitely formed an opinion of this Jasper. There's a family photo on the mantelpiece of Yolanda with a nondescript middle-aged man, a pretty blonde daughter of around twenty, and a floppy-haired youth I assume is Jasper.*

Donetti says, 'Where is your son? We'll have to speak to him, get the details of who he corresponded with.'

She nods. 'He's in his room upstairs and ready to show you it all. It's just some made-up email address and a PO box. I don't know if it will be any use, I'm sorry.'

Donetti stands, looks back at me. I shake my head – it's her I want to talk to.

She clears her throat once he's left us. 'You're Karen.'

'Yeah.'

'He told me about you.'

'He did? When?' *I thought you had very little contact once she left. I knew she sent cash on your birthdays and Christmas, but never actually had you over to visit. The money, always too much, was presumably intended to make up for the abandonment.*

'He came to see me. Just once. He said he was supposed to be with you that night, but something made him come here instead. It was all very odd, to be honest. He said a lot of things. I thought he was – ill. Not well mentally.'

'Did you do anything? Call anyone?'

She shakes her head. Her throat moves nervously. 'He drove himself here so I thought it couldn't be that bad. He seemed very upset, very guilty about something. I didn't understand. And then when I was making tea, he went upstairs and he was – looking in drawers and things. I only realised after.'

I digest this. 'You think he was looking for the card he made you?'

'Maybe. He sent me that I suppose about five or six years earlier. Around the time the other girl died. Your friend.'

'When was this that he visited? Could it have been 2010?' The night Nita was killed, when you arrived so late to meet me. Is it possible you actually had an alibi for that murder, because you were here in Nottingham, miles away from where Nita died? That you were trying to find the one copy of the symbol which could tie you to the previous murders? Maybe you were trying to stop. There had been three years between Alison and Nita. If you erased all traces of the symbol, there was a good chance you'd never be caught.

'Maybe. I can't remember.'

'Well, is there any way to check?' I'm impatient now too. 'You know, this is kind of important? We're trying to save a woman's life?'

'I can – get out my old diary. I remember Steven was away with the children at his mother's, so I happened to be alone. That's why I was – I was scared, to be honest. I just appeased him until he left.'

'Why did you do it?' I ask, suddenly. 'Just abandon him like that. You know his dad wasn't stable.'

'I didn't realise how bad Tom had become. Aaron hadn't told me things were like that.' I recognise the tone. She's defending herself, as I have done in the past. 'And honestly – well. I was scared then too.'

'Of Aaron's dad?'

She twists her mouth. 'A little. He had these blackouts, para-noias, after the Army. But that's not what I meant. I was scared of *him* too.'

It takes me a second to parse the pronouns. 'You were scared of Aaron?'

She nods, staring at the floor.

'He was a child. He was, what, ten when you left?'

Her hands are white, she's clasping them so tight. 'You know what he was like. Weren't *you* ever scared?'

Was I? Or was I too in love, too obsessed, to realise that the dark thrill you gave me wasn't healthy? I was certainly too scared to ask you whether you actually had been at home the day Jen died, like your father said, like I told the police. Then there was the last time, before they came for you, when I lay beside you, twitching with terror and desire. But if I have to admit I was scared of you, then I also have to say I could have, should have, known what you were. I have to say I could have stopped it all.

Donetti appears in the door to save me from answering, fol-lowing by a pale, frightened-looking boy, all good teeth and Jack Wills rugby shirt. The childhood you never got to have. I stand up, brutally. 'He was your son, Yolanda. Whatever he was, you shouldn't have abandoned him. And who knows, maybe if you'd actually done your job, we wouldn't be here.'

It's only when we're in the car that I realise I've done to her what the world has always done to me. Blamed a woman for the crimes of a man.

Chapter Nineteen

From *Becoming Bagman* by Karen Walker

After I was released without charge over the murder of Jen, on the arrest and conviction of Gareth Hale, I would not set foot inside a police station for another nine years. That was when I finally made the call about Aaron. Finally rang the tipline number I'd kept since the second Bagman murder.

It was a week after Emelia's shock survival, and maybe that was what finally made me do it. Someone had seen the Bagman now and lived. Surely it could only be a matter of time before he was caught, and I needed to do what I could to help with that. So I called and they told me to come in. I was met at a side door, ushered right through to a much nicer room than the one Dickinson had kept me in, with soft chairs and tissues on a table, a box of toys in the corner. This detective was young and female, with a high bun and grim manner. I thought we could have been friends in different circumstances. DC

Aisha Desai was her name. She's being played by an actress from a big Netflix show in the upcoming series.

'Karen? You were very brave to call us, thank you for that.'

My lips felt numb. 'I don't know if it's him.'

'Of course. And it might not be, but it's a strong lead. We need people like you to come forward, if we're ever going to catch this guy.'

She asked me a lot of questions, but not in the same relentless, tricking way of Andy Dickinson. More like a conversation. Active listening, nods. 'Oh did he? Really? That's so strange. And this was on the night of the fourth of November, you say . . .' She was sympathetic to my lapses in memory, finding them normal rather than evidence of lying. I outlined my suspicions – the mention of a mysterious symbol, the eyewitness descriptions of the long black coat, Emelia's report of the Bagman's accent and height. Aaron's interest in serial killers and the occult. His Army boots. His experience of killing and skinning rabbits. A smear of blood I'd maybe seen on his shoe once, the night Annie Andersen was killed. But it was when I alluded to Jen that she really seemed interested.

'I'm sorry – you're saying he was a suspect in a murder case as a teenager?'

'Well, not really a suspect. They questioned both of us, because she was my friend.' She was on her phone, thumbing through old news stories. 'Jennifer Rollason? That was your friend?'

'Yes. Jen.' I swallowed hard. This could get me in a lot of trouble.

'But someone was convicted of that – Gareth Hale? It says here you gave evidence against him.'

'I – I did see him that day near the woods. And Aaron, he had an alibi. I just told police what I knew. I was only trying to help.'

She focused on me very intently then, and I could see her trying to categorise me as oblivious woman or evil helpmeet. An Elizabeth Kendall, Ted Bundy's girlfriend, or a Rose West. 'You're saying you might have made a mistake accusing this Gareth?'

I counted my breaths in and out until my voice steadied. 'I just told the police I saw Gareth there that day, and that he had hurt Jen before. There was evidence – his DNA was on her. I just told them and they arrested him.' This was to become my mantra.

'You alibied Hughes?'

'Yes, but I . . . His dad told the police he was home. And I just . . . said that was true.'

She looked at me keenly. 'But you didn't actually see him.'

'No. N-not – with my own eyes.' I'd seen a hump in the bed, I thought, assumed his father was telling the truth about him being there. 'I was trying to help him. I was so scared – they thought I did it, or him, or both. And I really believed it was Gareth.'

'And now you feel, with these other murders, they might be linked?'

'I don't know. There was no symbol at Jen's murder. Nothing like that.'

She looked at me again for a long moment. 'Would you mind waiting here, Karen?' She left, and I sat in the warm, quiet room. Outside, I could see officers passing, glancing at me through the slatted blinds. I wondered what would happen if I got up and walked out. She couldn't stop me. I could change my story, say Aaron had been with me the night of Annie's murder, which was partly true. That I'd forgotten I really did see him on the day of Jen's death, silly me. I began to make a bargain with myself, that I would leave if the clock hands hit 2 p.m. and she wasn't back.

She was back at four minutes to. 'Would you come this way, Karen?' I didn't trust the over-use of my name, as if we were being recorded, which maybe we were. I followed her down the corridor, my stick-on visitor badge gradually unpeeling from my jumper, to another room, with no windows and a projector screen on the wall. She locked the door behind us. 'I've been authorised to show you the crime scene photos. If you're up for it?'

I could hardly say no now. 'What will they look like?'

'Not very nice. Can you bear it?'

I nodded. The screen turned blue, and there was a cranking noise as it warmed up. 'Sorry. Ancient equipment.'

An image had appeared. At first I couldn't tell what I was looking at, then I realised it was a woman's stomach. Ripped to shreds. 'You can see there's a kind of pattern there.'

I made a noise in my throat. 'I . . .'

Was it a pattern? All I could see was a terrible, brutal mess. I wanted to get up then. Aaron, the Aaron I knew, could not have inflicted such damage on another human being.

'Is this the symbol your boyfriend likes to draw?'

He's not my . . . I didn't say it. 'Um – I'm not sure.'

'Here's another version.'

This time it was a white wall in a house, something daubed on to it in a browning, running liquid. Blood. I could see it more clearly now. I blinked. The swoops, the whorls. I had only ever seen one thing like that. In that second my world turned upside down, like on a fairground ride, gravity no longer existing. I could have said no, I wasn't entirely sure – how could I be, looking at it drawn in blood on a wall instead of ink on white paper? I could have said no. I said, 'Yes. I think it's – yes, I think that's it.'

'Thank you, Karen.' She turned it off, mercifully.

'Wh— what will happen now? He'll be arrested?'

'I think we have enough to arrest if not to charge. We'll look for other evidence, of course.'

'So this isn't enough to convict him?' Maybe I could use the same excuse I had for Gareth, that it wasn't my fault. I just said what I knew and others made the choice.

'No. But do you have any photos of Aaron? I want to show them to Emelia Han, the girl who survived. She got a good look at her attacker, although it was dark.'

'Um, he doesn't really like . . .' I thumbed through my phone. It was before we all took so many photos, but I was sure I had one, and yes, there it was. Aaron was asleep in my bed, or he wouldn't have let me take it. I showed it to her.

'None where his eyes are open?'

'He doesn't like people taking his photo. But the school might have some? Or the police from last time?'

She nodded. 'Good thinking. Can you send me this anyway?' I did, and she thanked me again. 'We'll be in touch, Karen.'

'That's all?'

'That's all for now.'

I wasn't sure what to do now I had suggested my best friend, my sort-of boyfriend, might be a serial killer. I existed in a state of maybe but maybe not. Either everything was fine, or my life was ruined. What was I meant to do with that, go home and watch reruns of *Friends*?

I went home and watched reruns of *Friends*.

◆ ◆ ◆

You smile at me with genuine warmth again, across the same folding table in the prison. The darkened-over eyes, the shark-like blankness Emelia saw as you reached for her, there's none of it. 'Morning, Kar.' Your tone is chatty, you're crossing your long legs and folding your hands on the table. There's only one guard with us today, staring straight ahead, as impassive as the wall. 'I see they've finally worked out it's Gareth behind all this.'

'You knew?'

'Had a hunch. It's often the person shouting the loudest that has the most to hide. Plus, he has form, as you know.'

You could have told me this sooner, so that Lara can be rescued from wherever he's holding her – if she's alive – but you have nothing to gain from that.

'Do you know why he did it?' I risk.

You smile. 'I think we both know why, Kare-bear.'

Unfortunately, I have a good idea. 'He's on the run.'

The police have stationed an officer outside our house, which Arlene dubbed 'a load of fuss about nothing', but I'd certainly not slept much the night before, pushing a chair under the handle of my door, even. I remember the way Gareth looked at me in the station – pure loathing. Has he really done all this to get back at me, force me to return to Marebridge?

'He won't make it for long. He's soft. Thank you for the book, by the way.'

I gulp. 'You got it then.'

'I did. Some nice writing. You could always spin a sentence.' I wait. 'So you went with the story that my dad told you I was home that day, and you just believed him.'

I say nothing, just staring at the grain of the table.

'It holds water, I suppose. Just about. Unfortunately the book arrived too late for me to help you with Lara.'

'You don't know where she is?'

'How could I? I guessed Gareth might be involved, that's all.'

So I did all this for nothing. Then you say, 'Of course, I did ask you to do a few other things for me. I suppose that could help jog my memory further. So what did you find out for me? What's your conclusion about the old cases, Detective?'

'Nita Chowdry,' I say. You smile wider. 'I think that's the one that doesn't fit. I need the police to check it out still.'

'Why her?'

'Well, the MO was different, but that was often the case. I always suspected the husband at the time, and I've learned he was a cop, as were all his friends who alibied him. The police are looking into their story.' I have to be careful here. You don't want me to say directly that you carried out any of the killings, but the fact you have an alibi for that night is also highly relevant. 'Also – I saw your mum.' She checked, and the date you visited her matched the night Nita was killed, so you couldn't have been in two places at once. This is yet to be officially confirmed – once it is, the way is free for you to launch another appeal.

Only a second's twitch tells me this gets to you. 'And how is Yolanda? Enjoying her do-over, Waitrose-eating, Boden-wearing life?'

'I think she's pretty distressed. Her kid – the boy – he sold a copy of your symbol online. It was in Gareth's room.' I wonder if you have already worked out that this is how Gareth knew the symbol well enough to draw it on the wall. If you catalogued all copies of it. If Nita is the case you were thinking about that you didn't do. To ask you that would be to violate the most sacred part of our pact – that we don't talk directly about the murders, about Jen or what happened on that wet day almost twenty years ago. 'Is that – does that sound right? One of the families did have a copy too, but they never showed anyone.' I'm asking you to admit too much here. 'I mean – did anyone else have a copy?'

You think about this carefully. 'I can tell you she didn't have one.'

'Who?'

'Jen.'

Her name in your mouth is like an electric shock. I think of her that day, taunting me: *You aren't the only one he does drawings for.* 'She said she did.'

'She told a lot of lies, Karen. You know that.'

But what about the rest? Her supposed plan to meet you in the woods? I've never known, and I still can't ask even now. How could I, when for years the fact that you were home all day was my alibi too? That I never even went to the woods? 'OK. So that's – what I've found out.'

You nod. 'You've done well.'

You don't confirm if Nita is the one or not.

'So will you tell me where Lara is – do you know? I've done everything you asked for now.' And tore myself to pieces in the process.

'Not everything.'

My heart starts to race. 'What?'

You steeple your hands under your chin. 'I read the book, remember. You still haven't told the truth about Jen, have you? If you did that your entire personality – Karen Walker, the girl who didn't know, who sent the monster to prison – well, that would all crumble, wouldn't it? The nice black and white of it all. Me evil, you good.'

I'm shaking. 'I've never seen it that way. I know I made mistakes.'

'Well then, Kare-bear, I've given you everything I can for now.'

'Please, Aaron! Please tell me if you know where Lara is!'

'Why?' you ask, with what seems like genuine curiosity. 'You think if you can save her it will wash the stains away? It doesn't work like that, Karen. Anyway. How would I know where she is? It's nothing to do with me, as you've helped to prove.' You lean back in your chair as far as it will go, addressing the lone guard who's with us today. 'Oi. I'd like to go back to my cell now.'

I'm practically crying. 'Please. Please, you owe me!'

You laugh. 'You owe *me*, Karen. And you've never paid that debt. Not even remotely.'

And that, it seems, is all for now. The guard leads you away from the table with the glazed expression of someone listening to an engrossing podcast, though I can't see any headphones. In the absence of anyone to escort me out, I follow behind.

I'm on my way out when it happens. Lightning fast, so quick I have no warning even in the change of your expression or height-ened breath or widened pupils. Someone steps into our path – a hulking inmate with tattoos on his shaved skull and knuckles. I've seen him before, washing the doors the other day. He says to the guard who's ushering you, quite pleasantly: 'Gonna need you to step away, boss.'

The guard blinks. 'What the fuck's going on, Barry?'

'Breakout, innit. You're a decent lad, Damian, we don't wanna hurt you.'

Damian is reaching for his baton, but has to let go of you to do it, and you quickly move away. 'Fucking hell, how did you even get out of your cell? Who unlocked the doors?'

Barry taps his nose. 'One of your own, mate. So don't be a hero. Give us your keys.' The young guard freezes, looks at me, then at Barry. Then at you, standing there relaxed, and even smiling.

Then I see that Barry has a knife, tossing it casually in his hands. From the kitchen, perhaps. I see wheels spin in Damian's head. Slowly, he pulls his keys out and hands them over. You accept them graciously. 'Thank you, Damian.'

I've been speechless the whole time this has taken, which is less than ten seconds. Is this really happening? Aren't some other guards about to come rushing in? There are no alarms, no noises at

251

all. For once the prison is quiet. 'What's your plan? Even with keys you won't get out the front,' says Damian, petulant.

You point up, to the skylight we're standing under. 'We're going out that way. Thank you for your help, mate.'

Panic floods me as Barry takes hold of my arm, holding the knife close to my face. This is really happening. You are escaping. Was this the plan all along – you knew another appeal was unlikely even with new evidence, so you were using me to try and set this up? You pause for a moment and stroke my face. Gentle. The skin on your hands is rougher than it used to be. 'Don't worry, Karen. We'll see each other again. In her place. But remember what I said, OK? You need to be careful.' Then Barry drops my arm to hand you something from his trousers, a hammer of some kind, and you are somehow running up between the narrow walls, with surprising athleticism, a trainered foot on each side, bracing yourself to reach the top. Damian takes the chance to sprint away, cursing loudly. You have the hammer in your hands and you smash the glass with even, methodical blows. I crouch against the wall as it shatters around me, making a tinkling noise that might be pleasant in other circumstances. I don't even try to stop you – I'm frozen solid in fear. Then you look down once – your face outlined against the grey sky – and you're gone, as an alarm finally begins to wail. The burly prisoner drops the knife, holds up his arms in surrender. I can hardly speak. 'Wh— why?' I don't understand why he isn't escaping too.

Barry shrugs. 'Can't fit, can I? He'll do me a favour on the outside.'

'But – you'll be in here even longer now!'

'Don't care about myself. Just need to look after my family.' He brushes a shard of glass off my shoulder. 'You can go now, love. The alarm'll have been raised.'

I can't believe this is happening. 'He'll never get away. There's fences, guards.'

The big man laughs. 'Love, we've been digging under the fence for the past week, and no one's even noticed. You pay peanuts, you get monkeys. Not to mention that half the screws are on the take. He's got keys, he's got his phone, he's got money, he's got a tent and that waiting. They won't catch him.'

'But . . . but . . .' It can't be, my mind insists. Prisons are secure. Someone will find you – bring you in. But you have cash and a phone and you know how to survive out there, and someone is helping you on the outside, one of the guards, clearly. A woman, probably. I think of Sandra, her kind expression when she looked at you. Was it her? Has she been in my mother's house, all the while, scheming to get you out?

As the alarm keeps wailing and footsteps come running, voices raised, Barry stands to the side, arms raised in polite calm. I slide to the floor, my legs giving way beneath me.

The unthinkable has happened. The Bagman, who should have died in prison, is out and free to kill again.

◆ ◆ ◆

'This is bad, Karen. This is very very bad.'

I'm sitting in a different small room in the prison, no windows or decor of any kind. I've been checked out by the prison doctor despite insisting I'm fine, not even a scratch on me from the glass. I'm fine physically, at least. 'Yes, I know that, thanks. I was there.'

Donetti heard the news almost as it happened, and is here to interview me as soon as the doctor finishes. 'You see how this looks. He escapes while you're literally visiting him!'

I rest my head in my hands. 'It wasn't my fault, for God's sake. What kind of prison has only one guard for a man like him? It's lucky I wasn't killed, or that useless CO.' You could have done it then. There was a knife, there was time. But you spared me, once again. 'He's had help, clearly. But not from me.'

Donetti slams his hands on the table and I jump. He lowers his face to mine, glaring at me. I notice his eyes have a ring of hazel round the pupils. 'Tell me the truth.'

'I have.'

'He said he'd help find Lara if you did things for him.'

'Not this, for God's sake! Just – talking to the families. Letting him read my book. That's all, I swear.' But he's still glaring. I feel terror bloom in my stomach. This is even worse than you being free. Once again, I am a suspect. 'I didn't know. Of course I didn't know. Chris, it was me helped put him here!'

'But you have doubts. You're not sure he even was the Bagman.'

'I am sure.' But am I, am I? This escape surely proves it, doesn't it?

'You still have feelings for him.'

'I . . .' I'm speechless for a moment.

Donetti spins, and for a moment I think he's going to punch the wall. 'I thought you were coming here to help. Now I've got two criminals on the run, and I'm not one bit closer to finding Lara Milton.'

Eventually I'm allowed to go, and I insist on driving myself home. I rush through the front door, fumbling my key. 'Mum. Mum!' I'm no longer calling her Arlene, because something has changed between us. I'm thinking of her as my mother, who might be in danger because of me. The message I sent en route has remained unread, no blue tick. Has something happened to her?

'Hello, love,' a voice says. It's Sandra, who's in the kitchen washing up, looking very much at home.

'Where is she?'

Sandra is here. Sandra, who works at the prison. Sandra, who seems so fond of you and conveniently was not working when you escaped. 'Your mum? She's in the bath, love. I'm just clearing up here.'

I take the stairs two at a time. 'Mum. Mum!' All the while thinking – *Sandra is here.*

I hear splashing, and my mother opens the door, wrapping her dressing gown round her. 'Bloody hell, what's all that racket?'

'We need to get out of here. Pack up your stuff.'

Sandra has appeared now too, having followed me up. 'What's happened?' she says.

'Aaron has escaped from prison.'

I watch Sandra for a reaction. She blinks.

'You're joking, love?'

'I'm not. He got out while I was there and he must have had help from a guard. Any idea who that might be?'

She thinks about it, or pretends to. 'That Kerry, maybe, she was always talking to him. Christ, where's my phone? They'll be calling me in.'

'You seem very close with him too, Sandra.' I turn so I'm facing her, and she moves back slightly to the head of the stairs. 'Seems weird to me. You just happen to meet my mum, and you just happen to suddenly become BFFs, and you're working with him every day, talking to him, seeing him? Talking to him about me?'

'What's she on about?' Sandra says to Mum.

Mum sighs. 'Karen, you're being a bit of a bitch, to be honest. What's up with you?'

'Are you deaf? He's out of prison. He might be coming here, so we need to get somewhere safe.'

'Right, well, I heard that part, but there'll be coppers all over the place, won't there, so he's hardly going to come through the door waving a knife. What's it got to do with Sandra? You're saying she helped him get out or something?'

'Well, someone did. Seems like a coincidence you and her are suddenly all buddy-buddy.'

My mother gives me an exasperated look. 'Right, because someone wouldn't actually want to spend time with me unless they had another reason?'

'I don't know! Just get dressed, will you?'

'You need to tell her now, Arlene,' says Sandra.

'Tell me what?'

Mum sighs. 'Alright, don't get your knickers in a twist, Karen. Sandra and me are – well, there's a reason she's here a lot. She's my – we're together, like.'

I stare at her. Over her shoulder I can see into the bathroom, the new expensive toiletries I was surprised to find she owned. The two toothbrushes in the mug, which somehow I have not registered until now. 'Oh.'

Sandra rolls her eyes. 'I did say just tell her straight off, she's hardly gonna have an issue with it, she lives in that New York, doesn't she!'

'Of course I don't have an issue.' I'm just slightly speechless, having only ever known Mum to date men. Bad men, losers, or boring like Ash Rollason. Whereas Sandra is sparky, stylish, a fire-cracker. And Mum has seemed happier than I've ever known her. 'I – it's great. I'm happy for you. I just – it still seems like a coincidence, you being close to him and Mum too.'

Sandra folds her arms. 'Honestly? That is why I got to know your mum in the first place. I wanted to warn her he's still obsessed with you, talks about you all the time. I didn't know you were off in America, so when I heard that I didn't worry too much, cos what could he do, locked up inside? But by then we were friends, me and her. Then – more.'

256

Mum scowls. 'She don't need the gory details, San. But there you go, you know now. She's on our side, Karen.'

My head is reeling. 'OK. Fine. But he's still free, so we need to go somewhere else. Mum, can you get dressed, please? Pack some stuff?' Someone is meant to be coming to take us to a safe house. Better not be bloody Donetti.

'Bloody hell, give me five minutes to get my head round it.'

'I better go to work,' Sandra says, looking at her watch. 'It'll be bedlam. If we can find out who helped him escape, maybe they'll know where he is.'

I run into my room and throw my things quickly back into my case. I see that Emelia has sent me a long line of screaming-faced emojis and I don't even judge her. It seems the right response. *You're safe?* I type back.

At Matt's place. Police outside.

If you come for anyone, it will be Emelia or me. Or both. The ones with evidence against you. Even though you didn't touch me at the prison, it doesn't mean you won't come back when I'm alone. When I go out with my case, Mum is still standing in her dressing gown, dabbing at her hair with a towel. 'Mum!'

'Alright, alright. What do I need? How long we going for?'

'I've no idea! A few days at least.' How long can you stay hidden for? You used to camp in the woods, you know how to survive, thanks to your dad. It could be a long time before you're caught. I think of my years-ago plan to drive you to France or Ireland hidden in a car. Someone else might be doing that for you, maybe this Kerry. You've spent ten years trying to get out of prison, and now you have managed it you won't let yourself be found without a fight. It's possible you will never be caught again.

Chapter Twenty

From *Becoming Bagman* by Karen Walker

After I gave Aaron's photo to the detective, I heard nothing for two days. With each hour that passed, my terror eased. They would have arrested him by now if they had the evidence, so it must not be him. I would bury it deep and never think of how I had once suspected him of murdering seven women. I even spoke to him on the phone on the second night, our usual long and rambling chat that left my ear burning and my heart racing. The next morning the detective called.

'We'd like you to arrange a meeting with him, Karen.'

A lump was blocking my throat. 'But – why?'

'We're ready to make an arrest. It would be easier for all concerned if we knew where he'd be, and could control the environment. It's unusual, but if he runs we think we'd struggle to find him.' She was right. You knew how to disappear, how to live off-grid.

I was silent for a moment. With some sympathy, she said, 'I have to tell you, Karen, that if you alert him in any way, I'm authorised to arrest you for obstruction of justice. It could go further too. Assisting an offender. Joint-enterprise murder, even.'

'What? No! I'm helping you.'

'I know you are. And we need you to be brave for another last bit. You could save lives, Karen, if you do this.'

'You really think – you think it's him, then?' Even then, I had hope. Yes, they might arrest him, but he'd have alibis. He'd clear his name.

'We think this is the best lead we've had so far, yes.'

I had no choice. I texted Aaron and asked if he was free to meet at the weekend. It was Thursday morning then. Friday evening, I suggested. I thought about warning him at least every other minute during that time. Of running, the two of us, somewhere with no extradition treaty. Was his passport flagged? We could go via Ireland, maybe, or I could smuggle him in a car to France. The gate was slowly coming down, but there was still time to escape. We all know how the story went instead. I let the minutes go by, and suddenly it was upon me and I was waiting for him to appear in my flat. The police said it was the best idea – there was only one way in and out, so he wouldn't be able to run. They would be nearby, waiting to grab him.

All the same I was jumpy as hell. What if he picked up on my nerves and ran? Or he took me hostage, pressed a knife to my throat so the police had to let him walk me out? Then what would he do to me? I think even more than being hurt I was afraid of the look in his eyes when he realised I had betrayed him. The minutes ticked down. He was running late, and I was so jumpy I couldn't sit down, pacing around the flat. I was convinced he had guessed, that he'd fled, that I'd spend the rest of my life afraid of him turning up at my door. Or of never seeing him again.

Then, finally, forty minutes after I'd expected him, he was there. He came in the back way, through my little garden, unannounced. Long black coat and jeans, usual black grip bag. He had a cold and his nose was red. 'Bloody traffic,' he said.

I let him come in, take off his coat, settle. Then I texted DC Desai to explain he'd come the back way, the phone making a whooshing sound. It was way too loud. He must have known because he looked puzzled, but it only lasted a second or two before there was a thunder of footsteps, and eight police officers were suddenly at my door. He blinked. Looked at me. 'Oh, I see.' That was all he said.

The lead detective said, 'Aaron Hughes?' He nodded. 'I need you to come with us, Aaron. You're under arrest for murder.' He gave the usual caution that you hear on TV, which sounded so strange in real life, and then he said, 'Do you know what this is about?'

Aaron shrugged. 'I imagine everyone does.' And they took him away, and I was left alone. Shaking with nerves, I sank down to the ground.

It was basically over then, though I didn't know it. I kept expecting him to come back, released without charge, not enough evidence. But they had taken the time to build their case, and he was never to leave custody again. I didn't see him until the trial, six months later, across the floor of the Old Bailey. He looked different by then. He had put on weight from bad prison food, puffy in the cheeks, his buzzcut growing out patchy, as if he had some kind of skin disease. I would hardly have known him. As a key witness, I wasn't allowed in the courtroom until I had given evidence, so for the first few weeks of the trial I sat in an airless, wood-panelled room, slumped in an uncomfortable seat eyeing everyone else they brought in. Some I recognised, such as the parents of Alison Johnson. And Emelia, of course, who as the star witness was taken in right away. She held herself very erect, constantly fixing her hair. She looked at me and I looked away. Everyone knew who I was. The girlfriend, whether that was strictly speaking true or not. I felt that question whisper around me as I walked. *Did she know? How could she not?* And that has never ended, despite my hope of leaving it all behind that day.

◆　◆　◆

The safe house is a dingy two-bed flat on the outskirts of Doncaster, with a strong smell of boiled vegetables and drains. I raise my eyebrows at Charlene as she shows us in. 'Best we can do on short notice, sorry. And anyway the—'

'The cuts, yes, Jesus, I know. There better not be bedbugs.' I'm trying not to be annoyed that Donetti hasn't come himself; he has better things to do, and anyway I'm not really speaking to him.

Arlene has already installed herself in the bigger room and is putting on the (cheap, cracked) kettle. She was sufficiently composed on leaving to grab teabags and milk. 'Cuppa, love?'

Charlene shakes her ponytail. 'No time, sorry, Ms Walker. Now, there's going to be two officers outside the door at all times, in rotation. We've got an all-ports warning out for him, blocks at the stations and airports, so I don't think he can get out of the country.' That isn't much comfort. I'd prefer it if you were thousands of miles away. I wonder how the families must feel, seeing it on the news, that the unthinkable has happened and you are free.

Arlene folds her arms. 'You know this is all nonsense. There's no way he'll come after our Karen. Only person he ever cared about in this world, right there.'

'Maybe before I sent him to prison, Mum.'

She shrugs. 'I don't think he even blamed you for that. He wants fairness, right? The truth? So if he didn't do one of these killings he just wants that on the record.' And that extends further. You want me to tell the truth too, but I can't. Not after all this time.

Charlene checks her phone and swears softly. 'They've searched his cell – properly this time. Found a stash of love letters from one of the prison guards.'

'Who?'

'A woman named Kerry Farrell. Apparently she'd developed something of a – rapport with Hughes.'

Mum exclaims, 'That Kerry! Her with the bad skin. I knew she were trouble. Did you go to her house?'

'Oh, Kerry's already been caught, trying to get on a plane at Robin Hood Airport, using her own passport. No idea where Hughes is, didn't show up to the rendezvous she'd planned with him, unsurprisingly.'

'Bloody amateur hour over there. They need to put Sandra in charge. Bunch of clowns, the rest of them.' Mum pours hot water over teabags.

So where else could you be? I would know, surely, better than anyone. 'OK, so—'

'Sorry,' Charlene cuts me off. 'I really have to go. We'll check in later.' And she shuts the door, offering a glimpse of the uniformed officer out there, who looks no more than twenty, and it's just me and Arlene alone.

Apparently perfectly at home, she brings her tea over to the manky sofa and starts fiddling with the TV remote. The news comes on, and of course you are the top story, followed by the influx of murder tourists to Marebridge, taking pictures of the police as they comb through fields and dredge the river for Lara Milton. They even interview the owner of the terrible inn I stayed at, who's jubilant to be booked solid for once. Why are all these people heading *towards* danger? Our town currently has two criminals on the run and yet still they come.

'How can you be so calm?' I exclaim.

'Better than panicking. We're as safe as we can be here.'

'But what if he attacks someone else?'

'Well, that would be awful, but I can hardly stop him by fretting, can I?'

'You don't understand. This is all my fault.'

She sighs. 'It's not your fault, Karen.'

'Yes it is! I could have sent him away sooner, and I didn't! And all those women died and Ash broke up with you and look how we all ended up.'

To my surprise, Arlene laughs at this. She actually laughs. 'Karen, love, do you really think I wanted to marry Ash Rollason? He's a nice man, but come on, he's as dull as ditchwater. And not the sharpest tool, for all he has a big fancy job.'

I gape at her, the world rearranging itself in my head. 'You mean – you were *pleased* it ended?'

She tuts. 'I ended it!'

'What?' I'd always assumed Ash had dumped her, after I was questioned for killing his daughter. 'OK, explain yourself, please.'

She gives a long sigh, takes a drink of tea. 'I were never that keen on him, you must know that. I always knew I – well, I liked the ladies too. But you couldn't be like that, not back then. People didn't understand. And Ash, he were nice, he had that big house, took me fancy places. I didn't think it were going anywhere, but then he pops the question, out of the bloody blue! I had to at least think about it, for your sake.'

'Had you actually said yes? You were really engaged?'

'Hadn't said owt yet. I just wanted to give you a better life. But then, when it happened, you know . . .' She trails off.

'What?'

Then she says it. 'Come on, Karen. I knew you knew something about it. What happened to Jen. Something you never told the police.'

A tick of fear runs through me. 'Mum, I . . .'

She holds up her hand. 'Look, what's done is done. I knew you were afraid, that you were mixed up in it somehow. That you loved Aaron, and probably you didn't believe he could do a thing like that. No one ever does believe it. And I knew I had to keep you out of prison. Being married to Ash, living in that mausoleum – well, it'd all have come out at some point. Looking at an empty chair every Christmas, never living up to the memory of Jen and Saint Patricia . . . No, thanks.'

I'm stunned. My mother ended her engagement because she thought I had something to do with Jen's death. 'That night – you never came home. When Ash came round in the morning you weren't there.'

She sighs. 'There was this girl at my work. We – had a thing. I was trying to decide, you know, what to do about Ash. Then it didn't matter anyway.'

'I'm sorry.'

She shrugs. 'You were a kid. You were scared. You couldn't have known he did it, or that he'd do it again.' Then she says what I have waited to hear for so many years. 'Karen, you're not to blame for what he did. No one is except him.'

I give a shuddering sigh, leaning back against the warped plastic worktop. I want so badly to tell her the truth, the whole truth, but I still can't. As you said, I can't bear to lose that image of myself as Good Karen. A victim of sorts as well. Even though it isn't true. 'Mum, I'm so sorry. For all of it. Bringing him into your life, and leaving like I did. Not trusting you.'

She looks me in the eye. 'So maybe you tell me the truth now. What was it you knew? You knew he did it and you lied, said it was Gareth? You did see him that day too, maybe, down by the woods? Or you were pretty sure he'd done it, but you gave him an alibi all the same? You lied for him? That's what I always thought.'

I think of that day in the police station. After he told me Jen was dead, Dickinson had ushered me to a phone and I rang our landline. Arlene took a long time to answer, but at least she was finally home. 'Hello?'

'Mum, it's me.' I only said 'Mum' because the officer was listening.

'What did you forget?' She'd have assumed I went to school already.

'I'm at the police station.'

'What did you do?' She sounded weary.

'Mum, they've found Jen. Um – they're saying she's dead.' The act of saying it made me start to hyperventilate, in a strangely self-conscious way. Was I actually losing it, or doing it for Dickinson's benefit, to seem upset? No, of course I was upset. For all her faults, Jen was maybe the person who knew me best. My lifelong friend. Even when I hated her I loved her.

'What?' Arlene's voice cracked. I felt, unspoken between us, the same question repeated. *What did you do?*

'Can you come? They said you should come.'

'How am I meant to get there?'

'I don't know, Mum! Just come. Get a taxi.'

For once she made no complaint. At the station, they gave us a moment together. She stood in front of me, rain on her jacket and hair. I had never seen her so pale.

She hissed at me. 'Ash is coming. Tell me now, what do you know?'

I was stung by that. 'I don't know anything. I saw her at school today, that's all.'

'What about that boyfriend of yours? Hughes? Where's he?'

I turned away. 'He's not my boyfriend. And I don't know where he is.' And then Sinead Cowden came in weeping and wailing and that was all I ever told Arlene about it. Even after your trial I wouldn't talk to her, choosing exile instead.

'Well?' she says, now, asking me the same question as back then.

I stare hard at a patch on the wallpaper, mould blooming through. This place is falling apart. 'Mum . . . I . . .'

And maybe I would have said something, confessed it all, but I don't have time, because just then the teenage cop bursts in, radio crackling. 'Ms Walker? Eh, Karen, that is? I need to take you back to the station, please, there's been a development.'

'What? Have you found him?'

'No. But Rosalind Rollason has gone missing.'

For years I've had nightmares where the last two decades have all spooled away, and you are free in the world, and I'm back in that police station and Jen is dead.

I'm having one now, but it's real. I'm at a police station and Ash is there, and he's once again chalk-white and weeping. 'It can't be happening again,' he keeps saying. 'It can't be.'

Arlene insisted on coming with me in the police car. Now she walks right up to him in the family room and puts her arms around him. Miss Coxon, who's collapsed in a chair, doesn't even look up. 'It's gonna be OK, Ash,' says Arlene, her voice as tender as I've heard it.

'It wasn't OK last time! My little girl. Both my girls.'

'We don't know that anything's happened to Rosalind, come on. Maybe she's just run off.'

'She hasn't run off!' barks Miss Coxon. 'She should have been home at four and there's no sign of her. Her schoolbag was found on the road and her phone's out of service!'

'It's true,' says Donetti, grimly, coming into the room. He looks like he hasn't slept in days. I avoid his gaze.

'He's got her.' Ash falls into a chair, hands over his face. 'He took my Jen and now he's taken my Rosie too. Oh, why didn't I drive her to school and pick her up every day? I never learn. It's all my fault.'

Miss Coxon gives me a look of pure poison. 'This is *your* fault. He's been safely in prison for ten years and now you're back and he escapes. Did you help him? Tell us where he is!'

There's a certain logic to it. Rosalind is the image of Jen. Maybe you're recreating what happened back then, to draw me out, force me to tell the truth. Does this mean you've known exactly where Lara is all this time? That you and Gareth are in this together? I have no idea what's going on.

'She's not even answering me.' Miss Coxon is on her feet and lunging at me then, but Arlene, with her years of scrapping behind her, steps in and grabs her arm before Donetti can get there.

'Come on now, Lucy, no need for that. Karen doesn't know a thing. Some big lad pulled a knife on her and the guard, that's how he got away. We've had to go to a bloody safe house, she's that afraid.'

'Well, she must know where he'd go!'

'I . . .' I shake my head. 'I've been wracking my brains. The moors, his dad's old house . . . I don't know.' Her place, you said. I don't know what that means. Which her – Jen? What was her place – something only you and she knew about? Are you trying to taunt me?

'We've searched all those locations,' says Donetti. 'Karen, can I speak to you?'

Arlene eyes the grieving couple. 'I'll stay with these two. Get them some tea or owt.'

As if tea will do any good, when Ash is facing the loss of his second daughter. His replacement Jen.

Donetti's face is strained as he shuts the door to his office. I fold my arms, defensive. 'I've told you I know nothing about this. I don't know where he'd go.'

'I know. It's not that. Karen – we've searched Rosalind's room, and we found a number of books about the Bagman cases. We're afraid that she – might have tried to contact him. She wanted to know, understandably, what happened to her sister. Her search history is full of questions about murder, strangulation, the symbol. Karen – it was *her* who bought the drawing from Jasper, not Gareth. We found the account on her laptop.'

I stare at him. 'She was at that crime convention. I saw her there.'

'Right. She's obsessed with this stuff.'

'But *why*?' And how is this connected to Lara Milton?

'As far as we can tell, she was trying to – solve her sister's murder.'

'But it was solved.' I'm starting to shake.

'Karen, I'm not sure she believes that.'

Of course. There's plenty on the internet if you know where to look, that would 'prove' you didn't kill Jen, or indeed any of them.

'She thinks it was me,' I say.

He nods. 'I believe so.'

'And what does this have to do with Gareth?'

'We think they were in it together. She did the planning, he was the muscle.'

That makes sense. Gareth's never had the brains to organise something like this. And he too likely thinks I killed Jen, then framed him for it. He would be more than happy to see me brought low.

'So what's happened? Has Rosalind really been taken?'

'We're afraid she might have agreed to meet him. Aaron Hughes.' He looks at me, his eyes haunted. 'Is there anywhere you can think of that he might have brought her? Anywhere at all?'

My mind feels stalled. You warned me there was more to this than I knew. Had you figured out Rosalind and Gareth were conspiring against me – and is this you now trying to protect me, once again? By killing – again? I think about what you said to me at the prison. When you touched my face, the first time in so many years

I had felt the brush of your skin. Her place. Was 'her' Jen – or Rosalind? An idea starts to take shape. 'There is somewhere. Maybe. But I have to go alone.'

The pact, you said. I denied that there was one, but that wasn't true. Of course there was. We didn't have to say it out loud for it to be real. 'What? No, Karen! I can't let you do this.'

'How are you going to stop me? Arrest me?'

He says nothing for a moment, then I look down and see his hand has grabbed mine. He pulls it away. 'Please, Karen. Please don't do this. Tell me where and we can send a team.'

'No. It has to be me.' For another second I take in his face, the heft of his body, his anguished look, and I wrench myself away and I run from the station.

The day Jen died it was raining in the woods, the ground boggy and treacherous underfoot. Today it is equally cold, but dry, my breath showing as I stumble along. My head is full of missing girls, dead girls. Lara, Rosalind. Jen. All the others. This time I'm not in the woods, where Jen was found. The police have searched there many times. And you said *her* place, not our place. So I am here, stumbling my way down the field behind Ash's house, to the stable where Jen kept her pony, Applesauce. Long dead now, and apparently Rosalind isn't a horse girl, because the place is cold and deserted, smelling of the ghosts of hay and manure. All the same it's just like that day. The rain, the way it's turning dark already. The slide of the ground under my feet.

For a moment, just like back then, I don't think anyone is here. Then I see her, as before, in her school uniform and coat. Jen.

But of course it isn't Jen.

'You came then,' says Rosalind. She has her hands in her pockets, and I can tell instantly what has happened. Rosalind isn't in any danger, despite her frantic parents at the police station, despite Donetti's worries about you. No, it's me that's in danger. Behind her in the corner of the stable, I can see a lump wrapped in blankets. A woman with dark hair poking out. I can't tell if she's alive or not.

'You set this all up? Lara and – everything?'

She nods, briefly.

'Why – to get me over here?'

'Correct.'

'It has nothing to do with him – with Aaron?'

She shrugs. 'This isn't about him. This is about you. And how you killed my sister.'

I'm about to protest that I didn't kill Jen, of course I didn't, when there's movement behind her, and someone else comes out of the old building, stooping because he is tall, tall and broad. Gareth. He looks and smells like someone who's been sleeping rough for several days. So it's true. They are in it together. I clear my throat. 'I don't know why you'd think that. Did Gareth tell you? Did he also tell you how he half-strangled Jen himself, hurt her multiple times?'

Gareth puts an arm around Rosalind. 'Don't listen to her. She's a liar. She sent me to prison for something she did.' He nuzzles at her neck.

I can't help but exclaim, 'She's seventeen years old, Gareth! You're nearly forty, it's disgusting.' He always did like younger girls.

Rosalind arches her neck towards his mouth. 'I'm old enough to know what I want. It was me who tracked him down. And I want you to pay for what you did. I read her diary, you know. Long before you stole it. I know she hated you, that she wanted rid of you and your slapper mum. I know you threatened her. She stole your nerdy boyfriend and you killed her for it.' It was Rosalind who tore out the diary page, but not because it had your symbol on it. Because it incriminated me.

'I didn't kill her! She was my friend, my best friend!'

Even as I say it I know it's too late. Maybe it's being here, in the darkening light, or maybe it's the resemblance between her sister and Jen, but I feel like she's here with me. *It's time to tell the truth, Karen.* And yes, it's true she was my best friend, but that doesn't mean I didn't hurt her, or that I didn't lie. 'Is Lara OK?' I try, desperately. 'If I'm going to tell you what happened I want to know she's safe. You were dating her?' I nod to Gareth.

'Stupid cow. She had it coming. Broke up with me when she found out I'd been inside, for something I didn't even do.'

'So she's just a random girl. You wanted revenge on her for dumping you, so you staged this abduction to get me back to Marebridge. The two of you.'

Rosalind rolls her eyes. 'Get there faster, will you? Babe, do you have it?'

'Course.' Gareth pulls something from his puffa jacket and I see it's a knife. A large knife, reflecting back the dying winter light.

I try to keep my voice steady. 'So how did you do it without her neighbours hearing?'

Rosalind says, 'I went to her door and told her I'd met Gareth in a pub, that we were dating, and he was starting to scare me, so I needed her help. She came outside with me no problem at all. That's the thing, you know. If you get people to go with you willingly, there's no need for a fuss. Ask your friend Aaron about that.'

'And the blood?'

She shrugs. 'Syringe, Tupperware. Not very easy but it did the job.'

'So you hurt Lara, to get her blood for the symbol? Is she alive?'

'She's alive. I've been feeding her, don't worry,' sneers Rosalind, and I wonder how Ash and Miss Coxon could have failed to notice their daughter keeping a woman captive on their property. They must never come down here. And they'd never think their precious girl could do something like this. No one ever thinks it, until confronted by the evidence. Even then, many still can't believe.

'She's alive,' echoes Gareth, polishing the knife on his jumper. 'For now. Until you're dealt with, and you've confessed what you did to Jen, killed yourself from remorse, so sad.'

'The police know you're in this together. They're looking everywhere for Rosalind – they'll figure it out soon.'

Rosalind flicks her hair, in a gesture that's all Jen. 'Well, I'll tell them it was you who took me. Obsessed with Jen, trying to kill me too cos I remind you of her, to cover up what you did back then. It'll be fine. The police are well stupid.'

'They're not, you know. They found the flowers Gareth sent Lara. Proof he was stalking her.'

Gareth turns pale. 'What the fuck?'

'She didn't always collect her post on time. Didn't want anything from you, either. Downstairs neighbour still had one of the bouquets you sent her.'

'What?' snaps Rosalind. 'You said you weren't into her any more.'

'It was . . . a while back, babe,' he whines. Pathetic.

I'm counting on Donetti to join up the final dots and find us here. How stupid of me to just run off, trying to save the day. Still trying to cover up what I did. 'They'll be here, you know. Soon.'

'Shut up, will you!' Rosalind is losing patience. 'I've lived my whole bloody life with this, never as good as Princess Jen, so I need you to tell the truth for once. You killed her. Not Aaron Hughes. It wasn't even his style. I don't care about the others. But you're a killer and you should be punished for it.'

'And you stole my life,' says Gareth, weighing the knife in his hands. 'Sent me to prison for what you did. You need to suffer for that too.'

So this is their plan. Get me to confess, stage it to look like I killed myself down here. Maybe kill Lara too so she can't say who took her. Rosalind, tearful and angelic, tells the police I kidnapped her. Never mind that I was at the safe house when she went missing, or that Gareth's prints will be all over the knife he's holding in his bare hands. He never was the brightest spark. But none of that will matter if I'm dead.

Tell the truth, Karen. It's time.

I keep talking, delaying as long as I can. 'And Aaron – this is really nothing to do with him? You bought the symbol his mum had, copied it?'

Gareth looks smug. 'Got you here, didn't it?' So where are you now? It's not you I have to fear after all. You knew it, too. You tried to warn me. You must have guessed Lara was here. Maybe Jen brought you here, for secret meetings. In that moment, I decide. 'OK. I'll admit it. I did lie. And I'll tell you the truth, all of it, if you let Lara go. Come on, Rosalind, she's nothing to you. You don't want to kill an innocent woman. She's served her purpose.'

Rosalind looks at me and then Gareth. She's hesitating. Doesn't really want to hurt Lara. He whispers, 'She'll know it was us who took her.'

'She won't remember, she's so traumatised she doesn't know what day of the week it is.'

'She saw you – you went to her flat!'

'Well, she won't know who I am. And if she does I can always say it was true, that I did want her help. She won't remember who knocked her out.'

'Ros, don't be stupid! It's too late now. She saw too much.'

I lick my lips. 'Maybe I deserve this, but she doesn't. She's got nothing to do with this, she's innocent.'

Gareth tuts impatiently but it's clear the teenager is running this show.

274

'If we say yes, you'll confess?' says Rosalind.

'I'll confess. I'll tell the whole truth about that day. What I did to Jen.'

'I knew it! Give me your phone. Unlock it.' I fumble it over to Rosalind and she presses some buttons. Smarter than Gareth, she's wearing gloves. 'Talk into this.' She hands it back, camera flipped.

I swallow hard. Am I really going to do this, after all these years, confess my part in your crimes? Admit the thing I was so ashamed of that I alibied you to protect myself, leading to the deaths of seven more women? It's what you wanted, after all. The truth. And so I get ready to say what I almost said earlier to my mother. She asked if I had lied for you back then. But the truth is even worse.

The truth is that you lied for me.

I speak into the phone. Clear my throat. 'I suppose the easiest place to start is with all the lies I told.'

The Truth

The first lie – that Jen and I were best friends.

We were best friends, sometimes. We also, at times, hated each other. We jockeyed it out. She complained to Sinead that I was a know-it-all. I complained to you that she was an airhead, a narcissist with her boobs sticking out and ponytail swinging. When I told her to break up with Gareth, she listened, but she also resented me. Our friendship was full of depths and darkness. All the same, I imagine we'd have remained best frenemies, if Arlene had not got together with Ash.

Lie two – that Jen and I wanted to be stepsisters.

Neither of us could think of anything worse. Until the party, at least, we were united in our revulsion of it, refusing to go on 'family' days out or even listen to news of their relationship. I thought it would blow over, that they were just dating casually and would soon come to their senses. Jen was less prepared to risk it. It was the night of the party when it struck me, seeing the house all lit up, the marble entryway, the sweeping staircase, the outdoor pool. I realised I could live there too, in that beautiful mansion. I could have endless pocket money. I could have a car. I could get through university without a part-time job. I would only have to live with the two of them for less than a year and I'd be off. Maybe it was worth the aggravation.

Jen, unsurprisingly, did not feel the same.

Lie three – that the timing of Jen's death, two days after her Christmas party, was just a coincidence.

I almost wasn't even invited, that's the funny thing. Her so-called best friend. Despite our lifelong friendship I had never been cool enough to hang with her gang and she often did things without me. In the end Ash insisted, because he was taking Arlene to the Lake District for the night and worried about my safety alone. Which was a joke, given Arlene had been leaving me by myself since I was eight.

Jen approached me at lunch a few days before the party, with the reluctant invitation she'd been forced to extend. I said I'd only come if I could bring you, not that you would want to attend such a basic get-together with the normies, as you called Jen and the popular kids.

That was when she laughed and said, 'He's already coming, dummy.'

I didn't believe her. You and Jen didn't even speak, you barely knew each other. She'd always called you 'my loser Goth boyfriend'. When did you invite you? Why had you and Jen been talking without me? It was the first roll of a pebble that became a landslide.

Lie four – that nothing happened at the party.

There's so much I couldn't say about the party in my book. How Jen didn't wear a bra, so her nipples stuck up like bullets. How she flirted with every boy there and shunned Gareth, making him angrier and angrier until he screamed at Jen and stormed out.

When we arrived, the party was thronged already. Loud dance music blared out, and I could hear shrieking laughter and splashes. Despite it being December and the pool covered up already, people had opened it and were jumping in, drunk and half naked. It's a wonder no one died that night, actually.

When you and I went into the house, it didn't exactly fall silent on a record scratch, but people did look at us funny. I think some of them didn't recognise me at first, because of the job you'd done with my make-up and hair, which was backcombed and huge, talcum-powdered white in streaks. A witch, to match the terrible crime I would soon be suspected of. And you were the Grim Reaper, with a real scythe you'd taken from your dad's shed.

Jen was in the kitchen, in her slutty get-up, drinking Malibu from the bottle. 'Oh. You look different.'

'Aaron did it.'

'He's got some skills.' Her eyes moved over him, and I had the feeling something was going on under the surface, that I could not pretend to understand. Then Gareth was there in his offensive Twin Towers costume, already drunk and stoned, pawing at Jen.

'My little angel. Or maybe a devil?'

She rolled her eyes. 'Yeah yeah, you're hardly the first to say that.'

'Want to go for a swim?'

'It's like three degrees and full of leaves. No, thanks. Aaron. You want a drink?'

'If it's not coconut flavoured,' you said.

'Non-coconut drinks are available.'

'Your dad, he drinks whisky?'

'Yeah. Gross.'

You walked into the living room and straight to the cabinet, with a confidence that made me wonder if you'd been there before. But when? How? You selected a dusty bottle, took off the cap and breathed it in. 'That's the good stuff. Will he mind?'

'He won't notice. Not a big drinker, it's all for show.'

I can't remember every detail of the party, of course. It was nearly twenty years ago. I remember you had firecrackers in your pockets, and you set them off in the downstairs loo then laughed yourself sick as people ran, screaming. I remember you spiked the punch so people threw up. That you went out to the pool and pressed the button to roll back the hood, trapping the swimmers in there for a minute. Spreading misrule and fear. Jen seemed to find it hilarious, but Gareth was soon enraged. I left not long after, sickened by the sight of you and her laughing together.

'I want to go,' I said.

'It's too early.'

'Please, Aaron. Please.'

You were looking over my shoulder at Jen dancing in the kitchen. 'I'm not going to leave.'

'So what, I'll just walk home alone? Get myself killed?' You were always concerned about my safety before this.

You looked at me then. 'It's your choice, Karen.' That's why I made my last desperate stand. I grabbed your waist, reached up on my tiptoes and tried to kiss you for the first time ever. I still remember the unyielding pressure of your mouth, the way you took my arms and detached them. 'Kare-bear. Come on now.'

Desperate, I looked towards Jen again, her gleeful smirk. That's when I said, 'If you go near him, I will kill you.' Which she must have recorded in her diary for Rosalind to read. If the police had been more competent and found it back then, perhaps I would have gone to prison instead of Gareth.

I don't recall every detail of the timeline. I know that I went home alone, that Gareth also went off in a rage. I remember how I felt, like the edges of things had blurred, like everyday life was turned upside down. A medieval carnival, a day of the dead, like such festivals are supposed to be. Gareth drunk but grasping that something had changed, me struggling to keep up. Jen smug, the ballerina in the music box. And you, somehow pulling all the strings.

Jen was not wearing her angel wings when she died. That would have been a lovely image, and the picture of her drunk, her arm around you, has certainly done the rounds. Your deathly face, her glowing one, as if you're sucking the life right out of her. The truth, which is not the same as the best story, is that she died two days later, on a rainy afternoon, in her school uniform with her coat on, padded with fake fur around the hood. But all the same you were Death, stalking that party.

Lie five – that I didn't really talk to Jen the day she died.

It was true she didn't tell me anything concrete when we talked in the school lobby. But Jen was far too smart, in her own way, to say anything outright.

'Where've you been?' I asked, peevishly. 'You didn't answer my messages.' I had not heard from either of them all day Sunday, and you hadn't come to school on the Monday.

'Ask your little boyfriend.'

'What? What do you mean?'

She smirked. 'Not seen him today?'

'I'll – see him later.'

'You sure about that? I think he has plans. In the woods. With someone else.'

I couldn't help but yell at her, which someone likely reported to the police: 'What plans? What do you mean?'

'Just plans. You think you're the only one he talks to? Draws little pictures for?'

'Jen, what are you *on* about? Tell me, now, or I'll . . .'

She paused for a second and gave me a strange look. I have tried to dissect it many times over the years. Pride, perhaps? Triumph? I don't know. 'Gonna threaten me again?'

I begged. I wasn't too proud. 'Jen. Don't do this. You have everything and he – he's all I have.'

She just laughed, and she walked off, and I screamed after her, right in the lobby in front of everyone, including Miss Coxon, who came over to tell me off. 'You'll regret this, I swear!'

Lie six – that I went to your house the day Jen was killed.

What I wrote in my book, about the party and the next day at school, talking to Jen in the lobby, texting you both throughout the day to no answer, seeing Gareth's car by the woods – all of that is true. It's not a lie.

But lying is not the same as omission, and there is a part of the day I didn't mention. And that's how I went into the woods myself, to try and stop whatever might be happening between you and her. I didn't go to your house at all, so I had no way of knowing whether you were there or not. Your father, confused and edging even then into madness, probably confirmed that I came. And you told the police the same. That we had been together during the crucial time when Jen was killed. And so we saved each other. Either we were together or either one of us was a suspect.

How did we know, without even speaking, to get our stories straight like this? That was the bond between us. The pact, as you called it. You'd protect me and I'd protect you.

Lie seven – that I only saw Jen at school that day.

It was raining in the woods when I got there, coming down hard between the leaves and branches. The bird calls seemed to echo louder. I couldn't see anyone, but I knew you had to be here somewhere. 'Jen?' I shouted, howling into the rain.

Then she was there. Standing inside the old shed, apparently dry despite the weather. At the back were the blankets we'd brought down in summer, and I could see a bottle, a candle guttering bravely in the wind. 'What are you doing here?'

'You know what.' I faced her across the clearing. We were both in our uniforms, her with her coat over the top. Her face underneath it was smug.

'It's a free country. I can meet him if I want to.'

I still didn't believe her. 'Where is he then? Stood you up, has he?'

She looked at her watch, the pink one Ash had bought for her last Christmas. 'Not time yet. I came down to make it nice. Romantic.'

She smiled, and something tore through me, the claws of beasts and the roar of a lion. You were meeting her. You, my only friend, more than a friend, had chosen Jen over me. You were not different and special and discerning after all. Like everyone else, you only saw her pretty face, the curves of her body. 'So what, you're together now?'

She shrugged. 'I don't know. Since the party, things have changed.'

You must have stayed over with her on Saturday night. All those times I tried to ring you, when you wouldn't pick up.

'What's your dad gonna say about your rough-trade boyfriend?' I threw at her.

She laughed. 'Who said anything about a boyfriend? We don't have to be seen in public to do the things I want.'

'What about Gareth?'

She sighed. 'You were the one who told me to get rid of Gareth. He's a dick. He doesn't know how to treat women, and now I know he's also no good at – well, you know. Or no, you don't know, do you? Seeing as he's never touched you.' The rain was in my eyes and I could hardly see. The ground was boggy under my cheap shoes but suddenly I was right in front of her. 'Jesus, Karen, what are you doing? You're not even with him.'

'I – I . . .'

I couldn't explain what you were to me, what we were to each other. It went beyond stupid concepts like 'being together'. It's why I never know what to say when someone describes me as your girlfriend. I wasn't that, I was more. She would never get it.

Then she laughed. Her usual smug, Princess Jen laugh. And I snapped.

I can't remember exactly what happened in those few moments. I know I choked her. My hands pushed her hood aside, grasped at her pale neck. She stopped laughing. 'Karen!' She could hardly speak. She clawed at me, leaving marks with her long nails. The police saw them the next day and I said I had eczema on my hands.

Jen stumbled down, landing hard on her bum. Her voice was croaky. 'You're fucking mental. I'm telling my dad you attacked me. See if he wants to marry your skank mother then.'

'What the fuck?' Arlene certainly didn't have a ring the night before, or the happy expression of a woman who'd just said yes to a proposal. 'They're *engaged*?'

283

'Oh, you didn't know? He's popped the question, stupid twat. I reckon this might change his mind though. It's a crime, right? Assault? GBH?'

I was panting hard. I had throttled her. She was OK, she was breathing, but her neck was red and there would be more bruises on it. It was a crime, as she said – assault, if not attempted murder. It would be the end of Ash and Arlene, of the new life I had planned for myself. Of getting away to university. I might even go to prison. And worst of all, you would hardly want me now, after I'd lost control and hurt Jen just because you paid her some attention. I would lose everything. So I turned towards her, and in that second when her smirk darkened into fear, as my hands came up to her throat again – oh, in that terrible second, I came to understand exactly how it must feel to hold a life in your hands.

But I stopped again. Jen fell down into the mud with a splash. I didn't check if she was OK or not. I turned and ran back through the trees, panting and sobbing. It was all over now. I went home, took off my muddy shoes, tried to clean them as best I could, put my tights into the wash. Arlene was out, no one else saw me. I will have left traces – mud, leaves, something to show I'd been in the woods. But no blood. It was a bloodless death.

Did I kill her? I don't know. I've never known. I might have. But Gareth was there, a convenient alternative who might well have gone into the woods after I left, and finished the job. I told myself that this could be true, that I didn't have to be a killer. I let myself go free. Later, I thought you must have done the same. But I have never known for sure whether I'm a murderer or not, and you, you gave me a way out of the hell I'd walked myself into, like opening a door and ushering me back into my life.

Lie eight – that I told the police the moment you arrived at my flat, on the day of your arrest.

I did text them to say come and get you, that part is true. But you weren't late and you didn't come in the back. You were right on time, and I used those minutes to do something I had done only once before in all the time I'd known you. I stepped forward and pressed my mouth up on to yours. This time it was different. I felt you freeze again, but then you softened. You made a noise that was almost a sob. And I walked you backwards to my bed.

The truth is, this was the only time. That we kissed, that we lay together naked. We had hugged sometimes, slept in the same bed even, but we had never done that. I wasn't your girlfriend, but only because you didn't want me to be. I was a convenient shield, perhaps. To hide what you were.

When it was over and you were in the bathroom I sat up in bed and thought again about running. A whole other life, one with you. But I knew that it could never be. Because if you weren't a killer, then I certainly was. Because Jen was dead. Because we could never come back from that moment where we had lied to save each other. So I got up and dressed and I pressed send on my text to the police and a different life opened up. I wasn't even sure in that moment you were a killer – I was still hoping you would be cleared, that it was all a mistake. But when they took you away, part of me knew that we would never truly be together again.

The rest of the story is true – going home from the woods that day, Arlene out all night, Ash saying Jen didn't come home, telling me a body had been found. The stuff from my police interviews is all true as well. The transcripts are available for anyone to check. What I've left out is how fast my brain was turning all the while, trying to stay one step ahead of them. It felt like when you and I played chess, calculating how much to give up to save myself.

'Did you and Jen have some kind of row, Karen? People saw you storming out of the party at her house, and shouting at her in school today.'

So they had already spoken to Sinead and the others. I remember being surprised, impressed actually, at how quickly they had me in a pincer.

Defensiveness was a trap, I knew that. 'I wouldn't say stormed out. I just went home, it wasn't my thing. All that drinking. I saw someone puke in the swimming pool.'

'Can anyone vouch for you being at home yesterday, after school?'

'I walked back – maybe someone saw me. The neighbours, I don't know. I was home all night.'

'Alone?'

'Yes. My mother was at work.'

They made notes. Their names, which I didn't recall when I came to write the book and had to look up, were DS Andy Dickinson and DC Mike Cardew. Middle-aged white men. I couldn't remember which was which, but one was fat and smelled of cigarettes, and the other was thin and smelled of photocopier ink. The fat one – Dickinson – did all the talking.

'So no one can corroborate your story.'

'I guess not. I'm often on my own at home. But why does it matter?'

'Last time any of her friends saw Jen, she was walking away from the bus stop, towards the woods. Why would she be going that way in the rain?'

'I have no idea. I got a later bus.'

'Would Jen normally be on the early one?'

'She had a car. Or she'd go another route, the bus that goes over near her house.'

'So why did she get off by the woods? Why didn't she drive that day?'

'I don't know. I didn't ask.'

There were more questions, tedious repetitive questions, all about my routine that day, when exactly I had seen Jen and where. It was several hours before they mentioned your name, and when they did, it was with the air of a magician pulling a rabbit out of a hat.

'Tell us about Aaron Hughes, Karen. Good friend of yours, isn't he?'

'He's my friend, yes.'

'And where was he yesterday?'

'He didn't come in.'

'You didn't text him?'

They could most likely check this. 'I did, yes. A few times.'

'Twenty-seven times, Karen.'

'Oh.'

'That's a lot of times.'

'I didn't know where he was.'

'What happened at the party, Karen? Did you leave with him?'

'Well, if you can check my texts, you'll know I didn't.' That was a mistake. They wanted deference, fear, not some smartarse girl who thought she was cleverer than them.

'Texts can be lies, Karen.'

That wasn't a question, so I didn't answer it. I remember folding my arms. I remember I was very cold, except for in the cell, which was boiling hot. I was always taking my hoody on and off, even as it became stained and smelly.

Dickinson went on, 'In a sulk, were you?'

'Why would I be?'

He chuckled. 'Come on now, your boyfriend stays at the party, chats to your friend all night? Ditches you?'

'He's not my boyfriend.' The first of many times I would say that in my life. At times it would hit me that Jen was dead, and I would ask questions, some of which I already knew the answer to. *But what happened to her? Did anyone – touch her?* I couldn't say *rape*. They exchanged looks and said they 'couldn't be sure' but there weren't any signs of it, no. Was there any evidence – footprints, anything left behind? That seemed to annoy them. *Let us ask the questions, Karen.* They then asked a lot about my mother and Ash, and even Patricia, and I realised they were driving at some theory that my mother hadn't wanted a meddling stepdaughter. Was it true she had described Jen as an *uppity little bitch*?

I was careful there too, not to incriminate Arlene, who had allegedly been at work all night and yet not answered Ash's calls. 'I have no idea. But Jen could be rude sometimes, yeah.'

More questions about you. When you had come to town, how well you knew Jen, your father's service history and mental health issues. And then the kicker – that you had given me up. Accused me.

But as I walked down the corridor from the cell after that, I looked through to reception and I saw you there. We locked eyes for one second and it's hard to describe, but that told me everything I needed to know. What I had to do, what we would do for each other. The police were lying. You would never give me up, and so I would not give you up. As if we had agreed it between us, we both said we'd seen the other at the time of the murder, at your house.

And maybe it was true, and you were home, and Jen was lying, you'd never arranged to meet her. No one had seen me go in or out of the woods, the rain had washed away my footprints. No evidence against me. Or you. I gave them Gareth, and they snapped him up. Case closed. Luck was on our side again. In time I actually came to believe it was Gareth – not a leap, given what he'd done to her.

That story kept me safe, and you safe, for ten years. But not the other women you would go on to kill. I cannot go back now, to those days when I was seventeen and terrified, questioned day and night by unsympathetic male officers, and yet I held true. I believed you would not betray me, and I did not betray you. The one look in the corridor, that was enough.

What difference would it have made if I'd told the truth? Would I be serving time myself, for murder or attempted murder? I know that there's a good chance seven more women would still be alive. But how could I have known what you'd go on to do?

No one can live with crushing guilt all the time. I've done my best to make some breathing space under it, tell myself I couldn't have known, but the truth is that's a lie. The truth is I could have, and should have, known. And now you are out again, and no woman is safe.

Chapter Twenty-One

The story doesn't take long to tell. I committed a crime, indeed several – assault, attempted murder maybe, lying to police, perjury. Maybe actual murder. I could do a long time for this. But I find that there is a certain relief in admitting it all. My book will have to be pulped now. My career will be over, even if by some miracle I don't go to jail. But I don't care. If it can save Lara, save one more life, I will do it.

'You're still lying,' says Gareth.

'I'm not. This is the truth.'

Rosalind takes my phone and slides it into my pocket. 'Stand over there.' They're going to do it now. They have never killed before, I'm sure. Will they really murder me? If they could snatch Lara from her flat, daub her blood on the wall, they may be capable of it.

'You don't have to do this. I was going to confess anyway. I'll probably go to prison. Isn't that enough?'

Gareth is insistent. 'But we took her. Lara. We'll go to jail for that.'

'Not necessarily. If you just release her, would she know where she'd been?'

Can I really argue my way out of this? I see Rosalind is considering it. She's a kid, she doesn't want to go to prison. But Gareth is impatient.

'Let's just end this. Come on, Ros.'

'I'm thinking!'

'What's there to think about? She's a bitch, she deserves to die!' Then Gareth is running at me, and I'm so stunned I just stand there and let him.

But then you are here. You uncoil from the bushes behind the stable as if you've been there all along, with that absolute stillness that made you such a good hunter. 'I can't let you do that, Gareth.' You stand in front of me and push him back, though he's bigger and stronger than you.

Rosalind has blanched in fear. 'It's you.'

'Yes, hello, Rosalind. You really do look like your sister. I knew her well, as it happened. I know people didn't believe that after, but she was quite keen on me, for a time.'

I gasp. I can't help it. After all these years passed and blood spilled, it still hurts. 'It was true? You and her?'

You shrug. You look dirty, cold, but better than Gareth. 'I'm only human, Kare-bear. People don't believe that either, but it's true. I knew she was only interested in me to cause trouble with you, but I couldn't help myself. The pretty popular girl, and she wanted me. It made me feel – normal, for a moment. I'll never forgive myself for it. Being so – predictable.'

Rosalind is swaying on her feet. 'So you did go to the woods that day?'

'I did. And there was Jen, very much alive and absolutely furious. She wanted to go to the police, get Karen sent to prison. She wanted me to be the witness. I couldn't do that. We had a pact, Karen and I.'

The air seems to hang still. Rosalind is pale, terrified but needing the truth still. 'So you're saying . . .'

You admit to it so casually, as if you haven't spent years denying you ever hurt anyone. 'Yes, it was me who killed Jen. Karen's version of events is correct, except that Jen was fine when she left her. Winded, yes, but alive.' You nod to me. 'Turn the recording on again, Karen. You'll want to get this.'

I fumble for my phone. What is happening? I should be terrified, and yet the moment you appeared I only felt relief.

You are speaking clearly and loudly so there can be no doubt. 'This is Aaron Hughes here. I killed Jen Rollason to protect Karen, because I loved her, in a misguided way, I suppose. The irony is I didn't even need to. At the most Karen would have got a caution for what she did. Jen was barely hurt – just a catfight between girls. But here we are. I am the Bagman, and I'm responsible for the death of Jen Rollason, me alone. Oh, and the other women too. Not Nita Chowdry. I'd look at her husband again, if I were the police. But the rest I did. I killed them. Catherine Collins. Alison Johnson. Roshana Khan. Annie Andersen. Julia and Victoria. I tried to murder Emelia Han, and a few other women who never came forward and likely don't know they had a lucky escape. I don't think I can even say sorry, because what would that mean? I don't know why I did it. Why I kept going after I'd done it once, to Jen. I don't understand what's inside of me any more than the rest of us do. But this is the truth.'

Then there's more noise, and the metallic noise of radios, and a loudspeaker booms. 'This is armed police! Everyone there, put your hands up.' Donetti must have followed the clues, sent help.

'Oh shit!' yells Gareth, diving into the undergrowth with his knife.

You turn to me. You and I could always say what we needed to in the space of one second, one look, just like all those years ago

292

in the police station, the heartbeat that divided my life in two. I have lied all these times when I said we had no pact. Of course we did, and I broke it. The pact that any two people have when they know each other, when they love each other, when they see each other without lies. You never hid who you were. It was me who was pretending. This time is no exception. After ten years, after multiple life sentences, I still know exactly what you're saying with one look.

'Run,' you whisper, and I do. I'm halfway up the field when I hear the gunshot.

Chapter Twenty-Two

Serial killers don't get marked graves. No one wants their last resting place to become a site of pilgrimage, attracting the ghouls and fans that every gross act of violence stirs up. So I don't know where you will be buried. Only your mother has been told, and I don't know if she or your entitled replacement siblings will ever visit. Would I want to know? Would I stand by your grave, place flowers, talk to you as if you're still here, as if you weren't shot dead by police marksmen in the field that day? The truth is I don't know. And I don't need a grave to hear your voice with me, always, joining Jen's in my ear, and the voices of the other women who I never even met. Sisters under the skin.

It was a long night at the police station, sorting everything out. Watching the journey of Rosalind's parents from weeping relief to shocked horror as they learned their little girl planned all this, helped to abduct and hold a woman in a freezing stable just metres from their home. Lara was recovered moments after you were shot, brought to hospital and treated for hypothermia and shock. Apart from the wound to her arm, where they took the blood, she was alright. She got out of hospital yesterday, and I hear she's doing OK. I hope to meet her at some point, the young woman I've never spoken to but whose life I have pored over, looking for clues, who was used as a pawn to make me face my past.

There will be an inquiry, of course, into your death, when shooting by police is so rare in this country. Why you walked towards the armed officers, why you made it seem like you had a weapon. Why you ignored all warnings to stop. As if you wanted to be shot, almost. Like anyone, you will be afforded the right of having your death explained. But I don't think anyone will care much that you are gone.

I think you had worked it out from the start, that Gareth was mixed up in this, and maybe Rosalind too. You must have known I was in danger. I know you saved me at the end, even if you wanted to punish me too, to force the truth from me. You could have run but you came back for me, after seeing that Rosalind was supposedly missing too. You could have been free, in the wind, but you weren't prepared to let me die. Gareth is currently in custody charged with kidnap and assault, and the attempted murder of me too. He's looking at fifteen years in jail. Rosalind, being just seventeen and the sister of a murder victim, is facing much lesser charges. Not touching the knife was either a lucky accident for her, or evidence of a much more cunning mind than Gareth Hale will ever have.

I wonder what Jen would say about this. If she has, in some sense, watched it unfold, her sister's savage attempt to bring me to justice. What she'd think about it all.

How would I know? I never believed in any of that stuff, and Jen would have rolled her eyes at it and told me to *Get a grip, Mystic Meg*.

I was fully expecting some charges myself after I played my confession to Donetti, along with yours. Obtained with a knife to my throat, it was hardly admissible, but I was willing to sign a proper statement of what occurred on that wet day so many years ago. After some rumblings, it was agreed not to pursue assault charges for what I did to Jen. You had confirmed she was very much alive after I left the woods. That it was you who stepped towards her, and maybe she thought for a moment you were going to kiss her and she was excited, drawn in by you as I was, and then your hands were on her neck and your eyes had darkened and she must have known she'd made a terrible mistake.

Is it true? I will never know. Maybe I'm not a murderer, just a girl who lost her temper one day when her best friend tried to take the only boy she'd ever cared about. Or maybe I am and you decided to spare me that as well.

Nita Chowdry's husband was arrested the day after you died, and eventually admitted under questioning, after his former colleagues withdrew the alibi they had given him, that it was he who killed Nita, trying to cover it up by approximating a bloody symbol on the wall like this mysterious Bagman was known to do. One of his mates had worked on the case and shown him a sneaked photo of it. He will go on trial early next year.

My book of course had to be changed, but with some last-minute wrangling from April, it will be released as planned with an extra chapter added, where I tell the truth about what I did. She expects it to be a huge seller and is clamouring to get me on *This Morning*. Emelia and Matt are already making a podcast about all this, to be released in a few months and titled *After Bagman*. I saw his foot in a 'soft boyfriend launch' post she put on Instagram of her hiking on the moors, and I hope she can once again be in the north without being haunted by you. The Brains Trust are already on to their next project, the death of a whole family up near Scarborough. It seems like a straight-up murder-suicide to me, but I'm sure they will enjoy looking into it. They came to visit the other day. Jim and Arlene traded stop-smoking tips, while Janine badgered Sandra for stories of the criminals she's worked with. Mercedes shyly revealed herself to be 'heteroflexible' and praised Mum's bravery in coming out 'so late in life'.

To which Arlene replied, 'I'm not that bloody old, love, thanks very much.'

So what now? I'm still in Marebridge, still in my old room, Mum and Sandra keeping careful guard over me. I was so horrified to come back here, and now I find I can't quite leave. I keep extending my ticket home by a few days at a time. Santiago tells me he's watering the plants, and has brought Jane Pawsten to live with them for a while. Even Paloma has warmed to the beast. So there's little in New York for me. And here? There is Arlene. Mum. I can finally see her as she is, not the disappointing mother of my youth. Just a woman doing her best with a difficult, unhappy daughter. Who protected me as best she could, even from myself. There's Emelia and Matt, who are staying in Manchester to make the podcast. She came to the police station as I sat there in a foil blanket, trying to absorb what had just happened. She ran in, shoving aside paramedics and officers, kneeling in front of me, squeezing my hands.

'He's dead? He's really dead?'

I nodded, dumbly.

'I'm glad,' she said, fiercely. 'But I'm sorry for you, Karen. You loved him.'

As annoying as Emelia can be, I found that actually very moving. I may have even cried, but it was probably the shock.

And there's DS Chris Donetti, who has been coming round to check on me more than is strictly necessary. He's promised to give Sandra a reference when she applies to be governor up at the prison, the last one having resigned in disgrace after a vast ring of corruption was exposed among officers. Kerry wasn't the only one to have a love affair with an inmate, it turns out, or smuggle in phones and drugs. Donetti's been going to the gym with Arlene too, creating weights circuits for her. She and Sandra both give me lots of winks and nudges when he's round, which I ignore, but I can't say I don't look forward to his visits.

So who knows? Stay or go? Return to my half-life, safe and lonely and thousands of miles away, or stay here and face who I am? Live in the same town as the Rollasons, knowing I almost killed one of their daughters, and the other planned to kill me? I don't know, and some days the past feels too heavy to ever pick up again. I think of Catherine, who might have been a history teacher. Alison, who might have been prime minister. Roshana, who didn't even get to turn eighteen. Nita, her future snuffed out by someone she had loved. Annie, just trying her best to survive. Victoria, Julia, best friends who died together, maybe each hoping as the life left them that the other would survive, graduate, marry. All of the futures and children and loves and tears and life that might one day have been theirs. And I think of Jen, who will never leave me, who could have been so much and done so much. I can't take it, sometimes, knowing I survived, with all my sins and flaws and lies. Knowing it was me, not Jen, who was your real first girl, my life undone by you in different ways. Knowing I am perhaps the worst of them all, but for some reason I'm still alive when they aren't. It's not easy, and some days I can hardly live with myself. But all the same I find myself logging on to the airline website once more, and extending my stay by another few days.

BOOK CLUB QUESTIONS

1. Is Karen right to feel guilty for not figuring out sooner that Aaron was a killer? What should she have done differently, in your opinion?

2. What do you think you would have done in her situation at seventeen, after Jen's death?

3. Is Arlene a bad mother to Karen?

4. Discuss the novel's representation of the way social media fuels interest in crime. Do podcasts and documentaries create an unhealthy obsession with real-life crimes?

5. What do you think of the book being directly addressed to Aaron throughout?

6. Did Karen need to go back to her hometown in order to move on with her life?

7. Who do you think really killed Jen – was it Aaron, or was he still covering for Karen to try to protect her?

8. Discuss the different ways the families of the victims handled their loss.

9. What do you think of the character of Emelia – is she entitled to use what happened to her to make a career?

10. What are the differences between the main narrative and the extracts we read from Karen's memoir?

ABOUT THE AUTHOR

Photo © 2023 Philippa Gedge

Born in Northern Ireland, Claire published her first novel in 2012, and has followed it up with many others in the crime fiction genre and also in women's fiction (writing as Eva Woods). Writing thrillers for Thomas & Mercer, she has sold over a million books and has had several number-one bestsellers. She ran the UK's first MA in crime writing for five years, and regularly teaches and talks about writing. Her first non-fiction project, the true-crime book *The Vanishing Triangle*, was released in 2022. She also writes scripts and has several original projects in development for TV, as well as having had four radio dramas broadcast. Several of her novels are also in development as television series. She lives in London and would love to hear from readers via the methods below!

Website and email via: www.clairemcgowan.co.uk
X: @inkstainsclaire
Instagram: @clairemcgowanwriter
TikTok: @clairemcgowanwriter
Facebook: www.facebook.com/ClaireMcGowanAuthor

Follow the Author on Amazon

If you enjoyed this book, follow Claire McGowan on Amazon to be notified when the author releases a new book!

To do this, please follow these instructions:

Desktop:

1) Search for the author's name on Amazon or in the Amazon App.
2) Click on the author's name to arrive on their Amazon page.
3) Click the 'Follow' button.

Mobile and Tablet:

1) Search for the author's name on Amazon or in the Amazon App.
2) Click on one of the author's books.
3) Click on the author's name to arrive on their Amazon page.
4) Click the 'Follow' button.

Kindle eReader and Kindle App:

If you enjoyed this book on a Kindle eReader or in the Kindle App, you will find the author 'Follow' button after the last page.